Praise for the no
SWEETWA
(originally p

D0468849

"Sharfeddin has captured the family-like entanglements in a small community—by showing us what happens when those relationships begin to come apart."

—*The Philadelphia Inquirer*

"Superbly crafted...Characters are wonderfully drawn....Explores a wide range of themes related to sin and guilt, personal integrity, and the destructive power of prejudice. Essentially, however, this is a story about the miracle of love blossoming in unlikely places. Highly recommended."

—*Library Journal* (starred review)

"Comparisons will be made to Kent Haruf....Sharfeddin's... eye for detail...and her unsentimental compassion for her characters...will entrance readers. The stark terrain is beautifully rendered."

—*Kirkus Reviews* (starred review)

"Striking...A deceptively simple contemporary western about two loners who have learned from their mistakes and flaws, but not overcome them."

—*The Portsmouth Herald* (New Hampshire), in selecting *Blackbelly* as one of the top novels of 2005

WINDLESS SUMMER

"Heather Sharfeddin's characters are so complex and well-meaning and so frequently wrong you'll want to step in and hug the one you just slapped around. The woman can write. Imagine Annie Proulx taking on the Salem witch trials."

—Robin Cody, author of *Ricochet River*

ALSO BY HEATHER SHARFEDDIN

Windless Summer

Mineral Spirits

Sweetwater Burning
(originally published as *Blackbelly*)

DAMAGED GOODS

DAMAGED GOODS

A NOVEL

HEATHER SHARFEDDIN

Bantam Books Trade Paperbacks
New York

2011 Bantam Books Trade Paperback Original

Copyright © 2011 by Heather Sharfeddin

Published in the United States by Bantam Books, an imprint of The Random House Publishing Group, a division of Random House, Inc., New York.

BANTAM BOOKS and the rooster colophon are registered trademarks of Random House, Inc.

LIBRARY OF CONGRESS CATALOGING-IN-PUBLICATION DATA
Sharfeddin, Heather.
Damaged goods : a novel / Heather Sharfeddin.
p. cm.
ISBN 978-0-385-34188-2
eBook ISBN 978-0-440-33955-7
1. Auctioneers—Fiction. 2. Oregon—Fiction. I. Title.
PS3619.H35635D36 2011
813'.6—dc22   2010 046235

Printed in the United States of America

www.bantamdell.com

2 4 6 8 9 7 5 3 1

Book design by Diane Hobbing

*For Holli; thank you
for becoming a doctor.*

DAMAGED GOODS

PROLOGUE

A Tom Petty song seeped from the car radio, static-riddled on the vintage speaker. Hershel Swift punched the dash lighter in his Dodge Charger and drummed his fingers on the steering wheel. He bobbed his head in time with the music.

"Don't come around here no more," he sang quietly.

The car hummed over the bridge as he crossed the Willamette River, the dark Oregon countryside falling away behind him and the amber lights of Newberg winking into view. Another twenty minutes over Chehalem Mountain and down into Scholls and he'd be home. An empty house. A quiet retreat. A welcome bed.

He'd take care not to draw attention as he passed through Newberg; leave no witness to point out his car to a jury in some unimaginable courtroom in the distant future. No, he'd travel with caution.

"I'm a fucking genius," he said. He wondered if thinking that was a sign that he was actually crazy. He rubbed a dark stain on his jeans, still wet, and inspected his finger to see if it was blood. Too dark to tell.

The lighter snapped up hot and he touched it to the tip of his cigarette, drawing the woody smoke into his lungs and holding it there for a long moment. He rarely lit up anymore—the toll on his vocal cords too costly to business. But tonight he needed the nico-tine rush. It would calm his nerves.

He was keenly aware that the events of the evening had af-fected him far less than they ought to have. Perhaps another sign that he was crazy. He blew a thin streak of smoke against the windshield and leaned over to replace the lighter. His arms and shoulders ached deep down through the muscles. He straight-ened to relieve the pain, dragging the mud-caked sole of his boot across the floor mat, and rubbed his eyes.

He'd closed them for only a moment. He tried to make sense of the object in the road. Black and white. Huge. The impact flipped it onto the hood of the car, shattered the windshield, and then crumpled the roof. The car careened to the right and rolled as Hershel fought for control. Dirt flew into his mouth and up his nose. The ceiling cracked across his head with staggering force. His thoughts flickered, random images that made no sense, then went out.

1

"I can't believe all these people waited for him to open his doors again," Linda whispered. "It can't be because they missed him."

"They're here for the deals." Stuart scouted the cramped booth and plucked up grease pens. "There ain't no one here tonight that gives a damn about that asshole."

Hershel paused outside the door, listening as his staff gossiped. His stomach tightened at their words. Tonight would be the first auction Hershel had conducted since the accident, and his chest and hands tingled with nerves. A sensation he'd never known before, even when he was young and just starting out. What if he forgot the numbers? What if he couldn't remember the names of the things he would sell that evening? Lawn mowers and washers and hydraulic lifts.

A line of fifteen or so people snaked out of the building, into the weedy parking lot and the late-October chill. Bidders signed in and collected their numbers, glancing curiously in Hershel's direction. None smiling. Swift Consignment Auction was a Tuesday-night institution in the farming community of Scholls, and it appeared that people had missed the weekly event, if not him, these past three months.

He decided not to ask if Linda needed anything, but left the two employees alone before they saw him standing near the door. He poured himself a Coke from the concession stand and didn't bother to say hello to the teenage girl—another unfamiliar face— who was setting up for the evening. He thought he should know her. Was certain he should. There were only eight employees, and he'd hired each one personally. The smell of popcorn was rapidly overtaking the aroma of axle grease in the hulking warehouse building. The girl poured hot water into the coffeemaker without looking up. She was diligent in her duties, but seemed self-conscious in his presence. He assessed her more carefully. She was thin and wore a leather thong around her neck with a bear claw dangling at her throat. Red hair, long. Freckles, of course. A modern hippie or a greeny. She wore Birkenstocks with thick wool socks against the chill of the cement floor.

"Have everything you need?" he asked.

"Yes, Mr. Swift. Thanks." She was polite and soft-spoken. Wouldn't make eye contact, though.

What did *she* think of him? "Are you the runner tonight?"

Now she looked up, pale eyes catching the last of the sunlight through the cloudy window behind him. "I can't run tickets and do the concessions at the same time. I usually have a line."

Hershel grunted. "I thought you were just helping out the regular girl tonight."

She furrowed her brow at the stream of coffee trickling into the pot. "I . . . am the regular girl, Mr. Swift."

Hershel nodded. He gave her an awkward thumbs-up gesture, turned, his face hot, and headed down the corridor from the concession stand through the long, alley-like storage area beneath the bleachers. It ran the length of the building on the north side and was where the sold items were marked and shelved until their purchasers collected them. A dark catacomb of cubbyholes with numbers scrawled in permanent marker on bare studs—251-75, 226-50, 200-25 on down. He came out into a small room at the west end of the building, toward the glaring light of the open warehouse and the hum of myriad conversations. He nodded at the man who would accept and organize the sale items into their allotted cubbies. Hershel tried to remember his name. He had looked it up that afternoon. A balding fellow with broad shoulders and thick arms, who bent over his task of tearing off three-inch bits of masking tape and sticking them to the edge of the battered workbench in a neat row. The man's back pocket was crammed with grease pens ready to jot winning numbers on the scraps of tape. He looked up as Hershel passed. A wary eye, as if expecting something unpleasant.

"Walter," Hershel said, hoping he'd gotten it right.

"Boss." The man turned back to his task, but his eye followed Hershel out of the back room, out of his dark warren and onto the sale floor.

Hershel nodded to the life-size cardboard cutout of John Wayne near the bathroom. It looked so damn real that he thought it was an actual person. He felt thick and retarded when he realized what it was.

Out on the floor, he moved along the narrow path between the bleachers and a three-month backlog of ready-to-be-sold merchandise taller than his own head in places. He was the object of blatantly curious stares. As he edged by the three men working the floor—Stuart, Carl, and Henry—he repeated their names in his head. He'd been doing it all evening. These were the men he'd direct, and the ones whose names he most needed to recall on the fly. Stuart and Henry were in their late thirties, old enough to appreciate a good deal. They were pawing through the items even at the last minute, looking for treasures alongside other bidders. Henry examined a set of wrenches. He was a plumber and a family man who always looked for pipe fittings, sinks, and water heaters as they came through the sale. Stuart plucked at the strings of an acoustic guitar to see if it would hold a tune. He was a second-rate musician who played in a band down at the Elks Lodge in Salem. He was married—at least that seemed right to Hershel now. It was the microwaves and stereos he picked up here that kept him tinkering on the weekends and out of trouble.

Carl, the third man, was nearing sixty. He didn't poke at the merchandise like the others but looked out over the sea of items—shopping with his eyes. He still had a strong back, though, for moving washers and refrigerators.

Hershel let his eyes settle on Carl for a moment. Carl was the only one who had visited Hershel in the hospital, standing awkwardly near the door, asking if he needed anything. Hershel had vague recollections of the man recounting information about his business, his house, but the facts had dissolved in that drug haze of convalescence. Carl chatted sociably with the regulars in the front row tonight, illustrating his stories with broad gestures. A stream of laughter from that direction rose above the crowd, irritating Hershel's nerves. He'd seen Carl finally pick up an old box fan. Of everything there, he picked up the box fan, and that irritated Hershel as well. Carl was a ne'er-do-well Vietnam vet who bought whatever struck his fancy. Hershel guessed the man was a junkie.

The front row of the bleachers, where the regulars sat, most of whose names Hershel gratefully remembered, was filling fast. Number twelve, Bart Hanson, owner of Hanson Second Hand in Hillsboro. Number thirty-one, Winona Freehauf, an antiques dealer from Portland. Sixteen . . . Hershel couldn't remember his name. A Greek-looking fellow with a heavy mustache and dark eyes. The man nodded solemnly as Hershel walked by.

Hershel paused at the center of the sale floor, overwhelmed by the task ahead. The bright lights burned his eyes, and the noise made his head ache. Above him taxidermy moose and deer heads gazed down with dull eyes. He took his place on the platform.

His clerk, Marilyn somebody, sat on the stool next to his, bent over, testing out ballpoint pens by scribbling on the desk-size calendar that covered her work surface. Her eyes shifted in his direction, but she went on, silently separating the pens into piles of those that worked and those that didn't.

"Guess I should pick up some new pens this week," he said, noticing that the defunct pile was larger and growing.

She glanced up, seemingly surprised. "I can bring some in from the school like I always do," she said with a tone of apology.

Oh yeah, Marilyn Stromm. She worked as a secretary at Groner Elementary during the day. As he looked out over the amassing crowd, he noticed her sneaking glances at him from the corner of her eye.

It was five after six, and he picked up the microphone. His hand trembled as he turned it on, and he gripped the metal handle tighter to still his nerves. He cleared his throat and lifted the mike to his lips.

"Good evening, everyone. Thanks for coming. We're gonna get started now."

The crowd applauded, startling Hershel. His hand shook harder. A whoop went up from the group in the front row. Hershel smiled tensely, his breath catching in his throat.

"Make room up in the bleachers, would you?" he said, trying to appear calm. "We've got a lot of folks still getting numbers down here."

"What've you got, boys?" Hershel asked, and Carl thrust a toaster oven into the air. "Okay, let's open it up with a bid of twenty dollars."

The crowd continued to talk among themselves, keeping a half-interested eye on the item in Carl's hand. But this was the way it went.

"Give me fifteen, then."

No one bid, and Carl flipped open the little door and showed it around with a graceful sweep of his hand. "She's a good little toaster oven," Carl called, showing off his missing front teeth. "Just look at her. Practically brand-new."

"Give me ten," Hershel sang into the microphone, but he didn't get a bite until he dropped the opening bid down to two bucks. It was rapidly bid back up to seven dollars and sold to Bart Hanson for his secondhand store. As Carl ran the toaster oven back to Walter in the storage area, Stuart held up a sewing machine and Hershel began to feel the rhythm of his work once again as it rolled along in that smooth way. A rapid singsong of numbers: "Gimme five, five, five, who'll give me five? Three then, gimme three, three, three. There's three, how 'bout five now. Got five, gimme eight, eight, now ten, ten, now twelve. Who'll gimme twelve? C'mon, folks, it's a decent little sewing machine. Twelve, twelve, that's right, fifteen." And on until he'd sold it for seventeen dollars to a woman standing in the aisle.

At eight o'clock Hershel stared down at the still-full warehouse. They seemed to have made no progress in the mountain of things yet to be sold. His head ached above his eyes, a heavy throbbing in that place so familiar since the accident. He cupped his hand over the microphone and leaned down to speak to Marilyn.

"You need a break?"

She glanced up, her mouth open in confusion. "Who'll record the sale items?"

He scowled. "Don't...isn't..." Hershel waffled between trying to remember who usually gave Marilyn a break and the intense desire to sound as if he knew what he was doing. "Who usually relieves you when you take a break?"

"You don't let me take a break." She continued to stare at him, waiting for him to say something.

"What d'you mean? I make you sit here all night?"

"Uh-huh," she said, still not looking away. "When you hired me you asked how strong my bladder was, 'cause there wouldn't be a bathroom break."

He straightened up again, removing his hand from the microphone. A sea of expectant faces all looked back at him. They were waiting for him to move on to the next item.

"Guess you really did hit your head," she whispered to herself.

He stuttered out the opening bid on a rotary-dial telephone.

Marilyn spent the rest of the evening stealing furtive glances at Hershel as they worked their way through the heap of household castoffs, until the crowd in the bleachers had thinned to a dozen people and the line at the cashier's booth once again wound its way out into the cool and moist Oregon night.

Hershel thanked everyone for coming and slumped down on the stool with his aching head resting in his palms.

"Are you okay, Mr. Swift?" Marilyn asked.

"Yes, just tired."

"It was a good idea to keep it short tonight."

Hershel rolled his hand back and studied his watch. It was just past ten. He'd routinely run sales that went as late as one and two in the morning before. He couldn't imagine doing a marathon like that now. Even the smell of the popcorn had begun to wear on him.

"You'll get your speed back," she said as she gathered up the last tickets and shoved her pens to the back of the desk. "Some things just take time."

He sighed. His rhythm had been fine, even therapeutic, but he knew that he was moving through the merchandise at half his usual pace. As he surveyed the floor in front of the podium now, he saw that there were still large stacks of items he hadn't gotten to. The stove and dishwasher in avocado green, the sea trunk with its faded stickers and rusty lock, the cardboard boxes filled with books, and the antique banister rails salvaged from some long-ago architecture. It would all be here waiting for him next week. He could hardly face the idea.

He lumbered down onto the floor, and Stuart slapped his shoulder on his way past. "Good to have you back, boss." The sentiment rang empty, especially after the glare he had given Hershel the third time he couldn't articulate the name of the item Stuart had held up.

"Blender," Stuart had called out to the crowd with clear annoyance. "It's a *blender*, folks."

Hershel slept until noon the following day. He woke several times that morning, feeling as though he should get up and head over to the auction barn. People would be returning for items that they couldn't haul away the night before—unplanned purchases and miscalculated sizes. But Carl would be there. Carl always worked on Wednesday mornings, which Hershel knew only because it was included in the note taped to his refrigerator. A page of yellow legal paper with a tight and slightly backward slanting script. It had random bits of information, like what day the garbageman showed up, when advertisements needed to be submitted to the *Hillsboro Argus* or the Sunday *Oregonian,* the combination to his safe. It wasn't the only note like this, and Hershel was pretty sure he hadn't written them. But he'd added to the collection, decorating mirrors and doors.

Hershel briefly wondered if it was a good idea to leave Carl in charge of his business. Had he always done that?

He moaned as he sat up and held his head gingerly with both hands. He was so tired of the pain. He'd tried to return to work too soon; he wasn't ready. He was irreversibly altered by the accident. He'd suffered a serious brain injury. *Brain damaged,* they had called it. The doctors warned him that his cognitive skills might never return to the level where they had once been. Everything felt different and wrong. He thought back on the conversation he'd overheard between Linda and Stuart. Those words people associated with him. And those hostile looks he caught out of the corner of his eye from everyone. This morning he'd had other distractions to keep him from looking at the raw seed in the center of it all. Did people really dislike him that much? He felt vaguely nauseated. What had he done to earn such contempt?

Hershel had lost the context of his life. He'd returned home with only one recognizable aspect intact: a singular focus on making money. Though he couldn't remember the names of many of the items he'd sold the previous night, he could still assess their value with a single glance. It had comforted him at first, and made him believe he was ready to return to work. But last night had proved just how much was still missing.

Nothing came, and Hershel finally got unsteadily to his feet and wandered into the bathroom. He uncapped a bottle of painkillers and swallowed one down. The vanished days preceding his accident were particularly bothersome. The last thing he remembered was calling Georgine McClintock about doing an estate auction out at her mother's place in Gales Creek. That had been on Tuesday morning. His accident happened the following Saturday evening. He couldn't recall the sale that he held the evening after he made the call, or any of the days leading up to the wreck. He tried again, as he'd tried so many times in the past several months, to remember some small detail. Leaning both hands on the sink, he rested the crown of his head lightly against the mirror. Why was he traveling that road south of Newberg in the first place? If he could simply grasp one tiny recollection from that night, it would be like getting a fingerhold under the seam of this black shroud, and he could tear it away a little at a time.

After brewing coffee, he took his mug outside and sat on the front porch where the sun shone brightest. He'd suddenly become prone to cold spells, and this was a newly favored spot of his, especially on these cooling fall days. He gazed out across the field between his home and the Tualatin River, about a half mile to the north. Midway, a pair of buzzards ripped apart a carcass. A raccoon or a coyote. Whatever it was, it was big enough to have been a formidable opponent in life. Now its limbs were unceremoniously being torn from its body, stripped of muscle and skin.

The oak leaves were turning, but not with the flare of the maples along the river. These did not go bright yellow or red or purple before drifting quietly down, but simply began to brown on the branch. Dead before they've hit the ground, he thought.

As he tried once again to grasp any small detail of that night, he caught sight of the *Watchtower* magazine sitting at the bottom of the steps, tucked under the mat. He stared at it for a moment, then out at his long and very private driveway. His ears burned hot and he did find a memory, though not the one he sought. They had come here once before, a man and two women. Dressed in their Sunday clothes, with plastic smiles and polite gestures, they introduced themselves. Hershel was standing in the doorway in his boxers and a sleeveless undershirt, deliberately for the benefit of the women. It was what they deserved for dropping in on a stranger unannounced. He jutted his knee forward and his shorts gaped open, causing both women to pink on the spot.

When the man asked Hershel if he believed in God, he had responded with "I believe in my God-given right to run you off my property for trespassing."

That was when they drew out the *Watchtower* to leave with him in case he had any future questions about the faith. Hershel thanked them and said he'd be pleased to use it for target practice, pointing at the clean-cut young man on the cover. The trio retreated in horror, and Hershel had stood true to his word, taking the magazine out into the filbert orchard behind the house and pumping fourteen rounds into it until all that remained of the face was a ragged hole.

Today, though, he simply scooted down and picked up the magazine. He thumbed through the glossy pages, annoyed, but not as angry as he knew he would have been before. Perhaps it was that the people who had left it were the only souls to venture down his driveway since he was released from the hospital—a fact that brought a fresh stab of pain to his head.

2

Silvie Thorne slumped against the fender of her Volkswagen Rabbit. She gazed out across the field on the other side of Scholls Ferry Road. Golden wheat stubble rolled away from her in finely combed, nearly invisible rows, but for the blaze of evening sun lighting the bristly tips in white-blond. *Where the hell am I?* She turned back to her car, a battered relic.

"You piece of shit," she muttered.

She opened the passenger door and pulled out her jacket and backpack, then leaned over and locked the driver's door. She glanced at the backseat, wondering if her things—everything she owned in the world—would be safe. There was no taking them with her. Her eyes skimmed the laundry basket with barely folded sheets and towels waiting for a bed and a bathroom she did not have. Buried down along the floorboards beneath a bursting suitcase and hastily collected knickknacks was a metal lockbox. She stared into the backseat for a long time, her gut telling her to take everything out and bring the lockbox.

She straightened and surveyed her surroundings. The valley was narrow, and she could see several houses and farms fanned out along the base of the foothills, which were a deep, silky green, even in this late month. Silvie had never been to Oregon before, and the landscape reminded her of something from a fairy tale, with its ferns and mossy creek beds. The contrast of densely wooded hills and sweeping yellow glens. The road sign above her advertised Scholls two miles ahead. *Scholls.* Not a town she'd ever heard of. She'd been looking for Highway 99 en route to the coast. Now she stood on Scholls Ferry Road, wondering if there really was a ferry and what to do about her dead car.

"You're such an idiot, Silvie," she said. "A map. Why the hell didn't you bring an effing map?" She felt near tears, but bolstered herself against them. She could hear some long-ago voice. *What good will crying do?*

She decided to go for help first, then come back for her things, so she locked the passenger door and rounded the back of the car to make sure the hatchback was secured as well. She'd checked it a hundred times since leaving Wyoming two days ago, but she did so again just to make sure. Then she pulled her jacket tight, slung her backpack over one shoulder, and started up the road in the cool evening light.

She'd barely gone ten steps when a glistening black truck pulled onto the shoulder ahead, blocking her path. It was new. Still had its temporary tags in the window. The tailgate boasted its Hemi engine and four-wheel-drive superiority, and Silvie grimaced, even as she was grateful that someone had stopped. The truck itself felt like Wyoming all over again.

A man stepped out, but stood with the door open, as if he was still deciding whether to offer help. She tilted her head, smiled very slightly in an attempt to appear friendly without seeming helpless. He nodded a greeting and shut the door. He came toward her and she noticed that he was taller than she'd originally thought, with thick wavy hair the color of his truck.

"Car trouble?"

She gazed over her shoulder at the VW and shrugged. Wasn't that obvious?

He walked past her to the car, but didn't hide his sideways glances. "What's it doing?"

"Nothing. It's dead."

He looked back as if to see if she was playing with him. She smiled and shrugged again. He nodded, a faint smile of his own.

"What was it doing *before* it died?" He took the opportunity to stare at her as he waited for an answer. His eyes were black, and the longer he looked the blacker they appeared.

"It sounded like a sick lawn mower hacking concrete. Then it died."

His eyebrows went up and she slid inside to release the hood. After several minutes of fiddling with things in the engine, he asked her to try to start it. The car made a terrible crunching sound but fell silent again. Silvie joined him and peered down into the dirty engine, her fine gold hair ruffling in the breeze between them.

"Hate to say it, but you threw a rod." He turned and surveyed the road ahead where his pickup sat.

"Is that serious?"

"Yup. You can kiss this car goodbye."

"You're kidding me." She twisted in the soft evening air, looking out at the foothills now collecting a cap of menacing gray clouds along the western end. "What am I going to do?"

"Do you live around here? I can give you a lift home."

"Damn it! What am I going to do?" She glared at the ugly car.

He shoved his hands into his pockets and waited for her to answer.

"I'm on my way to Lincoln City. I—" She scuffed the sole of her worn-out leather shoe in the gravel. She didn't need to explain anything, especially to a stranger.

"Well, is there someone you can stay with?"

"I just drove out from Wyom—I mean Montana."

Her cheeks flushed hot. "I—I was living in Montana, then visited a friend in Wyoming...before I came out here," she stammered.

He stared down at the Wyoming license plate but said nothing.

"It's kind of a long story."

He nodded.

She tipped her head back and looked at the gray sky, then over at the car, then up the road again.

"What are you doing on this road if you're headed to Lincoln City?" His question sounded like an accusation.

"I got lost. I took a wrong turn coming through Portland and I just...I just figured southwest, go southwest and you'll find a main road or the beach."

"Navigation by dead reckoning, huh?"

"Works most of the time."

He laughed, and she joined in. She noticed how white and straight his teeth were. He was older than her—in his early forties, maybe. She glanced at his hands, but he had them tucked into the pockets of his jeans.

"Would've worked if your car kept running. Scholls Ferry turns into 219 and crosses over 99. There's a big sign telling you which way to the beach about six miles up the road."

They stood in awkward silence. She looked back in the direction she'd come. Portland lay behind a low band of hills, unseen from where they stood.

"What's in Lincoln City?" he asked. He tipped his head to the side and waited for her answer as his eyes darted intermittently from the pavement to her and back again.

"The sea," she finally answered with a little-girl smile she'd used too many times to know.

Another silence. The man eyed the oncoming dusk.

"Do you think I could maybe pay you to drive me there?"

"I...uh. Not tonight, I expect."

She waited. He was a guy, and the one thing she understood about guys was that if you gave one a problem he'd offer a solution. Especially since he'd already stopped to help.

"That's a two-hour trip down and another two back," he said quietly.

Silvie set her backpack down and returned to the car for her keys. She slammed the door harder than she'd meant to.

"Look—" he started.

She noticed that he had a habit of pressing the palm of his hand flat against his forehead, which was carved deep with a scar fresh enough to still have color. The outline of his expensive pickup loomed behind him. It was no indication of his status in her mind. She knew plenty of men who had thirty-thousand-dollar trucks and six-thousand-dollar single-wides, most with a vicious blue heeler chained to the front step.

"It's too late to go tonight, and tomorrow I have a sale." He stared off a moment. "Where did the week go? And Wednesday is always busy with cleanup, but I could take you down there on Thursday. You—" He kicked gravel at her pathetic car. "You don't have to pay me."

Thursday?

"There's a motel down in Newberg. You could maybe stay down there for a couple nights."

Silvie was already shaking her head. She'd left home with nine hundred dollars and had already burned through nearly a hundred in gas and food. After paying too much for a room at the Motel 6 in Boise, she vowed she'd sleep in her car until she found a place to stay. That money was all she had.

"I'll just—" She glanced at her car. She could leave most of her things behind. "I'll just take what I can carry and hitchhike."

"That's not safe," he blurted.

"Well, I can't really afford a motel."

"It's not the best solution, but—" He drew a breath as if already regretting his next words.

Silvie felt like a burden, and he hadn't even made the offer yet.

"There's a small apartment on the second floor of my sale barn. It's not really a barn," he added quickly. "We just call it that. It's more like a—" He seemed to search for the right word, pausing to stare down at the road too long. "A warehouse." The declaration was abrupt, awkward, and laced with an odd sense of victory. "You could stay there for a couple days." He looked at her apprehensively. "It's not…well, it's a bit of a mess. No one's actually lived there for a long time. But it has a foldout sofa and a bathroom with a shower."

Silvie fought the urge to say no. It had been drilled into her never to accept a gift the first time it's offered. Her mother's way of imagining they were humble, though the family routinely trawled for handouts. She studied the man's face. She guessed that he wouldn't offer a second time.

"That's really nice of you," she finally said.

"Don't say that until you've seen the place." He laughed. "I'll get a rope and we'll tow your car up there. It's just a couple miles. You don't want anyone to break into it during the night. And they will if it's sitting here on the road."

"Thanks."

He shrugged and turned toward his truck.

"I'm Silvie," she said to his back.

"Hershel. Hershel Swift."

3

Hershel reclined against the cold sofa in the soft shroud of darkness that encompassed his living room. The outline of his breakfast dishes loomed near his head on the end table. He gazed up at the ceiling, thinking about the girl he'd left at the auction barn. Pretty. Young. Twenty-four, twenty-five maybe? He knew she was lying about Montana. She'd answered the question too quickly, and the first story matched the plates on her car. *God, she was young.*

He pressed his hands against both temples, trying to push back the ever-present pain in his head. Why had he stopped to help her in the first place? That was the question he grappled with now. Before he'd realized what he was doing, he'd already pulled off the road. It wasn't until he'd gotten out of his truck that he figured he was into something he didn't want. He didn't believe he would have stopped before... before the accident. Hershel pressed his fingers in harder, making his vision go dark as he went back over his conversation with the girl. No, he was sure he wouldn't have.

What was her name again? Silvie? Is that what she said her name was? He guessed he might have stopped after all. But he wouldn't have left an attractive young thing like that alone in the apartment down at the sale barn. He'd have brought her home, made her a cheese sandwich or whatever he had in the kitchen, and then fucked her brains out. Hershel was a good-looking man—tall, with a full head of wavy dark hair and black, black eyes. A gift from his Nez Percé grandfather on his mother's side. Women had fawned over him from the time he was in junior high, and no matter how little effort he put into his relationships there were always plenty more waiting.

Hershel got to his feet. The pain in his head surged forward, trying to get out through the scar along his hairline. He paused to give it time to recede again. He didn't find the idea of fucking her brains out repulsive—in fact, quite the opposite. It was the idea that he wouldn't be able to sustain himself, or that the pain in his head would cause him to black out and crush her. Otherwise, he would have taken advantage. Instinct told him so. Was that who he really was at heart? Or who he had been? There were moments— palpitating moments—when he felt certain he'd lost who he was in the accident.

He clicked on the furnace and cool air blew dust through the vents. After a moment it warmed and he adjusted the digital display to sixty-eight degrees. Then he went to the kitchen, opened a bottle of painkillers, and swallowed two pills before making himself the sandwich he might have offered the girl. If he thought it would get him into her pants.

———

Silvie nosed around the dingy single-room apartment, looking for a heater. She found nothing. The place smelled of dust and mushrooms. She was coming to associate that rich organic aroma of rotting plants and dampness with Oregon. She peered into the dirty sink in the kitchenette, then ran water into it, creating muddy streaks. She opened the cupboard above the cracked brown counter and found a single coffee cup. She turned a circle where she stood and took in the whole of the tiny room. An orange plaid sofa that folded out into a bed, without sheets or blankets. In the corner stood a console television from the seventies. A small green dinette set was shoved up against the opposite wall, next to the bathroom door.

She'd been so worried that her Good Samaritan would turn out to be a rapist once they were alone in this place that she'd refused his offer to show her where things were, or to get her something to eat, or even to help her bring some of her things in. He couldn't remember which key opened the door to the building. She'd stood there as rain began to soak into her jacket, watching him fumble with the lock, cycling through a half-dozen keys—all very distinct in shape and color—until he finally found the right one. This can't be his building, she'd thought. But before she could get her wits about her and come up with a reason to leave, he'd opened the door and was leading her inside. She'd calmed herself by reconciling the name across the front of the building with the name he'd given her on the highway. SWIFT CONSIGNMENT AUCTION. Hershel Swift. But then anyone can pretend to be someone else.

She went to the only window in the apartment, a small one in the bathroom, and peered down at her car. A utility light cast a grainy yellow hue across the gravel lot, but the car was sheltered and out of view from the highway. The building sat alone on the road and was enveloped by a large filbert orchard on three sides. When she'd first seen the trees arching into rows of perfectly spaced tunnels, she'd marveled at its vastness: a virtual ocean of trees. It seemed to go on for miles. Now, in the dark, the place felt like the very edge of the world. What lay beyond it? How far was the next house from here? Could someone slip through the trees below and get to her? Would anyone hear her if she screamed?

The rain had dampened her clothes and she wanted the blanket in her car, but what might lurk in that orchard worried her too much for her to go after it. She returned to the sofa, where she pulled her legs up under her and wrapped her coat tightly around her shoulders, shivering.

After an hour or so, she got up to warm herself by walking around the room. Her toes felt nearly numb and her limbs were stiff. She checked the lock on the door again, chewing her lower lip at the thought of how easy it would be for someone to break in. So she shoved the dinette against it, imagining that it would give her time to find a weapon, or squeeze through the bathroom window. She thought of the two-story drop and the gravel below.

Her stomach rumbled with hunger and she dug through her backpack, coming up with a half-eaten Hershey's bar that had melted and re-formed as an indistinct brown slab shot through with creases and bubbles. She ate it slowly, making it last. She tried to get a channel on the old television, but nothing tuned in. She finally settled for the company of shadowy figures moving through a hazy picture like yetis in a snowstorm.

As she sat in the eerie apartment, her senses tuned to the sounds an intruder might make, rain began to pound down on the metal roof. It reached a deafening roar, and Silvie found that she could no longer hold back the tears that had stalked her all evening.

———

Hershel lay in bed listening to the torrent of rain on the roof and the splashing of the overflowing gutters. He contemplated going to see if she was okay—or even still there. He half expected that she'd packed what she could carry and hit the road as soon as he'd left. She had stared at him as if he were a complete imbecile when he couldn't remember which key opened the door. Then, when he'd offered to help her with her things, she acted as though he were going to attack her. He didn't know what to do, so he just left her there. Alone with no heat or food.

He tried to remember her name. Sandy? Sally? Neither sounded right. Sarah? He got up, stopping short to let the on-slaught of pain subside before going to the kitchen and pouring himself a glass of brandy. Sophie?

He put the glass down on the dining table, a finely polished walnut pedestal table with ball feet that he'd picked up at one of his many antiques sales. He ran his hand across the smooth grain, admiring the burl figuring, but it imparted something uncomfortable. Another lost story. All that remained of its history for him was that he'd paid one hundred dollars for it—a steal. This table, which might fetch a thousand dollars in an antiques store in Lake Oswego, was his to enjoy until he got tired of it and something more interesting came along. He had only to load it into his truck and take it down to the sale barn to dispose of it. He'd make sure he timed it well. Wait until the right crowd and economic circumstances would bring several times the price he'd paid. It was a beautiful prospect.

Hershel pointed at the table. "Dining table," he said quietly. He pointed around the room. "Glass. Newspaper . . . dining table." How could he look at an object and register its value in an instant but, too frequently, not its name? Or the names of half the people who would buy these things from him? He was like an Alzheimer's patient with moments of pristine clarity and stretches of hazy wordlessness.

He shoved aside the newspapers and magazines that littered the table, sending them cascading to the floor, and looked around at the house now littered with yellow notes. He had been a maniacally clean man before the accident, and the messy state of his home was a reminder that he wasn't right. It was a testament to his invalid condition. Besides the visual aids, he needed a housekeeper.

The idea brought back that he'd been married once. It was long ago, and had lasted only a few months. They were both just out of high school. Hershel had only recently attained his auctioneer's license and was working for a man out in Oregon City. The girl he'd married was local, someone he'd known since the seventh grade who had graduated from Sherwood High School the same year he had. Candice was her name. Tiny. Lovely. Homecoming queen. So enamored of Hershel that she would have done anything he asked without question. The marriage ended almost before it got started, though. He slapped her across the cheek when he came home one evening to find their breakfast dishes still in the sink, soaking in cold, gray water. What had she been doing all day?

"If I wanted to pay for a maid," he shouted, "I wouldn't have gotten married." He cringed now at those words. Hershel leaned forward on his elbows, staring down into the gold liquid in the glass. "Stupid bastard," he whispered. He'd revisited that moment at odd times in the intervening years. It was the most pertinent lesson of his life—perhaps the reason it was not lost, as so many others had been. The lesson wasn't that he shouldn't have hit her; he already knew that. It was the one and only time Hershel had ever hit a woman, and his meek little worshipper had found some cord of strength neither of them knew she possessed. Candice had had the good sense to leave him that very night, under the protective watch of her father. The lesson she taught him, though, was never to underestimate anyone. No matter how mild or weak she appeared.

Silvie couldn't stand the cold any longer. It felt as though the dampness had seeped into her bones, putting a freeze over her that she couldn't shake. She rifled through the single kitchen drawer, finding only a fork and a stubby little paring knife too dull even to peel an apple. But it was something. She took it, pulled the dinette away from the door, and peeked down the wooden stairway into the hulking warehouse. She felt along the exposed studs, tangling her fingers in sticky cobwebs and yanking her hand back. Finally, she found the switch for the bulb above the dusty stairs. The snap echoed, and she was certain that she heard someone downstairs. She stood unmoving as seconds passed, listening with every part of her body. But it was still and quiet, save for the continuous patter of rain on the roof. She gripped the tiny knife and stepped watchfully, letting her weight settle against each tread.

In the warehouse below, the cavernous room was packed with

junk—garbage, really. It smelled of dust and grease and stale pop-corn. She'd taken note of the odd assortment of tires and appli-ances, furniture and boxes. It seemed that this place had one of everything, no matter what it was. The path from the stairs to the front door was crooked and littered with strange objects at unpre-dictable intervals. She brushed against things she was afraid to touch, pulling her arms tighter around herself and walking with careful, tiny steps. Too many places for someone to hide, she thought. Near the front door, her foot caught an electric cord, dragging its nameless owner down from its perch with a metallic clatter. Her heart drummed at her throat. Her hands trembled as she fought with the lock, finally throwing the door open and stum-bling out into the parking lot.

She stood in a steady rain, panting, no longer cold.

"Everything okay?"

Silvie shrieked. It was *him*. He was standing beside her car, a black shadow against the filbert trees.

"Hey, I didn't mean to scare you. You okay?" He walked toward her.

She held up the little knife. "Don't come any closer," she shouted, her voice quavering.

He halted. Confusion worked over his face. "I'm not going to hurt you. I just..." He turned toward the orchard, then back to Silvie. "I just worried about you being here without any food or... or anything."

"Where did you come from?" Silvie demanded. "Where's your truck?"

Hershel held up a sizable flashlight, and shined it on a paper bag in his other hand. He cast the beam out across the murky orchard. "I came through there. I live on the other side. It's a shortcut—well, not really a shortcut. It's almost a half mile. But I take it all the time."

"A shortcut?"

"Yeah." He stepped closer, but stopped. "I've frightened you. I'm sorry."

"Or maybe you didn't want anyone to know you're here, that's why you came through the trees," she stuttered.

"See me here? I—" Hershel looked around again, as if there might be some explanation for her behavior written in the darkness. "I own the place."

He took a tentative step forward, holding the bag out to her as if she were a cornered animal. "I brought you a sandwich. I thought you might be hungry. I'll just be going. I didn't mean to scare you. Really."

She squinted at him, knife still poised. "A what?"

"A sand-wich," Hershel repeated. "It's . . . cheese. I think."

Silvie dropped her hand to her side. "I'm such an idiot. I'm sorry. I don't know what I thought. You just scared me. I didn't see you there."

"It's okay." He set the bag on her car and headed toward the orchard, clicking the flashlight on and off as he went.

"Wait," she called after him. "Please."

He turned back, but didn't come any closer.

"You've been so nice, and I've treated you awful. I'm sorry."

"You don't know me. It's okay."

———

Upstairs, Silvie wrapped herself in the blanket she'd dug from her car and sat remorsefully on the sofa, holding the soggy paper lunch bag on her lap.

"He must be wishing he'd never stopped to help me," she muttered.

In the morning, when it was light, she would pull everything out of her car to get to the box, then leave Hershel a thank-you note and head for the coast on foot. But she wouldn't go to Lincoln City. She'd already left a trail. She'd go north, to Astoria, cross into Washington, and head up the Olympic Peninsula. She'd have to risk it hitchhiking. She wouldn't stay here for two more days; she couldn't even imagine facing Hershel in the morning.

She opened the bag and pulled out a cheese sandwich on whole-wheat bread with mustard. She also extracted a Bosc pear and held it to her nose for a long moment, inhaling its sweetness. Pears were her favorite. She peered inside the bag and found at the bottom a small package of candy corn with a black jack-o'-lantern and HAPPY HALLOWEEN printed across the cellophane.

"He gave me candy corn." She held a piece up to the light, as if examining the man who'd brought it.

4

Silvie was awakened by a loud clatter below, and for a brief, panicked moment she couldn't remember where she was. A man shouted something, then the floor beneath her vibrated as the overhead door in the warehouse went up. She flew from the foldout bed into the bathroom, craning to see down to the parking lot below.

She'd overslept. The sun was well up, and two men were unloading some sort of combine or swather from a flatbed truck. A third shouted directions as they placed the hulking piece of green equipment so snugly against the rear of her car that she would never be able to get to the hatchback.

She forced the window open and pressed her face against the dusty screen, ready to shout down to them. Cool, moist air rushed in at her. Sweet with the scent of rotting cedar and mist.

"We'll put the Charger right there," one of the men hollered across the lot. He was stout, with a neatly trimmed beard, and he pointed at the space on the other side of her car. "It's what people will want to get a look at, I expect." He planted himself with a cocky, wide-legged stance and spotted the driver.

Silvie watched as another flatbed backed in. On its platform sat a ruined Dodge Charger. It must have been well cared for at one time—its paint still glossy red, though crumpled and distorted. The tires were intact and new. The roof had caved in and the windows had blown out, leaving ragged chunks of glass along the edges. Clods of dirt and dead grass were lodged into the crevices around the hood and the windshield. No doubt the driver was dead, she thought. The car's broken body seemed frozen in a scream of horror—unable to let go its last terrified breath.

The stout man whistled in amazement. "I'd say Mr. Dickhead is one lucky son of a bitch."

Another man came and stood next to the deformed car. He gazed up at it with a sense of awe.

"He ain't even here to witness its homecoming, the dumb fuck," the stout man commented.

The second man, a skinny, aging hippie with graying hair pulled back in a braid, turned and gave him a withering glare.

"Has he thanked you for taking care of things for him?" the stout man said, and proceeded to loosen the straps that had cinched the car in place. He looked at the hippie, waiting for an answer. "Bet he hasn't even paid you," he said, turning his attention back to his task. "You can't fucking trust him. That ain't changed. Besides, he screwed us both over. That recording unit was exactly what I needed—been looking for one for eight months, and he damn well knew it. Asshole calls Kuykendahl down here to run the price up on me."

"You're still working for him," the hippie pointed out as he collected the cinch straps and rolled them into neat circles for the driver.

The stout man shrugged. "All I'm saying is that he's lucky to be alive, and more than a few people wish he wasn't."

Hershel sipped his coffee and thumbed through the *Oregonian*, not reading it but simply giving his fingers something to do. The

Charger would already be there when he got to the auction barn today. He folded the business section and set it aside for later, then turned the corners back on the classified pages, reminding himself to read through them for prices. He didn't really want to see the car. But it had salvageable parts, and they were worth money. He couldn't let the prospect of making a buck, however small, pass him by. He blew across the surface of his coffee. His business was built on small profits. He would have to set his feelings aside, something he'd long ago become proficient at doing. He just needed to get through tonight, get the car sold, and he could forget about it forever.

Carl had called to find out where he wanted them to put the car. The conversation had sent Hershel on a deeper, but still futile, search of his memory for what sort of man Carl was. The tenor of his voice denoted concern—something Hershel hadn't felt from anyone else. But his only recollections of Carl were mere impressions of the man, like postcard snapshots. A derelict who lacked ambition or purpose. Old enough to be retiring and not a damn thing to show for himself. Hershel kept a folder for each of his employees. Carl's folder included a handwritten note about Campo Rojo, the migrant village tucked along the Tualatin River, far off the road—out of sight of the chartered limos carrying rich wine connoisseurs through the valley. Who would rent a single-room cabin for five dollars a week, including electricity? White people didn't live down there, except for Carl. Hershel didn't begrudge the migrants anything, because they slaved for what they got, but a white man could do better in this place without having to put a lot of effort into it. He guessed Carl had to work at being so destitute, and he had no idea why the man did it. If he'd ever known the reason, it was among those facts—significant and not—that were lost to him now. Hershel returned to his paper, imagining dark-headed Mexican children playing King of the Hill on rickety donated picnic tables and chasing after chickens and stray dogs. Was that a memory or an idea of the migrant camp?

These past weeks Hershel was coming to see that Carl minded the little things, though. When he called that morning, he'd very cautiously said, "The car is here. You want me to put it out back where you won't have to see it? We can get it in and out of here without you having to deal with it... except to sell it."

"Thanks" was all Hershel said. Knowing it was there now only made him think about it. Maybe he did want to see it, after all— stare death in the face one more time. And maybe not. The broken car stood testament to his damaged brain. Just as the car could not be restored, it was likely that neither could his life. He couldn't explain that to Carl. "Out back is fine."

There was a long pause on the phone. Hershel asked, "Was the place locked up when you got down there this morning?"

"Yeah, why?"

Hershel thought of the girl. Susan—that was her name. "I let someone stay in the apartment upstairs last night. I wasn't sure if she was still there."

"Haven't seen anyone." Carl seemed not to know what to say for a moment. "Want me to check on her?"

"No. She might be sleeping."

"Okay."

"If you run into her, her name is Susan."

He turned his attention back to the paper, pausing over the Living section and a story about a young woman who made filbert candies and desserts and sold them at the Portland Farmers' Market. His mother had been fond of filberts, too, but she called them hazelnuts, claiming that only filbert farmers called them filberts. His mother baked, too, but her specialty was cinnamon rolls, which she made every week for the Ladies Sunday School at her Baptist church. The thought of those sweet confections and the way she slathered them with creamy white frosting made him miss her. He hadn't seen his mother in... in... Hershel stared down at his hands. When had he last seen his mother? It wasn't the first time he'd asked that question, but it still surprised him that he didn't know the answer. She lived in Baker City; that he knew. So did his older sister, Rachel. After his father died, his mother had returned to eastern Oregon, where she'd grown up, and Rachel followed her there. But how long ago these things had happened was unclear. He'd had a strong sense of his mother during these past few months, almost as if he'd awoken from the trauma as a twelve-year-old boy.

When he was in the hospital recovering, he'd asked if anyone had called his family. One of the regular attending nurses, a harsh middle-aged woman, went uncharacteristically soft and said, "Yeah, we called them."

He had waited for her to elaborate, the silence gathering around him like thick wads of cotton.

Finally, she said, "They declined to come. I'm sorry."

Silvie peered down the dirty stairway at the patch of cement floor in the warehouse below. She had hoped she might dig the box out of her car, but a steady parade of people wandered past, gawking at the Charger sitting next to it. It would be trouble enough to take everything out with that combine blocking the back, but the last thing she wanted was an audience. Her stomach was rumbling with hunger, and her most pressing concern now was searching for something to eat. She'd watched for Hershel, hoping to thank him and apologize once again, but he was nowhere in sight.

With her backpack slung over her shoulder, she bolstered herself for strangers. As she descended the stairs she forced herself to her fullest height, and set her feet down with conviction. Charlie, the bar owner where her mother worked, had once instructed her not to look like a victim.

"Hold your head up," he had said with grave seriousness. It was just after she'd met Jacob, and Charlie was suddenly full of advice, most of which was too late by then. "Make people think you can kick ass, even if you can't."

To Silvie's relief, it was the hippie she encountered in the warehouse and not the other. The other was a familiar sort of man—someone she wanted nothing to do with. The hippie smiled as if he'd been expecting her. He was missing his front teeth, but his face was crisscrossed with laugh lines. His eyes sparkled.

"Good morning. You must be Susan," he said, setting a cardboard box down on top of a dented chest freezer.

"Sorry. My name is Silvie."

His smile broadened. "Leave it to Hershel to get your name wrong."

Silvie smiled, too.

"If you're looking for something to eat, I put some dogs in the cooker a few minutes ago. I'd make popcorn, but I don't know how that contraption works." He picked up the box and started toward the concession stand in the corner of the large room. "But if that's what you want, I can figure it out."

"No thanks. I'm okay."

"Oh, you gotta eat something." He turned and scrutinized her. "Course, you probably want real food. You can get a sandwich at the South Store, and they have some produce at the Berry Barn across the way."

An apple was what she craved. "Where is this place?"

He deposited the box on a stack of others that looked just like it. He pulled a grease marker from his dirty jeans, uncapped it, and scribble "67" on the flap.

"Gotta write the lot number down or I'll forget it," he said, sliding the pen back into his pocket. "The Berry Barn and the South Store are across from each other. 'Bout a quarter mile down the hill. North." He leaned in close and pointed in the direction of the auctioneer's stand. He smelled vaguely of patchouli oil and jalapeños, with an undertone of grimy buildup and unwashed clothes.

Silvie stepped back, but smiled. She entertained the idea of asking him to help her with her car. But it would only lead to questions about where she was headed, and why she was moving in the first place.

"Aren't you staying for the sale?"

She sized up the mountain of used goods all around them. It was odd, she thought, that she'd grown up in a farming community and had never attended an auction. Her father was always picking things up at estate sales—dressers, lawn mowers, used cars. Where others had kept neatly cut lawns, her family had amassed a dense junkyard—at least, that's how it was before the divorce. She could still remember the day she was finally old enough to understand that the school-bus game the kids played at her stop was not so much intended to be fun as to bring attention to the inordinate clutter. Count the Washers one day and Find the Stray Cats the next. Hanley, Wyoming's very own version of Where's Waldo. No one seemed to hold it against Silvie that she lived there, but that didn't change how she felt about it. After her parents' divorce, she and her mom moved into town and lived in the one-bedroom apartment above the old Sew & Vac store, where she relished the modest anonymity.

"I don't know if I'll stay," she said.

A growing number of people meandered through the warehouse, pawing through boxes, turning items under the light in search of defects.

"Oh, you should come," he said.

"I've got more than I can carry now. What would I do with any of this?" She laughed and gestured toward the stuff.

The hippie gazed at her, his eyes soft, his lips turned in a curious smile. "Hershel can use a friend tonight," he said quietly. The grimy man walked into a tiny booth with a Plexiglas window that had a small semicircle pass-through just above the counter.

Silvie didn't know whether to follow him. The conversation didn't feel over, though he'd walked away. Was this man implying that she could thank Hershel by staying?

He returned with a notepad and pen. "He's gonna be a little off tonight. My guess, anyway."

"Why is that?"

"He's selling that Charger." He looked around him and began to jot down the names of items that were in close proximity.

"Did he lose someone in that wreck?" she asked, curious now about her Good Samaritan.

"Could say that. That was the car he was driving the night of his accident." The hippie moved forward through the warehouse a few steps and scribbled down more items. There didn't seem to be any order or logic to what he chose to capture, but more like a random inventory.

"*He* was driving that car when it was wrecked like that?" Silvie realized, too late, that she was gaping at him.

"Probably why he messed up your name." The hippie glanced at her, then back to his page. He sketched out the warehouse and divided it into quadrants, then numbered them.

"That would explain why he couldn't figure out which key opened the door last night."

"He was doing almost eighty when he hit a cow full-on. Spent three weeks in intensive care." He divided the list of items into four brackets and labeled each with its corresponding number on the diagram. The hippie tore the page out and placed it on the auctioneer's podium. "You should stay for the sale," he said. "It'll be fun." Then he wandered away, leaving her alone in the midst of all that junk.

5

Carl had been working for Hershel exactly ten years this month. But Hershel wouldn't remember that, and it had nothing to do with the accident. Though Hershel's brain injury had been cause for Carl to take a hard look at life. The deaths, or near deaths, of friends and acquaintances always made him wonder why he was daily spared. He should have died in a jungle. He should have been dead now more times than he could count, but for some reason he trod on through like some well-armored insect.

Carl hadn't seen a doctor in decades. No need to. He listened to the people around him, especially the ones near his own age, talk about their aches, their blood pressure, their arthritis. It fascinated him, but it also repulsed him. He had abused his body in ways most people would never dream of, yet he rose every morning feeling more or less the same, worked through his day, and fell into bed at night with nothing more urgent or disturbing than a minor case of heartburn. And then only when Yolanda, his neighbor across the common courtyard, made extra-spicy tamales and shared them around Campo Rojo.

He had slowed a bit; *that* he had noticed. He couldn't quite lift the same amount of weight as he once had, but he was limber and hadn't bulked up around the middle like most people his age.

Carl had his eye on an old KitchenAid mixer this evening with Yolanda in mind. He picked it up and carried it to the concession stand. It would probably go for more than he could afford. They'd come back into fashion lately, and the older ones had a fifties sort of charm that made them highly sought after by secondhand dealers. He plugged it in and shifted the lever on the side. It spun the whisk attachment smoothly, so he turned it up to the highest setting, listening to it whir. It was built to last—a real workhorse for a serious cook.

Yolanda had been at Campo Rojo almost as long as he had, and longer than any of the other migrant workers. She'd become like a den mother, taking care of the entire village in addition to her own two boys, who were not actually boys but fully grown men. On Sunday afternoons, she whipped up Mexican wedding cakes, little round cookies smothered in powdered sugar, among other treats. She mixed everything by hand, though, and complained about bursitis in her shoulder. Carl had been delighted to find this mixer on the floor when he came in this morning, lying in the doorway on its side. He turned it off and pulled the plug, examined the cord for fraying. Satisfied, he placed it behind a chest of drawers at the back of the sale floor. He'd wait until the crowd was thin and the dealers had checked out, then bring it out for Hershel to sell. Most bidders wouldn't get back in line for the cashier after they'd paid their bill unless the item was particularly choice—the KitchenAid was missing its bowl.

Carl wondered if he'd persuaded the girl to stay for the sale. He'd never known Hershel to offer a kind hand to anyone, and Carl thought it was odd that he'd not only assisted her with her broken-down car but offered a place to stay. He hoped she'd be back. But then maybe she had a low tolerance for auctions. Lots of people were like that—a character flaw, in Carl's opinion. That anyone would buy new when the world was chock-full of perfectly good, inexpensive necessities was an affront to Mother Nature. A raping of natural resources. A shortsighted, selfish act.

Hershel took the muddy shortcut through the filbert orchard at three o'clock, getting himself mentally ready for the evening auction. He'd decided to walk through the sale barn and memorize the names of items that he wanted to sell while the crowd was good, rather than leaving it up to his floor men to randomly pull merchandise from the nearest heap. He could maximize his commission on the premium items if there was more competition for them. He also suspected that his employees hid some of the best stuff until the end, then picked it up for a fraction of what it could have brought. He'd taken to running up the price with a fictitious bidder, which sometimes forced him to buy the item and resell it later.

Hershel paused mid-stride to think about that. It was a common practice in the business—shill bidding, they called it. But also one that could get an auctioneer boycotted if he did it too often, or poorly enough that the bidders caught on and realized they'd never get a bargain on anything at his sales. And auction-goers were hopeless bargain hunters.

The fall air and the chilly temperature gave him energy as he trudged along under the low canopy of tree branches. The filberts had already ripened and fallen to the ground. Steve Thompson, the farmer who leased the orchard from Hershel, had sucked up the nuts with his giant vacuum-like machine, separated them from the leaves and debris, and moved them to his drying plant in McMinnville to ready them for sale during the holiday season. Thompson took good care of the trees he leased, as if they were his own. Still, Hershel ran his hands along the bark as he went, poking around for signs of blight. It was an old orchard, nearly thirty years. It wouldn't produce like this for much longer, and then it would need to be replanted. Soon enough Hershel would have to make the decision between replanting filberts and moving into the newer crops of wine grapes that were rapidly transforming the landscape of the Willamette Valley. He loved the glorious yellow display of those hillside vineyards in the fall before the leaves fell. They were much prettier than filberts, which weren't especially showy. The clean lines of the vineyards brought an orderliness to the valley that he enjoyed. He didn't imagine he'd go in that direction, though. Not because pinot noir didn't interest him but because the filberts provided a wide berth of privacy between his house and Scholls Ferry Road that grapevines would not.

He thought of the girl as he neared the sale barn. "Sophie," he reminded himself. He should have checked on her earlier, but he doubted that she was even still there. She didn't need him, and she wasn't his responsibility. She was a big girl, traveling solo.

At the edge of the orchard, Hershel walked out of the trees and into the gravel parking lot. At the sight of the Charger, the air rushed from his lungs as if he'd been slugged hard in the gut. He'd forgotten about it. There it sat, like a wadded-up piece of bright, glossy paper. Hershel flexed his hands. The feeling had momentarily left his body, yet his forehead throbbed.

"Floyd," he growled to the wreck. "You look like hell."

Hershel pressed his palm against the painful scar at his forehead, feeling betrayed for the second time by the car he'd saved from the wrecking yard. This hunk of metal harbored the secrets of that night forever lost to him. For all Carl's efforts to spare him, Hershel had forgotten and stumbled right onto it. He shoved his shaking hands into his pockets and strode past like a man with a million important things to do.

"Hey, boss," Carl called from across the warehouse as Hershel entered the building.

Hershel waved, then ducked into the cashier's booth and slumped down in the chair, still struggling to get his bearings. Trying to let go the image of Floyd's spidered windshield, wondering if his own head had made it so.

A dozen people wandered around the warehouse, looking things over in anticipation of the sale. Hershel always opened his doors at noon on Tuesdays to give bidders a chance to preview the offerings. The more time they had to think about any particular item, the more likely they were to convince themselves that they couldn't live without it. Through the Plexiglas window where people collected their numbers and paid their bills, Hershel listened to a pair of farmers talking about the combine.

A tall, familiar-looking man wearing coveralls and a John Deere hat approached them. "You get a look at that Charger out there?"

The two nodded a greeting, as if they all knew one another. "Yep," the slighter of the two replied. "Belongs in the U-Pull-It, you ask me."

"My son wants it," the other said. "Thinks he can restore it."

The second man laughed. "Yeah, with a new body, a new rear end, a new transmission, and probably a new engine, he might be able to make it roadworthy again."

All three laughed.

"I suspect he wants it for its legend. The two tons of metal that tangled with Swift, and who comes out on top?" He shook his head and whistled.

"I can't believe that bastard survived," the third man said. He lifted a grease-stained ball cap off his head, ran his fingers through his thinning hair, and replaced the hat.

"Tougher than any goat I know. Hardheaded and mean," the familiar man scoffed. "People like that are hard to die off."

Hershel waited for them to laugh again, but there were grunts of agreement all around and then silence.

Hershel listened, amazed by the contempt people carried for him. He didn't feel as mean as a goat. In fact, he felt downright charitable. He thought again about Sophie and got to his feet. He should check on her. But he had to wait for the throb in his head to recede before he walked out into the warehouse and past the three men. They nodded at him as he passed, looking slightly ashamed. Hershel didn't make eye contact or acknowledge them. "*Fuckers,*" he muttered when he was far enough away.

He found Carl and helped him push a dusty riding lawn mower out into the aisle for another man to inspect.

"That gal Silvie left a little while ago," Carl said. "She wasn't interested in the dogs I threw in the cooker."

"Silvie?"

"I think that's what she said, boss. Said her name was Silvie."

"That's right, Silvie. She coming back?"

Carl shrugged. "I invited her to stay for the sale."

Hershel wanted to ask Carl about the comments he'd overheard, not just today but last week between Linda and Stuart and others. He pressed his hand idly to his forehead.

"You okay, boss?"

Hershel jerked his hand away. "Yeah. Fine." He busied himself straightening boxes and picking through items, looking for treasures to sell early in the night. He stepped up to the lectern, looking for a pen and some paper, but found that someone had already listed the best items for him. He turned to Carl, who had followed him but turned away when he saw the page.

Carl said in a low voice, "I put that Glock on your desk in the back office. I see you didn't have it in the ad this week."

Hershel vainly searched his spotty memory. He stared at Carl as if seeing him for the first time. "What Glock?"

"Came in right before your—" Carl lifted a shoulder in a half shrug, as if that filled in the missing words. He scribbled numbers on boxes, making himself too busy to look at his employer.

"Thanks," Hershel said.

He stood outside the office door at the rear of the building and fumbled with his wad of keys, looking for the right one. Irritated, he studied them. He needed to spend an afternoon identifying and labeling each key. The sixth key fit the lock and snapped the latch open. He glanced over his shoulder, but Carl was nowhere in sight, and the men browsing the floor were too busy picking through the sale merchandise to pay attention to him.

Just as Carl had said, the gun lay in the middle of Hershel's wide oak desk. Hershel picked it up and inspected it. It wasn't in top condition. The metal was pocked and dull; it had seen some hard use. But that didn't matter. It would bring a nice price, and Hershel knew it. Out of the haze of his past life, the ritual connected to this and many other firearms came back to him. He stared down at the cold gray steel of the German pistol and finally remembered something. Carl had scanned the ad in the *Hillsboro Argus,* and the conspicuously missing reference to such an easy-to-sell weapon served as his instructions to leave it on Hershel's desk.

He'd been selling guns through his auctions since he opened his doors. Though he couldn't recall their names or faces, his sales drew a wide network of buyers. Hershel would collect his commission and pay the consigner with a single check and a vague receipt that failed to specifically list the gun. This gun would have to be part of a larger lot that included the mundane articles of daily life. Furniture, farm equipment perhaps, tools, whatever. And because Hershel hadn't advertised this gun the buyers would understand that he had no intention of filing the paperwork stating that it had been sold through his business. If it was ever traced, it would be traced back to the consigner, not to the buyer. And, if questioned, Hershel would shrug and state that a lot of things came through his auction business. But if there was no paperwork on a Glock, a Glock had never been here. He kept deliberately careful records of other items, antiques and appliances, and especially the guns he advertised. His business was credible in all the ways it needed to be. If a single gun was consigned, or a group of guns without the usual junk that accompanied them, he advertised them in the paper and publicly notified bidders that he would file the paperwork. No official could look through Hershel's records and prove dishonesty. He had followed the letter of the law enough times to make sure of it.

He laid the gun down in the mess of papers that had accumulated over the months. Carl was the only one with a key to the office; Hershel realized that he trusted his hippie employee that much. Carl collected the mail, sorted the financial stuff out for the accountant, and stacked the remainder here in this chilly, dim room. Carl, it seemed now, was like a loyal servant caretaking business as Hershel struggled first to survive, then to regain some recognition of his own life. It was Carl who had given him the forecasted tonnage for the filbert crop that year. Carl was the one who had reported the number of delinquent units at the mini-storage Hershel owned over in Sherwood. Hershel picked up the diagram of merchandise he'd found on the auctioneer's lectern. The backward-slanted script familiar. It was Carl who had gone out to Hershel's house to check the locks, cut the grass, pick up the newspapers. And paste notes to the refrigerator with simple information like garbage day. He let the paper float back to his desk.

The gun, however, had snapped a more significant puzzle piece into place, and it left Hershel with a new and uneasy sense about himself. He lifted the piece again, let it settle into his palm, snug and comfortable. An icy pall had settled over the dusty room like a specter. On its surface, the practice was simple enough. Not harmless, but also not the worst thing a man in his line of work could be involved in. An uncomfortable indication of his character at worst. But the gun put a bad taste in Hershel's mouth, an ominous clue, just beyond his reach, to the night he could not remember.

6

Silvie sat at a tavern table in the old South Store, running her toe up the barley-twist leg and staring out at the Berry Barn across the road. The two buildings had charmed her. The Berry Barn truly was a barn as advertised, surrounded by neat rows of berry canes now devoid of foliage, carefully labeled with hand-painted signs: BLACKBERRIES, RASPBERRIES, MARIONBERRIES, and the like. Painted red on the outside, the building had had its interior gutted, leaving only the worn wood floor and weathered walls. Instead of animal stalls there were shelves of gourmet jams, jellies, candied nuts, and regional sauces on one side; a potpourri of soaps and lotions on the other. The soft but pervasive smell of lavender greeted visitors. In the back stood a deli case with exotic cheeses made from sheep's or yak's milk, with herbs folded in. Silvie had stood on the front porch admiring the superb produce until she saw the prices. Inside, she made a quick meander through, feeling as though she didn't belong. She couldn't fathom having the means to pay twelve dollars for a three-ounce bottle of sweet pepper sauce.

She decided to try the South Store, on the other side of Scholls Ferry, but spent an eternity standing on the shoulder as BMWs, Acuras, and luxury SUVs raced down the hill, tailing one another impatiently. The average speed on Scholls Ferry seemed well over sixty, despite its tightly curving topography. Hillsboro Highway, which came in from the west, ended at the South Store, further complicating her crossing. During a pause in traffic on Scholls Ferry, Silvie had stepped out and nearly been run down as a driver darted out from behind the stop sign. It didn't seem that he had even noticed her as he sped off. Silvie moved up the road to stand directly across from the next car, where she could make eye contact with the driver. Then she tore across at the first lull. When she reached the store, her heart was racing double time and her breath was short.

She stood outside the South Store, peering through the window. The building reminded her of an old photo of the Hanley Hotel, with its tall, narrow structure and white clapboard siding. The front doors sat so close to the road that any of the drivers she'd just encountered could easily take out a patron or two. But the interior looked warm, with yellow walls and a buttery pine floor. She entered to the welcoming smell of roasted coffee beans and pastries. It enveloped her, and she wanted to sit down and never leave. As she gazed out the large front windows onto Scholls Ferry, she realized that the entire building was askew. The door frame was so far off true, a minor quake would bring the second floor down on her head.

A robust woman wearing a flour-sack skirt set a menu and a glass of water down in front of Silvie and smiled. "You must be thirsty after that run."

"Did you know that your building is crooked?" Silvie asked, pointing at the front door.

The woman nodded and joined Silvie in admiring the tilted structure. "It's a great building, but I had a hell of a time getting the county to grant me a business permit. I finally just sweet-talked the inspector with a lot of double-caramel lattes and grilled cheese sandwiches. He lives around the corner and comes in on his way to work."

"Doesn't it worry you?"

She shrugged. "Not as much as Mount St. Helens or Mount Hood deciding to erupt and bury us in ash."

Silvie ordered a sandwich, and the woman ducked back into the kitchen for a moment. Silvie looked around at the empty dining room. It didn't seem as though the locals frequented this place. When the woman came back Silvie asked her, "Have you ever been to the auction here?"

The woman leaned against the table behind her and adjusted her ponytail. She had soft laugh lines around her eyes, and her hair was a deep chestnut with a sprinkling of gray. "I'm not from Scholls. I bought this place a few months ago, after coming out to the valley with friends on a wine-tasting tour. I just fell in love with it. The building, the valley, everything. That auction was closed until last week."

"So you don't know the guy who owns it?"

The woman shook her head, then added vaguely, "Heard he's kind of a jerk. But I've never met him personally." She shrugged, as if that was all she wanted to say about it. "Where are you from?"

"Wyoming," Silvie said, realizing that she ought to have lied, but it was too late. And glancing around the empty diner she began to wonder if this place was obscure enough that she might be able to hide out until she had a better plan.

The woman went back to the kitchen and returned with Silvie's sandwich, presenting it to her with a flourish. Silvie admired the heaping Reuben, with its huge dill-pickle wedge—a luxury she knew she couldn't afford. The woman caught her look but didn't pry, taking a damp rag from the counter, which she used to wipe crumbs from the tables around Silvie.

"Is business slow?" Silvie asked. She hadn't realized how starved for company she'd become.

"Always is on weekdays. Stop in Friday night. We've got the Chehalem Shockwave playing. It's a Spanish guitar trio—no idea about that name other than they all live in the area. Then Saturday and Sunday we get the wine tasters. I do a good business for breakfast and lunch. It's downright hopping this time of year."

Silvie considered the place again, trying to imagine it filled with people. It made her a little homesick for Hanley. She and her high school friend Laree spent lots of weekends at Rick's Red Pies, the local pizzeria. Rick was relaxed about the drinking age there, and most of the high school kids, whom he knew by name, had had their first beer at his restaurant before they'd attended their junior prom. He metered it out carefully, though, and no one went home falling down drunk, but she'd caught a buzz there plenty of times.

"You just move here?"

"Uh...yeah. Well, I'm on my way through. Just stopped for a few days."

The woman glanced up, compelling Silvie to elaborate.

"I haven't decided, I guess. I might stay around the area awhile."

"Ever wait tables?"

Was this woman offering her a job or looking for someone to commiserate with? "Well, not tables exactly. But I was a carhop at A&W for three years while I was in high school."

"With skates?" The woman's eyes sparkled and she seemed to delight in that idea.

"No. The asphalt was cracked and torn up." Silvie smiled. "The whole place was kind of a dump, actually."

"Well, I could use a waitress for the lunch shift on Fridays and Saturdays if you might be interested. It could work into more hours if you were a good fit."

"How do you know I'm looking for a job?"

"You got that look about you, hon. Like you could use something reliable. I could use some help. Just thought it might be something you'd be interested in."

"I'll keep it in mind." Silvie nodded as she finished half the sandwich and wrapped the other half in the waxed paper it had been served on. She slipped it into her backpack while suffering the urge to take the job on the spot. She'd spent enough time looking for work in her life to know that it wasn't always available when she needed it. She'd once believed she would go on to college and study veterinary medicine, but Jacob wouldn't hear of her leaving Hanley. She'd floated between poor-paying jobs where she could find them but mostly lived on the money he gave her.

Hiding here for a while appealed to her. And she contemplated the idea that if someone could track her here they could track her to Lincoln City or Coos Bay or San Francisco. Perhaps this was, in its way, a good place. Off the beaten track. She studied the crooked windows at the front of the building and the way the floor sloped to the left. She ran her fingers over the worn walnut table-top and noted that it didn't match the others. Along the far wall was a long church pew with three oak tables shoved together to accommodate a large group. Mediocre oil paintings of historic buildings, slightly off in perspective, were carefully spaced along the walls, white price tags in the lower left corner of each canvas. Probably a local artist, a friend of the proprietor's. It was such a small-town thing to do, Silvie thought.

"How soon do you need someone?" she asked.

The woman smiled warmly, as if she'd found her new employee. "Friday at the latest."

This is crazy, she told herself. "I've been thinking about staying a couple of days anyway. I'll stop back if I decide to make it longer."

"What's your name?"

"Silvie." She thought again that she ought to have given a dif-ferent name. How many Silvies were running around in the world? She wasn't very good at hiding. She would need to get a lot better if she was going to survive.

"I'm Karen Gibbs. Consider it. I know it doesn't look like much now, but it's a fun place on the weekend."

———

Hershel's ringing cellphone startled him. He'd begun to wonder why he had one, because no one ever called it. He looked at the name: Kyrellis. Familiar, as so many things were, but not remem-bered.

"Swift," he said, picking up his keys and starting for the office door.

"This is Kyrellis," a man said. His voice was smooth and deep, but that did nothing to put the name in context for Hershel. "You're selling that Charger."

"Yeah."

"I guess that's one way to dispose of it."

"How can I help you?"

"Hope you're also planning to part with that Glock tonight. Expected to hear from you last week."

A hot prickle skated across Hershel's arms. He twisted and looked at the pistol sitting benignly on his desk. A gun dealer; Kyrellis was a gun dealer.

"Haven't decided," he said. "Might put it through the sale."

"What's the problem? I've got a guy who wants it."

"Maybe," he said, stalling for time. "We'll see how the crowd looks."

"You want a bigger cut or something?"

Hershel's head pounded. He was taking kickbacks.

"You're not exactly in a position to demand that, now are you, Swift?"

"I said maybe." And he hung up.

He returned to his desk and picked up the gun again. His life seemed to belong to someone else. Who was this man who ran up bids, provided untraceable firearms to God knows what kind of people? Whoever he was, he was out of his league.

———

Silvie sat alone in the upstairs apartment, listening to the din of Hershel's auctioneering below. She'd returned to a packed auction house and a line of people winding out the door, into the cool rain, waiting to sign in and get their bidding numbers. The hippie was busy helping people preview merchandise. The room was lit up like a football stadium, with enormous fluorescent lights that cast an unforgiving scrutiny over the assembly of junk and bidders. Small groups stood around, snatches of their conversations coming at her like sound bites.

"Joe's after that set of tires for his truck."

"Cold snap coming. You get your water turned off?"

"Hazelnuts were good this year. Better than expected."

Silvie drifted through, listening, but keeping a keen eye out for anyone who might be looking for her. She'd always be glancing over her shoulder. The reality of that was setting in like an infection, and crowded places were the worst.

Smokers stood in the doorway near the back of the building, where a small awning provided a stingy shelter. Good-natured swearing seasoned the myriad discussions swirling around her.

The smell of fresh buttered popcorn gave the whole place a carnival atmosphere as the stands filled. Two middle-aged women in the front row squabbled over a seat that each claimed was hers and always had been.

"Out of the way!" The stout man she'd seen in the parking lot that morning came through the narrow aisle lugging an ornately tooled western saddle. He leered at her on his way by.

She slipped upstairs and locked the apartment door behind her. There was nothing Hershel would sell that could interest her, even if she could take it with her.

As she sat alone on the sofa, the warmth of the sandwich shop and the woman she'd met there waned into nothingness. She was homesick for her mom's tiny apartment. She could be making plans to drive into Casper with Laree right now. Silvie unlaced her shoes and tossed them into the corner, then dug through her backpack in search of a second pair of socks to put on. She wished that she had never found the box that was now snuggly tucked into the floorboards of her Volkswagen Rabbit. Failing to find a second pair of socks, she shoved the backpack into the crook of the sofa and used it as a pillow.

She considered how she'd gotten here. It had happened so fast. She hadn't paused to think it through. She'd been looking for cash while her boyfriend—if she could call him that—showered. He sometimes kept hundred-dollar bills in his underwear drawer, and on a few well-spaced occasions she'd taken a single bill out of the roll.

Silvie pulled the blanket over her, knowing it was too early to sleep. The irony was that she didn't need the money that badly not this time, anyway. And he'd have given her the cash if she'd asked for it. That night he'd brought flowers. Some nights he took her to dinner. There were other occasions when he bought her new clothes or paid her mother's electric bill when the power company threatened to shut the service off. There were many things about Jacob that were likable. He could be a very generous man.

The rhythmic flow of Hershel's auctioneering lulled her. She closed her eyes, trying to imagine that she was still in Wyoming. The cadence of Hershel's song, which was punctuated by the whoop of bidding, was an unfamiliar barrier between this place and her home. Silvie sat up again and stared at the snowy television, present like a quiet cat. She'd thought the same thing of her mother not more than a week ago. A woman hiding in the shadows, never drawing attention. Silvie thought she should call, but her mother couldn't be trusted with the knowledge that she was safe, let alone somewhere in Oregon.

———

"Bring up that Fostoria crystal, boys. Let's get that sold."

Stuart cursed audibly as he squeezed down narrow passageways to find the requested stemware.

But Hershel hadn't seen the KitchenAid mixer and didn't call it out from its hiding place behind the refrigerator, and Carl was able to pick it up for five dollars late in the evening. It was when Hershel started auctioning off the vehicles that his concentration faltered. He stumbled with the combine, pausing three times and waiting for someone on the floor to holler out the last bid.

"We've got twelve hundred from bidder three ninety-eight, now," Carl sang. He glanced at Stuart, whose face had gone hard, the blood coming up in his cheeks.

"Stupid fucker," Stuart mouthed to Henry, the plumber. Henry just shrugged and rolled his eyes.

But the Charger was almost a non-sale for the number of times Hershel started over. Carl watched as the poor man shook his head and stared down at the microphone, apologizing twice and beginning again. His hands trembled, and silent tension rippled through the crowd as bidders waited with expressions of disgust and frustration. At last he sold it to Kyrellis for a mere two hundred dollars—almost what he'd paid to have it towed up here from Newberg. Carl moved rapidly on to the Volkswagen Rabbit, calling out to the crowd the details that Hershel would normally provide.

"It's locked, but no one has the key. We don't think it runs. As is, folks," he shouted. "But, then, so are they all." He smiled broadly at the crowd.

As Hershel started the bidding on the Rabbit, stumbling from fifty dollars to seventy-five, Carl eyed Kyrellis. Why would a gun dealer buy a wrecked Charger? He'd rarely known the man to buy anything but firearms, except for one antique mahogany bureau six or seven years back and a few other small odds and ends Carl could probably count on one hand. His purchases had been primarily guns in the ten years that Carl had worked at the auction. So it surprised him even more that Kyrellis picked up the Rabbit, too, for a hundred dollars.

———

Hershel stumbled through the filbert orchard toward home, his flashlight cutting a sharp yellow path ahead of him. The rain had stopped and the moon shone down now, but he took no notice.

His mind wasn't on the trees, or the mud that oozed beneath his feet, or the starlit sky above. He went back through the night, reliving the sale of the Charger and the embarrassment of forgetting his place. He didn't care if people forgave him this because of the trauma he had suffered, though seeing their faces he didn't believe that was the case. He could never forgive himself such a grotesque show of ineptitude.

Inside his century-old farmhouse, he went immediately to the kitchen and poured himself a brandy without removing his coat. He slumped against the counter and sipped the liquid.

You're so fucked up, Hershel, he said to himself. You're like a child. A pathetic little boy. Incapable of doing a man's work. You're worthless.

He swallowed the whole of the glass and poured another. "You shouldn't have lived," he said quietly.

7

"Where is my car?"

Carl flinched as Silvie rushed past him, nearly knocking him over. He'd forgotten that she was staying in the apartment. He hadn't seen her at the sale. Carl lugged one end of a sofa-sleeper out of the warehouse to a waiting pickup truck. The man on the other end grunted under the strain of it. He was younger than Carl, by ten years at least. "Hold on," he called to her. "Let me get this gentleman taken care of and I'll be right with you."

"Where is it?" she shrieked, rushing out into the parking lot.

He found her turning circles in the gravel lot where the Charger had been.

"It's gone," she cried. Her cheeks were flushed, and Carl could see the telltale signs of tears coming. He braced against them. "What have they done with it?"

"What car?" he asked.

"Rabbit. It's gone."

"The little green one?"

"Yes!" She looked hopeful. "Yes, the green one."

"We sold it. Last night."

"*You what?*" She stepped toward him as if she might punch him. "You have to get it back! It has everything—*everything* in it."

"Okay," he said, patting the air between them as if that might calm her. "It's just a mistake. I'm sure we can fix it."

She seemed unable to stop her tears now, sniffing hard. "I have to get it back," she said with her face tipped skyward, as if speaking to God himself. "Oh, please *please please* get it back."

Carl put a hand on her shoulder and guided her back into the building and to the door of Hershel's office. As he unlocked it, he thought of the Glock. Hershel had been so distracted with the sale of the Charger that Carl doubted he'd done anything with the gun. "Wait right here," he told Silvie. Inside, he found the gun exactly where he'd left it and slipped it into the top desk drawer, then went back for her. "You just wait here while I call Hershel. He'll get this straightened out."

"How could he sell it when it wasn't his?" She ignored Carl's instructions and sat down across from him in Hershel's office, her brows pressed together.

"We have twenty-four hours to convey title." Carl picked up the desk phone and punched in Hershel's home number, keeping a wary eye on the girl. "That means whoever bought it will be back today."

She nodded, sinking her teeth into her lip and staring at the floor.

"Boss, it's Carl," he said. "We have a situation down here. That green Rabbit we sold last night—"

The receiver was loud enough for Hershel's disembodied voice to carry into the office. "I didn't sell that Rabbit. It belongs to Sophie."

"Silvie."

"Yeah, yeah. Silvie."

"Uh...actually, we did sell it." Carl waited for Hershel's response, going back through the sequence of events and realizing it was his own mistake—he'd put the Rabbit up as Hershel struggled to get his bearings. "Boss?"

"Shit."

"I'll look up the buyer," Carl said. "You maybe wanna come down here and let Silvie know that we're gonna get her car back. She's pretty upset."

"Fuck!" Hershel said.

"Boss?"

"I'll be there in ten minutes. Get the buyer's name and phone number for me." Hershel hung up before Carl could respond.

"He's on his way," Carl said to Silvie. "He'll get this straightened out. Don't you worry."

She lurched forward out of her chair. "Oh God, please get my car back. You have no idea how important this is."

To Carl, that seemed like the truest statement ever spoken.

Silvie shivered as she waited in Hershel's office. She rocked out of nervousness, telling herself the car would be returned. She pictured strangers digging through her things, finding the box and spreading its contents across the hood. There was no way to know what they would do with their find. They could keep the car, she didn't care, but the box... She closed her eyes, tears slipping through the lids and blazing down her cheeks. "Oh God, please," she repeated.

Hershel came into the office, flinging the door so wide it banged against the wall. "How did this happen?" he asked Carl, who followed close on his heels.

"I... well, you were..." Carl's voice trailed off as he regrouped. "It was my fault. You seemed a little off after selling the Charger. I put the Rabbit up to keep the sale moving. It was in the lot. I assumed—" He handed Hershel a piece of paper. "Kyrellis. Here's his number."

"Kyrellis what?" Hershel glared at Carl.

"Kyrellis bought the car." Carl blinked several times, but kept his gaze on Hershel. "Bought the Charger, too."

Hershel took the note. He stared down at the number as if confused. Finally he glanced up. "Are you sure?"

Carl nodded.

Hershel turned to Silvie with an apologetic expression. "I'm really sorry about this," he said. "We'll get it back."

"Oh God, you have to," she said. "You have to."

"If we can't get it back, I'll pay you for it. I'm—"

"No! You don't understand. I need to get it back. You *have* to get it back."

Hershel eyed her, then picked up the phone and dialed the number. After what seemed ages, he spoke to leave a message. "Kyrellis, this is Swift. There seems to have been a mistake last night. My floor man—" He turned to Carl, who stared down at his worn leather boots. "My floor man put up a car that wasn't for sale. The little green Rabbit you bought . . . we need it back. It belongs to someone else. Wasn't for sale. Call my cell so we can arrange to come get it."

She stared at him through tears, his image a dancing blur. He handed her a neatly folded handkerchief from his jeans pocket. It smelled faintly of bleach, and she held it against her face a long time, letting it soak up her tears.

Carl disappeared out the door.

"I'm sorry about this," Hershel said again. "Why don't you let me buy you breakfast? There's nothing we can do but wait for him to call back, anyway."

She opened her mouth in protest, but he put a hand up to stop her.

Something about his gesture reminded her of Jacob. The car had been a gift he never let her forget, as if accepting it had somehow enslaved her for life.

"You can't buy me like that," she snapped.

"Buy you?" Hershel looked confused.

"I'm sorry. You don't know how important it is that I get that car back."

"It doesn't run. Why not let him have it? I can look up the sale price. I won't take a commission. Just let him have it. I'm sure he'll give you your personal belongings back."

"I don't want anyone going through my stuff!"

Hershel sighed heavily. "This is my fault. I was off my game last night. I'm sorry. I don't remember selling your car."

"Carl told me about"—she immediately regretted starting down this path—"the car. The Charger." She looked down at her hands, feeling self-conscious. "It was a bad wreck, huh?"

Hershel nodded and looked out the window, as if to escape the conversation. "Yup. Pretty bad."

They sat in awkward silence for several moments; then the phone rang, startling them both.

Hershel swiped it up in his fist. "Swift." He held it away from his head as the man at the other end shouted.

"I'll reimburse you for your trouble. It was a mistake. C'mon, don't be an ass."

Silvie studied Hershel's face, but he wouldn't look at her.

"Is this because I didn't sell—" Hershel glanced at Silvie, then away. He lowered his voice. "Is this because of that other item you were after last night?" He rubbed his eyes. "Fine. It's yours," he said in a hushed tone. "Just bring the fucking car back." After an extended pause, he set the phone down. "I guess he agreed; he hung up."

Silvie felt no sense of ease at the news. Now she waited with mounting anxiety about whether the angry man on the phone had ransacked her things and gotten his hands on Jacob's box.

"Please, let me buy you something to eat," Hershel said. "To make up for all this. Please."

Silvie shook her head. "How soon do you think he'll bring it?"

"What's in your car that's so important?" he asked.

She looked away.

"I should fire Carl for this."

"He's a nice man," she said. "I don't think you should fire him."

"No, you're probably right."

"Has he worked for you long?"

"A couple of years. Tell me again why you're going to Lincoln City. Are you going after a job?"

Silvie bit at her lower lip. "I'm just . . . I just want to be near the ocean, that's all."

He studied her. "So what's all the fuss about the ocean?" he asked.

"I've never been."

"You don't have to move to the coast to see it for the first time." She kept her eyes on the floor, her mouth now set in a hard line.

"You're not from Montana. Not with Wyoming plates on your car. You should take the money. It's more than you'll get for it anywhere else." He sat back in his chair, looking suddenly confident. "So why would a girl who can't even afford a motel room prefer a dead car over a little extra cash?"

"I'm running from an abusive man."

He blinked.

"It doesn't matter," she went on with venom. "Now that I've been here and you know my name and what I look like, I'll have to find some other place to go. It won't be Lincoln City. It won't be anywhere that you can tell him about, that much is for sure."

Hershel opened his mouth to speak but didn't.

"If—*when* he shows up looking for me, just tell him you never saw me. Okay? Tell him you found my car somewhere in Washington. Tell him—" She began to cry. "Tell him whatever you want." Her narrow shoulders shuddered violently and she buried her head in her lap.

8

Carl pulled his jacket collar up to keep the morning rain off his neck as he stood on Yolanda's step. The siding was rotting away, and he could see where water had seeped down into the seam and buckled the plywood. Mold covered the entire structure. All the cabins had been painted bright turquoise three summers back. The landlord had offered a week of free rent to tenants who painted their own, and everyone took him up on the offer. They complained bitterly about the color, though, saying it was "omosek-swal." The landlord had gotten a deal on the paint down at Columbia. An order that was never picked up—probably because the customer had come to his senses at the last minute.

"It's too much," Yolanda said, her face alight with surprise. Yellow light glowed through Yolanda's open door, and the smell of fried tortillas wafted out into the damp Oregon morning. "It's too much. I can't take it." Her frame took up the entire doorway as she clutched the KitchenAid to her chest with her doughy fingers. Her dark eyes twinkled with delight, and she held it out again to inspect it.

"You can. It's for you." Carl's voice was strong, stern even. He had to work to hold back the smile that was fighting its way up from his center.

"No, no," she said in her heavy Mexican accent. "I can't pay you."

"Have I ever asked you for money?"

"Carlos," she said, resigning herself to the fact that he would agree to nothing but total acceptance. "Santa Carlos."

"Make some cookies or something," he said, throwing his hand up and stepping off the stoop. She would, whether he supplied her with a used mixer or not.

"You are so kind," she called after him. "I will make you wedding cakes."

Carl trudged through the muddy yard between the cabins, scattering large spotted hens and gaining the attention of an enormous gray rooster. They eyed each other balefully for a moment, the rooster's guard feathers rising in preparation for attack. But Carl rushed the bird and sent it retreating behind one of the shacks before it could make its move.

A small boy was huddled on the step of the same shack with a blanket wrapped around his shoulders against the cold morning. He watched apprehensively as Carl intimidated the rooster.

When Carl noticed the boy he said, "That one's mean. Don't let it get the upper hand. Chase it off before it thinks it can take you."

The boy stared, and Carl knew that he didn't speak English. His face was dirty and his jeans were torn at the knees. The warmth Carl had carried from Yolanda's porch dissolved as he was reminded of the overwhelming need in this place.

He nodded at where the bird had gone and flapped his hands, making the child smile. The door came open suddenly and a short, work-worn man with a hard expression stepped into the light behind the boy.

"*Adentro,*" he said, and the boy rapidly scuttled past him into the dark interior. The man leaned against the doorjamb and lit a cigarette, appraising Carl.

Carl nodded a greeting. When the man didn't respond, he turned toward his own shack, just past the picnic table, across the small yard.

"Cabrón," the man said in a barely audible tone.

Carl walked on without looking back. A new crew had arrived the previous day while he was working. The ten shacks at Campo Rojo were full again, and a handful of tents were set up in the adjacent field. Fresh from who knew where. California? Arizona? Straight from Mexico? They were here for the fall pruning of fruit trees and vineyards. It was always this way when a new bunch of workers arrived. Suspicious stares and muttered racial slurs. They assumed that he worked for Arndt, the landlord. They believed Carl was stationed there to keep an eye on the goings-on in camp. Yolanda would fill them in. They wouldn't believe her at first, thinking she'd been duped, but over time things would bear out and they'd see that he was just a resident, the same as themselves. Then they'd move on and a new crew would arrive, and it would begin again.

Inside his one-room house, Carl shook the rain off his jacket and hung it on a peg next to the door. A small potbellied wood-stove put out a generous heat, and he kicked off his muddy boots and warmed his fingers.

He craved. Today it was severe—worse than most.

He tried to shut the thoughts out of his mind, turning them to Silvie. She'd been constant on his mind since he discovered the terrible mistake he'd made in selling her car. But it wasn't his screwup that weighed on him, though he harbored a strong desire to somehow make it up to her. No, it was her fear that bothered him. Kept him up most of the night thinking about it, in fact. He could understand her frustration, anger even. But the overriding emotion she'd shown upon discovering that her car was missing, a car that Hershel told him didn't even run, was terror. And that, Carl could not shake.

Silvie found Hershel in the cashier's booth the following morning, poring over receipts. She'd wandered every square inch of the warehouse the previous day as she'd awaited the return of her car, and had discovered a back hallway leading to the room where they cataloged merchandise. She had pawed through boxes of weird and incongruent things like hair dryers next to poultry feeders. There was a life-size cardboard cutout of John Wayne leaning against the wall next to the women's bathroom, and its realness unnerved her every time she passed it, giving her the sense that she should say "Excuse me" as she went by. She kept up her energy with small cups of Coca-Cola from the fountain in the concession stand. But hunger never found her.

Hershel looked up when she appeared at the window, as if she were a customer waiting to receive a bidding number. "Hello," he said. "How did you sleep?"

She shook her head. "When do you think he's going to bring my car?"

Hershel picked up his phone, scanned through, and held it to his ear. "Kyrellis. Swift." He listened a moment. "Silvie is wanting her car back. How about you let me come get it?" Another long pause. "Okay, but if it's not here in an hour I'm coming over. She needs her things."

He hung up and looked at Silvie. She tried to smile, but the expression eluded her.

"He says he's on his way shortly. Give him an hour."

"Did he go through it?"

"Let me buy you breakfast," he said. "I know you haven't eaten. You have to eat something."

She shook her head and glanced around at the mostly empty warehouse. "How does this work? Your business."

Hershel lumbered up from the chair and came around to stand next to her. "It's simple," he said. "People bring in anything they don't want anymore and I sell it for them. I take thirty percent of the sale price as my commission. That's it."

"How do you remember whose stuff it is? Was everything you sold Tuesday from one person?"

He laughed. "That was about twelve different consigners. We

track it with lot numbers. A lot number is assigned to each seller."
He picked up a cordless drill set that had come in that morning
and pointed at the "22" scrawled onto a piece of masking tape
stuck to the plastic case. "Twenty-two is Greg Westerman—at
least this week it is."

"How much money will you make on that?"

He glanced over it briefly. "It's worth about fifty bucks. Probably sell for around thirty. I'll make ten."

"How do you make a living on that?"

"Three hundred items a week, give or take. Some big, some
small like this. The trick is to never lay out your own cash. Bring it
in and get it out within a few days. Volume."

"What if it doesn't sell?"

"The seller takes it back. It's in the contract."

She studied him, watched his eyes survey his kingdom. "It's the
perfect business. Really," he said. "When times are hard, people
sell. They also buy used instead of new. Business booms. When
times are good, people have extra cash. And business booms."

She tipped her head back and let her eyes roam the drab warehouse with its open beams, adorned in dusty cobwebs. He wandered down to the merchandise room at the other end of the
building, and she followed. He called out the value of items they
passed: seventy-five dollars for a chrome dinette set from the
fifties, twenty for the darkroom supplies, eighty for large tractor
tires that were taller than she was.

In the catacombs under the bleachers, she asked, "Don't you
ever buy anything for yourself?"

He pulled a yo-yo from the box she'd found the previous day
and threaded it clumsily over his finger. "Only if I know it can
bring several times more than anyone bidding is willing to pay.
Then sometimes I pick it up and resell it later." He released the
yo-yo and it twirled down smoothly to the top of his shoe and
back up again, causing him to grin. "It's simple. Anyone can do it.
But to do it well you have to be able to tap into people's greed."

She turned abruptly and looked at him.

"Seriously," he said, watching the yo-yo spin. "They call it a bidding contest for a reason. There's a winner and a loser. A good auctioneer keeps that war going as long as possible. We pit bidder against bidder like fighting cocks."

"You're proud of this?"

"I'm not ashamed of it. I don't force anyone to buy anything. I simply leverage what's already there." He tossed the yo-yo back into the box. "C'mon, let's get breakfast. We'll go down to the South Store. It's close, and we have time."

She shuffled her feet. "Can we drive?"

"Of course. How else are we going to get there?"

Finally, she relented and followed him outside to his truck. The interior had warmed, despite the lack of real sunlight, and for a fleeting moment all Silvie wanted in the world was to lie down there and rest.

Hershel took a table at the front of the store, where Silvie could watch the road through the plate-glass window. He inspected the old building, trying to conjure up some memory of it, but he wasn't sure he'd ever been inside. He knew its name from driving past on the road. He somehow knew that they served potato-pear soup with roasted hazelnuts and Parmesan cheese on Sundays, and he had a vague recollection that he liked it, but the interior of the building was as unfamiliar to him as any place he'd never been before.

He pulled out the chair, scraping it loudly along the warped pine floor. A woman appeared with menus, chatting with Silvie as if the two were old friends.

"Have you decided to give the job a try?" she asked.

Silvie looked up at the woman as if coming out of a trance. "Uh . . . I haven't decided. Can I think about it a little longer?"

"Don't wait too long, I've got swarms of people wanting to work here," she teased.

Silvie laughed, and Hershel smiled at the sound. He hadn't heard her laugh since they'd discussed her uncommon form of navigation the afternoon he found her on the road. It seemed like weeks ago, but it had been only three days. Today was the day he had promised to take her to Lincoln City. The subject hadn't come up.

"I'm sorry I pried yesterday," he said when the waitress had left. "If this guy comes looking for you, I won't tell him you were here."

"Thanks." Silvie pressed her lips together, turning them white. "I didn't have a chance to thank you for letting me stay. It was really nice of you. You didn't have to do that."

"Yeah, and then I sold your car."

"It was a mistake."

"I'm still sorry it happened."

She peered out the window at the road.

"So you have a job offer? Are you going to take it?"

"I should. Jobs don't usually come along this easy."

"I think you should, too. You know, if there's a guy following you it wouldn't hurt to be somewhere that you know some people. I mean..." Hershel fidgeted with the salt shaker. "Between Carl and me, we could keep an eye out."

"Do you think this building is safe?"

"Nope."

"So if my ex doesn't get me the building will."

"Oh, it's been here a hundred years. It'll probably last one more."

Hershel mopped up the drippings from his fried eggs with a piece of whole-wheat toast. The food here was good; he'd be back. Silvie hadn't touched her breakfast. She tilted her head, looking up the road toward Hillsboro, and leaned in toward each oncoming car, then pressed back against her chair with each disappointment. Finally, she jerked forward.

"It's him," she said, and gathered up her coat. "It's him. Let's go."

Kyrellis drove past with the green Volkswagen on the back of his flatbed. Silvie was already standing with her backpack slung over her shoulder, waiting.

"You want a go-box for that?" Hershel gestured toward the bacon-and-egg sandwich. She didn't answer, and he scooped up the plate, unwilling to leave it behind, untouched.

Silvie was headed out the door.

She drummed her fingers on the armrest, her entire body rigid. Her door was open before Hershel had parked, and she'd swung down and started toward Kyrellis, who was removing the straps from the vehicle. Hershel followed her at a distance, noticing the way Kyrellis paused and appraised Silvie. The man smiled to himself and went back to his task without saying a word. She walked around the flatbed, inspecting the car.

Once he'd unloaded, Kyrellis turned to Hershel and said, "You have something for me?"

The two men went inside, leaving Silvie with the hatchback open, digging through her belongings.

In Hershel's office, Kyrellis examined the Glock. "It's not much. You led me to believe it was in better condition."

Hershel couldn't recall that conversation about the gun; it had been before the accident. "It is what it is. You want it or not?"

"We'll call it even for the car."

"You paid a hundred dollars for the car. The gun's worth more."

"Consider it compensation for my trouble. I could've made your life difficult over the car and I didn't."

"It was a simple mistake."

Kyrellis assessed Hershel with deep-set eyes, as if appraising a piece of merchandise. The man was short and stout. As stubborn-looking as Hershel instinctively knew he could be. He wore a gray wool coat with large black buttons, and dark jeans. "I'm surprised you sold that Charger."

"You said that before."

Kyrellis waited for further explanation, his dark gaze unwavering.

"You think an auctioneer is going to let an opportunity to make a little money pass him by?"

"Looking at that car, it's amazing to see you standing here, conducting business." Kyrellis took a handkerchief from his pocket and blotted his nose. "You're a survivor, Swift." He carefully folded the cloth into a precise square and slipped it back into his coat. "I never asked you where you were coming from the night you wrecked that car. Do you remember?"

Hershel's cheeks burned like coals. "Does it matter?"

"Never know."

"I was coming up from around St. Paul. On 219."

"So you don't recall *what*, exactly, you were coming from?" Kyrellis stepped forward, looking into Hershel's eyes.

Hershel turned away. "Are we square on the gun and the car?"

"Sure," Kyrellis said, and put the gun into his pocket.

As they walked toward the door, Silvie rushed in. "You went through my stuff," she blurted.

Kyrellis paused with his eyebrows raised. He looked at Silvie in a way that could have been interpreted as kindness or sympathy. "No. I went through the car I bought, before I found out it wasn't mine."

"You've taken a box. It was on the floor in the backseat."

"You must be mistaken."

"I'm not. You know what I'm talking about."

Kyrellis moved past her, and she grabbed his arm.

"Give it back!"

"Please, dear. I don't know what you're talking about." He patted her hand.

Silvie followed him into the parking lot, where her things were scattered about on the rain-soaked ground. She shouted at him to return what he'd taken, but Kyrellis ignored her, climbing into his truck and pulling away with all the urgency of a toad. She turned to Hershel, her eyes wild, then collapsed on the ground sobbing.

9

"He's lying," she said for the twentieth time. "He has it."

"Are you sure you didn't just misplace this box?" Hershel said, holding up a bath towel and picking gravel out of it.

"I didn't *misplace* it! He *took* it."

"Why would he take it? What was in it?"

She began to cry again, and he wanted to shake her, slap some sense into her. She was being completely irrational.

"You can buy something new. Everything has a value." He stood back again and folded the towel. He stared down at the other things, clothing mostly, smeared with dirt. "You need to wash these. You can't use them like this, they're filthy."

She didn't answer, and for a moment he thought she was having a seizure the way she rocked back and convulsed, unable to get her breath. He recoiled, then realized that she was crying so hard she was gasping.

"Whoa," he said, crouching beside the sofa where she sat. "It can't be that bad."

"It . . . is," she sputtered. "You . . . don't . . . know."

"You can say that again," he whispered. "Was it some kind of family heirloom?"

"It's just . . . I can't say. But it's important. It's—" She looked at him through tears, her eyes pleading. "It's personal."

Hershel went downstairs to see if Carl had come in. Carl had a softer touch and had guided many of Hershel's past consigners through the illogic of material attachment when they regretted the decision after their treasures were gone. He would know just what to say in this situation. But the place was deserted. No one was due to return here until tomorrow, when a new lot was coming in from Vancouver, Washington. He stood in the quiet warehouse, wondering how the hell he got himself into this situation and what he should do to get out of it.

Upstairs he found Silvie nearly recovered, but her eyes were swollen and red and her nose was running. When she saw him, she turned away. He paused at the door and considered leaving her alone for a while, but that didn't seem like the right thing to do, either.

"C'mon," he said, picking up the laundry basket and gathering up the soiled items. "Come with me."

She shook her head.

"It's not a request."

She looked at him, alarmed, then got to her feet and pulled on her jacket. "Are you kicking me out? I don't have any place to go."

He sighed. *That would be a good idea.* "No, I'm taking you to my house, where you can get yourself together. Use the washer. Get warm." Hershel grabbed her few things that were strewn around the room. "You can eat the breakfast that you didn't eat this morning."

After turning onto an unmarked dirt road a half mile north of his auction barn, Hershel wound deep into an orchard of gray, dormant trees. The truck bounced over ruts and potholes along his driveway, and Silvie clung to the handle above the door for stability. He noticed and slowed.

"I need to have the road graded," he explained.

She peered down the quiet tunnels formed beneath the trees where their canopies touched, searching for the other end. But they simply disappeared into a haze of branches. The orchard seemed to go on forever. She struggled between the sense of protection it provided, away from the road to a place where Jacob was less likely to find her, and her apprehension of Hershel. Now he was taking her somewhere that no one could find her. Was that good or bad?

"The mud in the winter just swallows up the gravel. I need to put down some road fabric," Hershel elaborated, mostly to himself.

At last they approached a house tucked along the foothills and flanked by two wide, symmetrical oak trees. His home sat atop a knoll, with a sweeping view of the orchard and a green sliver of wetlands to the north. To the east, Mount Hood's white volcanic peak loomed over a bank of clouds as if floating there in the sky. But Silvie preferred the view of the lower-slung coastal mountains to the west. They receded in layers of blue, one behind the other, eventually merging into the blank sky.

"It's not much," Hershel said, as he parked in front of a detached garage too small to hold the truck.

Silvie's eyes skimmed every corner and angle of the farmhouse as she dropped out of the truck onto the mossy ground, her backpack in her hand. The place was meticulously maintained. The gutters straight and even. The windows true. He should see some of the places she'd lived in.

"How old is this place?" It sounded rude the moment she spoke it. "I mean, it looks nice."

"This?" He glanced up at the pale-yellow building, with its overly tall, slender windows and Italianate cornices. "I don't know, exactly. A hundred years. Maybe older."

"Was it your family's house?"

Hershel's expression darkened and he shook his head. "Bought it a while ago from a guy whose wife had passed."

He pulled the laundry basket down from where he'd stashed it behind his seat, and Silvie grabbed it from him, dragging a towel out of the pile and covering the jumble of shirts and underthings, now muddy. He pointed at a trail that led past a small brick outbuilding and into the orchard.

"That's the trail to the auction barn. It's a hike, but I prefer it over driving, unless the weather is really bad. Just remember where the well house is and you'll find the trail."

She wondered how long he expected her to stay here.

He led her inside, through a door at the back of the house, and paused in the small mudroom. "There's the"—he seemed to search for the word—"the machine to clean your clothes. Soap is in the cupboard. I'm gonna heat up this food you didn't eat, and after you've finished your breakfast you're going to tell me what Kyrellis took out of your car that's so damn important."

Silvie stared at Hershel in disbelief.

He stared back. "I'll be in the kitchen," he said.

She watched him lumber away, his head barely clearing the door frame between the two rooms, and her blood came up hot and fierce. Her hands shook as she emptied the basket into the washer. If he thought she was going to tell him what was in that box, he was out of his mind. Once the wash cycle was under way, she leaned against the machine and listened to Hershel clank around in the kitchen, wondering what she was going to do. The room was decorated with yellow notes. One on the back door, another above the washer, and a third over the utility sink. She squinted at the page nearest her. Did he really need to write himself a note that he'd turned off the water to the outside spigots or replaced the battery in his pump heater?

"Your food is ready," he called.

Silvie bit her lip and contemplated walking out the back door with just her backpack. She turned to the small window overlooking the backyard, working through her options as she stared at the closely cropped deep-green lawn. Wyoming would be brown or under snow by now. It was simple. She would have to offer Kyrellis something in exchange for the box; that was clear. And there was only one thing she had.

"Do you need help?" Hershel called.

"No."

"Your food is going to get cold."

"I'm not hungry."

He appeared in the doorway. "I can't force you to eat, but if you don't keep up your energy you'll never get this thing back from Kyrellis."

"Do you know him well?"

Hershel went back into the kitchen without answering. Finally Silvie found her way to the table and began to pick gingerly at the soggy sandwich he'd reheated in the microwave. There were more notes pasted around this room, too.

Hershel noticed her looking around at them and seemed embarrassed. "How much did Carl tell you about my accident?"

"Just that it was bad and that it took a long time for you to get back on your feet."

"Well, I don't remember everything. Not just from that night but from life before it. So if it seems like I don't know things that I should, like . . . names and words, it's because my memory isn't the same."

Silvie pulled a slice of bacon free and nibbled on the end. "I'm sorry."

He watched her for a long moment, as if trying to divine whether she was being honest or patronizing. "I knew Kyrellis before the wreck, but I don't remember him."

She swallowed the greasy meat, trying not to gag. "So you don't know if he'll give me back the box?"

"What kind of box was it?"

"A small metal lockbox."

He rolled his eyes. "What was in it?"

"I don't have to tell you that. It's private."

Hershel crossed the kitchen and sat down at the table. He looked Silvie straight in the eye. "Okay, you don't have to tell me. But if I don't know what's in the box I can't help you. You leave me no choice but to assume it was something that you shouldn't have, something illegal probably. Was it drugs?"

She shook her head.

"Look, I can draw all kinds of conclusions about the contents of that box and about you in the absence of honest information. You can pretty much assume that the ideas I come up with will be far worse than the truth."

"You don't know that."

He sighed and sat back in his chair. "Fine, have it your way. When your clothes are washed, I'll give you a hundred bucks for your car. It's double the price you'll get from any wrecking yard— probably more. You can sign the title over to me so I can sell it legally this time, gather your stuff, and I'll drop you off in Lincoln City or wherever you want to go. I feel really bad about what happened, but I don't have time to play games. If you want to get your box back from Kyrellis, I guess you can file a police report."

Sylvia pushed her plate away. "The box has pictures of me . . . *naked* pictures."

"That's what this is about?" He got up and went to the window, flexing his hands impatiently. "I thought it was something serious."

She wished Jacob were here. He might understand if she told him she was just scared. He would forgive her, wouldn't he? She wished he could wrap his arms around her and pull her onto his lap. She needed him now.

"Geez, you had me thinking this was a big deal."

"It is a big deal."

"What did you expect would happen? Letting some guy take nude photos of you?"

"You think this was my fault."

Hershel stared out the window, the muscles of his jaw working back and forth.

"It's not like I *let* him."

"What? Did he tear your clothes off?"

Silvie stood and gathered her backpack, slinging it over her shoulder and heading for the door.

"Where are you going? Your things aren't done."

"You keep them."

"Stop it." He grabbed her arm as she reached the back step, halting her beneath a waxy camellia bush. "Don't be silly. Where are you going to go? You have no car. You're leaving everything. C'mon."

"You just think I'm some kind of slut running away from my boyfriend. I don't need this shit from you."

He let go of her arm.

"Those pictures were taken when I was twelve," she said quietly, staring at her feet.

They stood in silence for a long, awkward moment, neither knowing what to say. Finally, Hershel said, "Come back in the house. I'll fix you some tea."

Silvie felt raw inside from having exposed her secret to this near stranger. She was confused and angry and unable to decide what to do. At last she followed him back into the warmth of the kitchen.

Hershel busied himself heating water and searching the cabinets for tea bags. He obviously didn't drink the stuff himself. Silvie wondered what was going through his mind now that he knew precisely who she was.

"You could go to the police," he suggested.

She laughed bitterly.

"They might help."

"Those pictures were taken by the sheriff of Walden County."

Hershel stood on his front porch, watching a rain squall drift over the valley from the west, backlit by the setting sun. A rainbow arced a quarter of the way up the sky and disappeared into thick lavender clouds. He considered what to do about Silvie, who was upstairs using the shower. What was the price of nude photos? He needed to get rid of this girl. This was no business to be tangled up in. He was not responsible for what had happened to her; he'd simply stopped to help.

He considered how much money was enough for Silvie to get on her feet somewhere else, away from her abusive sheriff. Away from here. But as he worked through the math his gut tightened. He didn't want to be responsible for her—he *wasn't* responsible for her.

The door opened behind him and Silvie stepped out onto the porch. Her feet were bare and her hair was wet, hanging in soft curls around her shoulders. She pulled her jacket around her and looked out at the evening. "It's pretty here."

"You'll catch a cold standing out here with wet hair." He couldn't help looking at her.

"Colds are viruses. Having wet hair won't make me catch one."

"You'll catch something. It's not healthy."

"In Wyoming, on January first, the old people go down to the Hanley reservoir and go swimming. There's ice all around the edge of the lake, but they just plunge in. They call themselves polar bears."

"Yeah, we have crazies like that here, too."

"Their lips are blue when they get out. But they claim it's good for their health."

"Good way to hasten a heart attack, if you ask me."

"Are you from Oregon?" she asked.

"Yeah, I grew up one town over. In Sherwood."

"Do you have family here?"

Hershel shook his head and started inside, mourning his lost privacy. "Are you hungry?"

"I need your help getting that box from Kyrellis," she said. "You know him. Maybe you can talk to him. He might listen to you."

Hershel shrugged. She wasn't his responsibility. "I don't know. I'll see what I can do."

Silvie ran her fingers over the polished mahogany night table. Its red grain glowed in the soft lamplight. It was part of a set—bed, dresser, nightstand. It was antique, but she didn't know enough about that sort of thing to calculate how old it was or how valuable. She could tell it was fine, though. Just like the matching bed set she'd dreamed of as a child, only this one didn't have tall spindly posts at each corner. Everything was polished to a high gloss, and she guessed Hershel had a housekeeper. There wasn't any way she'd believe he kept it like this himself. Men were mostly slobs, and the ones that weren't hired women to clean. Either way, he had a little money. Not as much as Jacob, but Hershel also seemed more modest about it, like he had it and it was nobody's business. Jacob liked to flash wads of cash bundled in his sterling money clip. He ordered the finest bottles of brandy at the bar, or steak and lobster at Hanley's only upscale restaurant, and made a loud display of commenting on its superiority. For Silvie, the taste of fine food would always be laced with dreaded anticipation of the coming night with Jacob.

She lay back on the bed and listened to the quiet of Hershel's house. It was too early to sleep, but her admission about the pictures had left her raw and unable to stand his silence. Hershel was markedly reserved, even nervous, in its wake. She could imagine what he thought. Hanley was a small town, and as soon as word got out that she was Jacob's girl she only ever got two reactions. The decent people behaved like Hershel. The others... well, the women gossiped and the men leered. One of her schoolmates' dads tried to trap her in the alley between the bar where her mother worked and the bank next door. If she hadn't been so skinny he would have succeeded, but she slipped through a gap in the chain-link fence at the other end. As she ran down the back street behind the buildings, her heart thudding in her throat, he shouted, "You'll be back. I know what kind of girl you are."

Carl stretched out on his bed and listened to the music blaring across the yard. The lyrics were in Spanish, as always. He worked to make out the words over the rapid picking of guitar strings, but after all these years he didn't understand much of their language. How could he have lived here so long and not learned more? He craved again, the way he always did at the end of the day, and especially when the people around him were having fun. He scratched at his forearms, a phantom itch that never went away, though he'd been clean for twelve years. He reminded himself of that polarizing moment when he finally sought help. He'd awakened under a freeway overpass in Portland, a stinking wool blanket from the homeless mission wrapped around him. As he'd come to his senses in the wet and icy January morning, struggling out of a drug haze, a rat gnawed at his leather shoe. He'd shit his pants, and the pavement around his head was wet with vomit. He couldn't recall if it was his or someone else's. But since he'd woken up alone he guessed it was his.

Carl closed his eyes against the humiliating memory. His descent into homelessness had happened so rapidly following his discharge from the army after his second tour in Vietnam, and it lasted nearly twenty years. That pathetic morning, he was certain he would die. He'd wished for death many times, but wishing for it and recognizing its imminence are two different things. He didn't really want to die.

The drug habit he'd picked up in Asia had consumed him in the absence of military structure and some sense of purpose, real or imagined. And now, more than a decade later, to be clean and alive and working still amazed him. So did the daily struggle to remain that way. It confirmed for him that there was a higher power, something greater than himself. He focused on that power, silently reciting the addict's prayer. When the craving diminished, he said a prayer of thanks, then reminded himself of his purpose here—to provide for those with less.

He was roused from his contemplation by a knock at the door, and he scrambled up and into his jeans. "Just a sec," he hollered.

When Carl opened the door, he smiled instinctively. Yolanda was standing on his stoop, holding out a plate heaping with small, round powdery cookies.

"Well," he said, trying not show his delight. "What's this?"

"Wedding cakes." She was beaming with pleasure. "Just like I promised."

"So you found some use for that mixer, huh?" He looked off toward the festivities.

"I made these special for you."

"You shouldn't have done that. I didn't bring it for you to make me treats."

Her joy vanished into confusion. "You don't want?"

"Of course I do. You know I love your cooking, Yolanda."

"Come, join us," she said, gesturing toward the crowd in the courtyard.

"No."

"Oh, Carlos." She shook her head. "They're harmless."

"I'm not afraid of them," he said truthfully. He'd simply grown tired of making friends who would inevitably move on to the next job. Friends he'd likely never see again. People he would hope for and wonder about for years to come. "Where did this group roll in from?"

She pushed the plate at him, her eyes searching his face. "Sacramento. They think you work for Arndt."

"They always do."

"If you join them, they will see."

"No. I have to work in the morning. I need a good night's sleep. But I'll enjoy these cookies." He took the plate from her. It was familiar. He'd given her a box of mismatched dishes the previous summer. "You are a divine baker, Yolanda."

"Divine?"

"Heavenly."

She waved him off, grinning, and stepped down from the porch, heading toward the crowd of men at the picnic tables. There weren't many children in this group, and Carl knew that was a bad sign. The presence of families always served to keep the peace. There was less drinking, less swearing, and fewer racial slurs shot in his direction when they brought their children.

Carl watched Yolanda's broad hips swish from side to side. She had a fluidity about her that defied her abundance. He wanted to call her back, invite her into his home, and touch that warm dark skin.

Hershel pulled his coat on and trudged across the spongy ground to his pickup. He felt like a stranger in his own home, and he cussed himself for bringing the girl there. How could he ask her to leave now? He'd be an asshole of monumental proportions if he put her out on the street after what she'd told him.

He went to the sale barn, standing on the cement stoop in the dull light, trying key after key. When he found the correct one he held it up, staring at its contours, its color. Why couldn't he recognize this simple key when he needed it? He shoved the wad back into his pocket and stomped inside, slamming the door closed behind him. He turned on the overhead lights and squinted against the sudden, painful glare.

This place had once been a source of immense satisfaction for him. From the outside it didn't look like much. The casual observer wouldn't appraise this business very highly, and that was beautiful. He'd found ways to make money—lots of money—without the appearance of money. But now it represented the ugly words people called him. Their sentiments echoed between the walls long after they'd gone. Who was this man they valued only for what he could sell them? This person they seemed so wary of?

Hershel stood in the doorway of the cashier's booth and let his eyes roam the cramped space. There had to be clues here to who he once was and to his relationship with Kyrellis. He stepped in and pawed through a stack of dog-eared papers—advertisements from past sales, old calendars, and handwritten notes. Bidding numbers turned in, new ones ready to go for the next sale. He pulled open the drawer and examined the mismatched pens and pencils. A pack of chewing gum so ancient it was calcified. He didn't know what he was looking for, but he was certain he wouldn't find it here. He sat back in the squeaky chair. Had it been a sale item, too? Of course it had. He wandered into the concession stand, running his fingers over the torn vinyl of the twin bar stools on his way past. Five dollars for the pair he'd paid, because they didn't need to be attractive. The popcorn machine, secondhand from the liquidation of the Fox theater in some nameless town. Twenty-two dollars. Had he cleared a nest of mice from the grease pan? The idea seemed too real not to be true, and that soured his stomach a little.

He had no particular destination in mind as he pulled out of the gravel lot onto Highway 219. He'd just roam around awhile, think about things. Try to figure out what to do about Silvie. He'd been through the scenario too many times now, and he couldn't see how she would take any amount of money for her loss. She was afraid, and fear changed the value of things. Her price, if one could be reached, would be too high—higher than Hershel was willing to pay, anyway. It was Kyrellis he needed to focus on if he was going to get this box back and get rid of the girl.

These weren't his photos. And if anyone discovered that he'd paid for them he'd go to prison as a sex offender. He let out an irritated growl. Was he really responsible here? He'd sold her car. But he'd also taken her in. Where did things balance out and his obligation end? He should just give her a couple of hundred dollars and drop her off in Lincoln City as she'd asked him to. Let her worry about Kyrellis. Wash his hands of the whole thing.

"That's what I'll do," he said. "Fuck 'em both. I don't need this."

Darkness had overtaken the landscape, leaving only the moist pavement with its faded yellow stripe to unfold before him. The overcast sky hid what stars he might have seen. And the farms along that stretch of Washington County were set back away from the road, tiny yellow dots in a sea of black.

He wound along southward on 219, its curves coming fast and sharp, the engine straining against the steep grade. He drove faster than he'd done since the accident. How things change, he thought, remembering the way he'd raced his Charger down back roads at speeds of up to a hundred miles an hour in places. Finally, he topped the summit of Chehalem Mountain and dropped into Yamhill County. He took the hairpin turns on the other side a little slower, the city of Newberg twinkling up from the valley through leafless trees and blackberry thickets.

He cruised into town, past George Fox University, then left on First Street. Downtown was quiet, and he picked up 219 again south of Newberg. He headed toward the tiny hamlet of St. Paul, not because he had business there but because that's where the road led. As he neared the site of his accident he slowed and looked for signs of that terrible night, but everything had been restored. Even in the dark, he could see that the fence he took out had been rebuilt, the grass he'd gouged up grown anew. The milepost marker that had skewered his radiator had been replaced, too. The car behind him flashed its lights impatiently, and Hershel resumed his speed. He took a left at the turnoff to Champoeg State Park, mostly to rid himself of the growing line of traffic trailing him. The road twisted ahead, running between dairy farms and nurseries, through mossy creek beds and up onto the smooth straightaway of French Prairie. Where was he coming from that night? Kyrellis's question had simply echoed his own maddening query of what he could not remember.

After a time, the rancid odor of pigs reached him, and he had a fleeting memory of staring down into a muddy sty filled with enormous dark hogs. He struggled to piece the memory together, but it was fractured, the way so much of his past was. He hadn't raised pigs as a kid, or kept them as an adult. Where did this random image come from, and why did it carry such an overwhelming sense of foreboding?

Silvie crept downstairs a few minutes after midnight, sleepless and thirsty. She peered out the kitchen window to the spot where Hershel had parked his truck that afternoon, but it wasn't there. She looked around, pondering how long he'd been gone. What small comfort she had found there evaporated with the knowledge that she was alone. Hershel's presence, though not warm, at least provided a sense of security. She needed the shelter he offered, and she'd come downstairs prepared to show him that she could be warm, friendly...whatever he needed her to be.

She filled a glass at the tap and took a slow sip. Oregon well water tasted coppery and sharp compared with the water in Wyoming, and she liked it. She finished the glass and refilled it, then made a quiet inventory of the windows and doors. She tried the sash on the living-room window, but it wouldn't budge. She checked the front door and found it secured with a dead bolt and a chain.

When she returned the glass to the kitchen she found Hershel's cellphone plugged into an outlet near the refrigerator. She glanced around, double-checking that she was alone, then scrolled through the contacts. When she found Kyrellis, her hand suddenly shook. She set the phone down abruptly and stared at it as if it were a poisonous snake. But it held the only connection to the man who had Jacob's pictures. She took it up again and quickly pressed the call button before she lost her nerve. It rang only twice before he answered.

"Swift. 'Bout time you called. You finally figure out what that girl is hiding?"

"Th-this is Silvie," she stammered. "You have my box."

"Silvie," he said softly, as if committing her name to memory. "What a beautiful name."

"Just give it back. Please."

"I can see why you don't want anyone to see these pictures." He spoke softly into the phone, a sympathetic, fatherly tone. "Who took them?"

"You have no idea what kind of trouble this will bring," she said.

"Yes...yes, you could be right." He paused over the idea. "Was he kind to you, the man who took these? Even a little?"

Her mind swam with conflicting answers. "He'll come after you for them." Silvie knew what Jacob was capable of, because she'd once witnessed his confrontation with a man behind the outhouses at the Hanley reservoir. It was dark, but she caught the flash of silver in the beam of the headlight before the man collapsed at Jacob's feet. When he returned to the truck, wiping the blade of a knife with his handkerchief, he eyed her balefully.

"He should have done as I asked," he said matter-of-factly. The next morning, the sheriff was called out to investigate a murder at the reservoir.

"Who will come after me?" Kyrellis asked. "Who is the man in this photo where you're—" He paused a long moment. "Well, I don't need to say exactly. I'm sure you know which one I mean." He sounded sad.

She flushed, imagining precisely which picture Kyrellis held.

"That's a fine-looking house—what I can see of it. He has some money, this man. Doesn't he, sweetheart?"

"He'll kill me," she pleaded.

"Listen, my dear, he may have told you he would kill you if you told anyone, but men like that are not murderers. You're not in as much danger as you've been led to believe."

"What do you want for them?"

"I hate to admit it, but that is the question, isn't it? How about the name of the man in the picture?"

"He *will* kill me. He'll kill you, too. You don't know him."

"No, I don't know this specific man. But I know men *like* him. Tell me his name and I'll make sure he never bothers you again."

Silvie hung up the phone and stood in the dark kitchen, exhausted. She had no way of knowing how far Kyrellis would go. There was something approaching kindness in his voice, and it confused her. Maybe he had a soft spot that she could appeal to. He wouldn't go as far as Jacob; she was certain of that.

She wiped the sweat and oil from Hershel's phone and returned it to the exact place where she'd found it. She went back upstairs to the bedroom and sat with the light on, trying to forget the memory of Jacob Castor slicing down a man with all the concern of someone ridding himself of a rabid dog, or the things he'd made her do afterward.

11

Carl was nearly to the highway when a white van pulled onto the rutty road leading into Campo Rojo. The driver slowed to a stop and leaned out the window.

"You the landlord here?"

"Nope." Carl pointed to where the road forked to the left and disappeared into a stand of noble firs once intended for Christmas trees but long overgrown. "Jimmy Arndt owns the place. He lives back there."

"He got anyone that speaks English down at Camp Rojo to tell me which units get satellite TV?" He pronounced the name phonetically, with a *j* instead of an *h*.

"No idea," Carl said. "Just don't put one on unit five. That's mine, and I'm not paying for it."

The man scrutinized Carl as if he were joking. It was a common response, as if no white man would truly be living in a migrant camp. And it always put the short hairs on the back of Carl's neck straight up like a mean dog's. When Carl didn't smile, the man drove on, taking the left fork into Arndt's driveway. Carl trudged onto the highway and turned south toward the auction barn, shaking his head. How did these people expect to save money if they spent it on television? He knew from experience that when he returned home that evening every cabin in camp, with the exception of his and Yolanda's, would sport a satellite dish directed at the southern sky, each like a proud American status symbol.

A car whizzed past, spraying an icy mist across him. He zipped his jacket and picked up the pace. In the summer the mile-and-a-half walk past berry fields and filbert orchards to the sale barn was pleasant. The old houses in Scholls proper—a short strip of road that started at Groner Elementary and ended at the South Store—were a sight to behold in spring. Hundred-year-old magnolia trees, wisteria, rhododendrons, and generations of wild daffodils brought a charm to the place that new money couldn't. The mini-mansions that had sprouted up along the ridgeline of Chehalem Mountain looked garish and self-important in the steely drizzle of winter. This time of year, the walk was simply a chore to be gotten done with.

—

Hershel sipped coffee at the breakfast table, spying an oil painting at the bottom of the stairs in the other room. He half listened to Silvie talk about the greenness of Oregon. She was charmed by it in a childlike way. The painting, an Impressionistic view of a canal and a fishing boat in muted colors, had been in his family and it was Rachel's favorite. A Dutch painter, he thought. Six thousand dollars? That appraisal seemed right. His sister had wanted it, but he'd gotten it. How?

Silvie rambled almost nonstop about the camellia bush outside his kitchen window and how pretty it would be when it bloomed, making him question whether he even knew what a camellia bush was. Could he see the buds already forming there? He turned and gazed out the window at the bush. She wanted to know if it was pink or white, but he couldn't remember it at all.

"Pink," he said. She wouldn't be here long enough to know if he was right.

He experienced a flash of Rachel's anger over the painting, but he couldn't bring the memory together. Tears. Shouting. Name-calling. He thought she'd sell it; that was why he'd taken it. It was a glaring lie. He was the one who would sell it. He simply hadn't yet come into the right situation to catch top dollar. It suddenly seemed like the most precious thing he owned. It connected him to his family, however tenuously.

"Have you called Kyrellis yet?"

Hershel snapped back to Silvie. "I'll call him now." He'd been putting it off, hoping she'd decide to just leave on her own.

"Swift, is that you?" Kyrellis answered.

"Yeah, it's me. We need to talk." He glanced at Silvie, then stood and walked into the living room for privacy.

"Did she tell you about the pictures?"

"That's why I'm calling. What do you want with them?"

Kyrellis sighed into the phone. "How much do you think a man would pay to keep these pictures quiet? I mean, if it were you in one of these shots, how much would you pay?"

"I wouldn't know. It's not me." Numbers had flashed through his mind, but this was one object—or collection—that he could not appraise. And Hershel's dislike of this man, despite his refined mannerism, was growing more precise. Whatever they had been to each other before the accident, he wanted nothing to do with Kyrellis now.

"Well, that's how we're going to determine the value, so think about it."

"Let it go. You got the gun. I offered to pay you for your trouble. Why are you doing this?"

"Why did this man take these pictures? Why did you sell your Charger? Why didn't she put oil in her car?"

"She's a victim. She was twelve when those photos were taken."

"Mmm, that young?" He was quiet for a moment. "Yes, she *is* a victim. She is indeed." Kyrellis whistled to himself as if amazed by something he saw.

"C'mon, Kyrellis, you want me to call the police?"

"I don't think that would be a wise move on your part, Swift." Kyrellis's voice went suddenly hard. "You really don't remember where you were the night of your accident, do you?"

Hershel's scar prickled.

"Does the name Albert Darling ring a bell?"

The prickle turned to pain, and a man's face flashed through his mind, then was gone just as quickly. He couldn't recover the details.

"Think hard on that before you get the police involved. You wouldn't want to bite off more than you bargained for." Kyrellis hung up, leaving Hershel standing in the living room with the name Albert Darling bouncing through his brain, seeking recognition, begging for a home.

"What did he say?" Silvie asked from behind him.

Hershel didn't answer straight off, but worked at recalling the face that had faded back into his muddled past.

"Is he going to return the box?"

"Not that easily, it seems."

"What am I going to do?" Her eyes remained on Hershel, as if he could fix this for her if he would just try a little harder.

Hershel rubbed his hand over his head and stared at his feet. He couldn't stand the way she looked at him. Like he'd disappointed her. "I don't know."

"How much money does he want?"

"He hasn't said. But . . . I can imagine it'll be a lot."

She watched Hershel, and he wondered if she was figuring his net worth. Would she expect him to pay Kyrellis's price?

"How much are these photos worth to the man who took them?" he asked.

Her face went dark. "He won't be blackmailed. That's where Kyrellis is wrong."

"He's the sheriff. Would he rather the media got hold of them?"

"No. He'll find Kyrellis and kill him. Then he'll kill me. And maybe you, too. That's the way he works. He won't be blackmailed."

"Listen," he said, "why don't you take that job down at the South Store?"

She looked up, astonished by the sudden change of subject.

"I think it's going to take some time to work through this. It'll give you something to do, and you can earn some money."

She simply stared at him as if he spoke in a foreign tongue. Finally she said, "How will I get there?"

"Well, it's not far to walk from the sale barn. You can stay there."

"Oh," she said, as if suddenly understanding that she was the butt of a joke. "You want me out of here."

"I didn't say that."

"No, but it's what you meant."

"Wait, be fair. I . . . you're welcome to stay here. I just thought, well, it's closer. That's all. I wasn't asking you to leave."

She eyed him suspiciously. "I can't stay there. It's scary. I'll go. I'll find a place to stay somewhere." She disappeared, and he heard her footfalls on the wooden stairs.

Hershel rubbed the pain in his scar and struggled with letting her just leave with no place to go. She wasn't his responsibility. Wasn't it enough that he'd offered her a place to stay?

"*Goddamnit!*" He walked to the bottom of the stairs and hollered up. "Silvie, I didn't mean for you to go."

She emerged from the bedroom with her backpack over one shoulder and the laundry basked with her folded clothes on the other arm.

"Put that stuff down. You'll stay here until we get this mess sorted out."

Without a word, she returned to the bedroom.

Hershel heard a backpack hit the floor, followed by a basket. He sighed, vacillating between relief and irritation.

By noon Carl had inventoried and organized three large deliveries for the upcoming sale. The first two consisted of various farming implements: ladders, pruning tools, and tractor parts. One cider press that was old, but still in good condition, and several boxes of household items. Boxes that Hershel would probably sell off for a buck or two for the entire contents of each one in a "take one or take 'em all" deal. But the third load had been full of antique radios and televisions from the estate of a man who had made his living repairing and selling them. Carl had spent twenty minutes trying to tune in the AM country-and-western station but, losing patience, ended up listening to Clark Howard instead. He liked Clark's philosophy about money, but not the calls from people who were on the brink of investing everything they had in scams that played on their desires to be rich. He knew it was easy to criticize other people because he'd never had any money of his own to invest or lose, but this didn't stop him from shouting "You idiot" at the radio every once in a while.

Hershel arrived shortly after lunch and silently went to work marking lot numbers on pieces of masking tape and putting the radios into the order in which he wanted to sell them—least to best. Sometimes with specific collectibles he could frenzy the crowd, like sharks after meat. Another load from an architectural salvage yard came in at about two o'clock, and they worked side by side, moving the nicest items, like the brass andirons in the shape of eagles, to the front of the staging area, where people could look them over and see other people looking them over, too. Hershel was a master at fostering competitive wars among bidders. He had an innate understanding of human nature and had once told Carl that most people will pay more than an item is worth, and often more than they can afford, simply to make the others around them believe they're well-off. Ego. Everything was driven by ego. All he had to do was tap into it. That same night he'd sold a Mission-style library table with fake-wood veneer for six hundred dollars. It might have been worth that had it been oak, but the two bidders were inexperienced at assessing antiques and had behaved like sparring roosters. One man surely awoke the following morning relieved, despite the momentary sting of defeat. Hershel laughed about and retold that story for weeks.

"You remember anyone by the name of Albert Darling?" Hershel asked, breaking the silence and startling Carl.

"Yeah," he said cautiously. "He came round here looking for you a couple of times."

Hershel paused in his work and waited for Carl to elaborate.

"Didn't we liquidate his storage unit over in Sherwood for non-payment?" At times it felt as if his boss was testing him, checking to see if *he* remembered. Of course he did.

"Sherwood," Hershel mumbled, and returned to his work.

"Yep."

Hershel placed the stained-glass pieces behind the auctioneer's podium in the grimy window, where they might catch a little light. But the dusty cobwebs and dead flies made them seem more like junk than treasures, and Carl climbed up after him and wiped the debris away with a dirty rag.

As he unpacked a box of nineteenth-century door knockers, Carl sensed Hershel's eyes on him. "Need something, boss?"

Hershel shook his head and ripped the tape from another box, revealing tin ceiling tiles with Victorian-era stamping.

"I think he was in prison or something."

Hershel scowled.

"Albert Darling. Claimed you sold a gun that was his while he was in the big house."

Hershel squinted at Carl. "What do you know about the guns?"

"I don't know anything about that, boss."

12

Karen Gibbs put Silvie to work that afternoon on a trial run. "Things start to pick up on Fridays," she said. "But Saturdays are downright busy. If I like what I see, you can do the lunch shift from eleven to two."

Though Silvie hadn't waitressed much, she'd spent long hours at the bar watching her mother. She donned an apron, slipped a new pad and pen into her front pocket, and hoisted a fresh pot of coffee off the burner. She greeted her first customers, a couple wearing matching fleece vests in bright orange. The man had on a flannel button-up shirt and jeans. The woman wore a turtleneck and leather ankle boots. Her straight blond hair was trimmed to a perfect blunt line, and she wore expensive sunglasses tilted up on her head even though it was pouring rain outside. They looked so freshly scrubbed that Silvie was afraid to stand too close.

When she slid the couple's order into the queue, Karen smiled approvingly. "So far so good," she chirped, and began grilling onions for the patty melt.

After three hours, Silvie had collected twenty-two dollars in tips and her feet were beginning to throb.

"That'll do for today," Karen said after Silvie had wiped all the tables and started a fresh pot of coffee. It had been a half hour since the last customers left, and things seemed to be slowing. "My sister is coming over to help with the dinner shift. But I'll expect to see you tomorrow." She smiled warmly. "You did great. I'm glad to have the help."

Silvie grinned, feeling suddenly needed and useful. "Tomorrow, then."

As she stepped toward the front door, Karen called her back and tossed a bag of Kettle chips at her. "Come take a scone, too. It's not much. I should've fed you. Tomorrow you'll get lunch. Come thirty minutes early and eat before you start. You can have anything on the menu, but if you want something else you'll have to cook it yourself."

"Thanks." Silvie pocketed a lemon–poppy seed scone wrapped in cellophane and tore open the bag of chips. She hadn't felt hungry all morning, but now she was ravenous.

Outside, she paused on the walkway in front of the South Store and watched a woman at the Berry Barn across the road placing fresh fruit out on the covered front porch. Rain was still falling, though lighter now, and Silvie realized that she would have to buy an umbrella if she planned to stay in Oregon very long. She started walking toward Hershel's auction barn.

The idea of staying was too foreign to entertain, and unrealistic as well. There was no point in spending what little money she had on something as extraneous as an umbrella. She would never be able to stay in any one place with Jacob Castor looking for her.

It had been a long time since she'd thought about him the way he was the first time she met him. Jacob found her at a bar where Silvie was keeping her mother company and writing an essay for sixth-grade Wyoming history. It was late afternoon and the place was quiet yet. Silvie had taken up residence in the main lounge, in a booth along the back wall, because Charlie was chopping onions in the kitchen. He'd become disgusted when she wouldn't stop sniffing back stinging tears and sent her into the dining room, where she'd never been allowed. After a time, he brought her a

Coke—a little truce to let her know that he wasn't really mad. Her books and papers were spread across the wide corner booth, so rather than kick her back to the kitchen he let her stay where she was. She'd marveled at the coincidence of that single event, how it had changed everything. Was it her destiny or just shitty luck?

Jacob strode in with purpose, and Silvie was instantly polarized by his presence, though he didn't notice her for a full twenty minutes. He wasn't particularly tall, but he was rigid and tightly wound. He looked as if he could suddenly spring several stories into the sky without warning. She understood that he was an important man, even though he wasn't in uniform at the time. She would later learn that he was the county sheriff. But that day he wore a cowboy hat and boots, jeans, and a western-style shirt. He looked like the other cattle ranchers who frequented Charlie's bar. His face was set hard, and he was the first person she'd met who could smile without really smiling. He walked straight in and slapped the bar. Everyone scrambled. Charlie himself greeted the man, setting a draft beer on the counter before Jacob could ask for something different. Charlie poured drinks only when the bar was so busy that his staff couldn't keep up. He preferred to do the cooking. The change of roles did not escape Silvie.

She tried to refocus on her essay, but the man had changed the air in the room. She was already certain that she didn't want him to suddenly realize she was there. After he'd finished one beer he started on another, drinking alone while Silvie's mother and Charlie buzzed in and out of the kitchen.

He turned. Silvie ducked back into the booth and fastened her eyes on her paper, but she could feel him staring. The setting sun made the opaque window behind him glow white, and his figure was silhouetted, his hat warped and large in the odd light. When she glanced up he was halfway across the room, coming toward her. She pretended not to notice and shuffled her papers. In her fluster, one slipped off the table and floated to the floor in slow motion. He bent and retrieved it for her, placing it on the table in front of her. She stared at his large fingers and neatly trimmed nails.

"Thanks," she said in a small voice.

"And who might you be, young lady?" His voice was smooth and warm.

"Silvie."

"You don't look old enough to be hanging out in a tavern."

She flushed. Would Charlie get in trouble for this? Would her mother get fired? "My mom works here. I...I usually stay in the kitchen, but Charlie was chopping onions."

"Mind if I join you?"

She shrugged, still afraid to look the man in the face.

He slid onto the red vinyl bench on the other side of the booth. "What are you working on?"

"An essay."

"About what?"

"The Oregon Trail."

"Ah, that's a good topic. You must be what? Fifteen?"

Silvie blinked. "Twelve."

"No way," he said, letting his head roll back a little and showing her his long white teeth. He had blue eyes, and they seemed to scour her. "You look much older. Did you know that?"

She shook her head, not knowing what to say. She'd never been a very pretty girl. No one ever fawned over her the way they did other girls. The boys at school didn't tease her or send her notes as they did her friend Laree.

"Hey," he shouted toward the bar. "Someone bring this young lady a burger."

"No! I don't need anything," Silvie said, certain now that her mother would be fired.

Charlie emerged from the kitchen and stood for a long, strange moment, as if he had no idea what a burger even was. He looked pained as he stared across the room at the two of them. Silvie shook her head, hoping he'd see that she didn't need anything. She hadn't asked.

"Coming up," Charlie said, his voice quieter than usual.

"I don't need one. Really," she said to the man.

"Of course you do. A girl needs her energy for brainy work like this."

When the burger arrived, it was her mother who served it. "Can I get you anything else, Sheriff?" She sent Silvie a withering glance.

"I'll have another beer. And a Coke for this young lady." He nodded at Silvie while keeping a level eye on Melody. "She's yours, isn't she?"

Melody nodded, but she gave no proud smile or compliment about Silvie the way she usually did when she was identified as her mother. "She should be at home working on that. Not here. Not in a bar."

"Oh, she's fine," he said, waving Silvie's mother away.

When Melody left, he leaned in and winked at Silvie. He had soft wrinkles around his eyes, and graying hair. He looked a little like her math teacher. "Don't you worry," he said. "You're not in any trouble. I'll make sure of it."

In that simple exchange, Silvie had understood his authority. Her mother and Charlie never said a word about that strange evening when Sheriff Castor discovered her and lavished her with burgers, Coke, and ice cream. No one mentioned how unusual it was that a grown man would spend the entire evening in a booth chatting with a twelve-year-old. Silvie came to like him that evening. She hoped she'd have a chance to see him again.

Hershel rummaged through his desk drawers. Nothing here revealed itself as relevant to his past. He was looking in the wrong place. The clues, if they existed, were not on paper but in the objects he sold. How could he find anything relevant when nothing stayed? Things came in and things went out, but nothing stayed.

He stood and wandered out into the corridor between the concession stand and the sold-merchandise area. The building was full of strange little nooks and hideaways, all harboring their own intriguing things: boxes of old clothes, broken tools, ancient books. But these were simply the castoffs of his business. The left-behinds in the cycle of recycle. Valueless, but not so much so that he should round them up and take them to the dump. He picked up a tractor manual for a 1948 International. It wouldn't bring two bits in the upcoming sale, but to the farmer out there looking for it, it was priceless. For the man with a disassembled machine in his barn and a nagging wife at his shoulder, it would easily be worth twenty dollars. Hershel tossed it back into its dusty tomb. Everything has its price, and he was the man who innately knew what that price was. But these forgotten pieces didn't explain why he dealt in guns, why he needed to avoid the police, or why people hated him.

Back in his office, Hershel picked up the phone and dialed the manager of his storage facility in Sherwood. He'd spoken to him only twice in the past three months. His name was Woody McClintock. The first time Hershel called was to thank him for the get-well card with the looping handwriting too feminine to be Woody's. Woody had sounded embarrassed, and said he'd pass that on to his wife. It had been a one-minute call. The second time was to get an accounting of delinquent units. Woody usually gave the renters ninety days before he locked them out. Another thirty days to come current. And, thirty days after that, he liquidated the contents. Generally, he hauled everything over to Hershel's sale barn, because holding auctions on the premises wasn't good for business. But they'd had occasion to liquidate multiple units before, and then it was more efficient to hold a special Saturday auction and simply start at one end and work down the rows.

"Hello," Woody said, breathless. "Sherwood Mini Storage."

"Woody, it's Hershel Swift."

"Afternoon, Hershel. What can I do for you?"

"You remember a guy by the name of Albert Darling?"

There was a long pause. "Yeah, I remember him."

Hershel waited for Woody to continue, hating that everyone could remember things so effortlessly when he himself struggled to piece together the simplest information.

"We liquidated after a hundred and eighty days of nonpayment. Six months or so back."

"You remember anything else about him?"

Another silence. "He was a mean one. Came round here threatening everybody. You don't remember him?"

Hershel scowled. Why would he ask these questions if he did? "Vaguely."

"He was doing time for armed robbery when he lapsed on his payments. We sold his stuff after repeated attempts to collect. It was all legal. He doesn't have a leg to stand on. He knows that—we've been all through it."

"What does he look like?" Hershel regretted asking the question. He'd only meant to think it.

"I don't know...short. Long hair. Goatee. Tattoos on his arms."

Hershel closed his eyes, remembering the tattoo now because it was unusual. It was the face of a child—a little girl with cherub wings. It looked like something from a Renaissance painting, and the peaceful face was out of character with the spitting, swearing man that Hershel could now see storming into the auction barn.

"We did it by the book," Woody said. "He's got no legal claim. I thought we'd gotten rid of him. He still coming over there harassing you?"

"No. No, I just came across his name and couldn't remember the details, that's all."

"Hard man to forget, that one." Woody's comment sliced through Hershel with a sharp sting. "Haven't seen him around, though. I'll let you know if I do."

"Thanks, that's all I needed."

"Anytime." Woody hung up, and a splintering pain blossomed across Hershel's forehead.

Silvie opened the door, an unexpected smile on her face. Her cheeks were rosy and her hair was damp from the rain.

"You should've called me. I could've picked you up. You didn't have to walk." He couldn't take his eyes off her. She looked suddenly alive and vibrant.

"That's okay," she said. "I wasn't sure if you were ready to go."

"Yeah, I'm finishing up here." He took his jacket from the coatrack and picked up his keys. What was so different about her? "How did it go down at the South Store?"

"She hired me. I worked the lunch shift for a trial, and she wants me back tomorrow." Silvie's smile widened. "It was a good idea. I kind of enjoyed it."

"Good." He tossed her the keys. "I'll be right out. I have something I want to show you."

Hershel followed her out into the warehouse, and then located Carl in the cashier's booth.

"Be a good sale this Tuesday," Carl said. "We've got some nice stuff. It'll draw a big crowd, but you need to get the ad in this afternoon."

Hershel had forgotten about advertising. There was so much routine business that was anything but routine now.

Carl gauged Hershel, as if understanding. "Want me to call it in? I've made some notes: antiques, stained-glass windows, brass knockers, tin ceiling tiles. We'll put the good stuff right at the top. Could do a headline in bold this week."

"Thanks," Hershel said. "Yeah, do what you think will draw the best crowd."

"Will do, boss." He turned back to his papers, but paused. "That gal Silvie looks like a million bucks today. All smiles."

Hershel looked off toward the door where she'd gone. "Yeah, she does. I'm taking off. You'll lock up?"

"Course."

Silvie felt Hershel's eyes on her as they pulled into the driveway. He'd glanced over at her repeatedly on the short trip from the sale barn. The sky was a patchwork of multicolored clouds and breaks of clear blue. The rain had stopped, but she could see a new storm building over the coastal mountains.

"The weather can't make up its mind to rain or not," she said, trying to break the growing tension.

"Welcome to Oregon. It'll be like this until the Fourth of July."

She already missed the vast cyan sky of the Wyoming winter and the blinding white of fresh snow. She could lose her sunglasses here in Oregon and not miss them until summer.

Hershel parked the pickup next to the well house today instead of in its usual place in front of the garage. Silvie slid out, always feeling as if she were leaping off a tall ledge with no way of knowing how far down she'd have to go before she hit solid ground. He didn't walk toward the house but went to the garage and pulled its double doors wide. They gouged the mossy ground. The small building was dark and musty inside. Dust motes floated in the still air. A small window at the back, opaque with dirt and cobwebs, failed in its mission to provide light. Her eyes slowly adjusted, but she couldn't make out what she was looking at. Hershel shoved a lawn mower back against the wall and picked up a rotting cardboard box, lifting it over his head and lodging it into the rafters.

"It's not much, but it'll get you where you need to go."

As he spoke she finally saw the oxidized orange hood of a small car. It sloped down at a smooth angle, and she could see that the headlights were the kind that popped up when on and disappeared into the hood when off.

"It's a...a 914," he said, squinting at it.

"A what?"

He scratched his head and stared down at the car. She'd grown accustomed to his long pauses as he searched for words and names. She busied herself inspecting the paint, pretending she didn't notice that he hadn't answered the question.

"A Porsche," he finally said, as if committing it to memory once again. "It's a Porsche 914."

She'd never actually seen a Porsche, except in magazines and movies.

"Don't get too excited. It's vintage 1974. But it still has spunk."

"You're going to let me drive this?"

"Sure. If we can get it running."

Silvie looked doubtful. She knew nothing about cars, but joined him in clearing the junk off the hood. Slowly the car materialized. It was dull and dusty, but she didn't care.

"The top comes off."

"Cool."

"Not that we'll get any decent weather for that. But it's fun in the summer."

They both went quiet. She figured he was hoping she'd be far away from Scholls and the rest of his life by summer. She pulled the door latch, but it was stuck. Hershel stepped in behind her, and as he reached for the handle he brushed her forearm, sending a surprising jolt of energy through her. She turned. He was close, just inches from her, smelling of linseed oil and something mildly sweet, like dates. She could feel his breath on her neck and glimpsed a fleeting smile before it disappeared and he stepped away.

"Sorry," he said.

She stood aside, and he jerked up hard on the handle, freeing the latch. The door creaked open, and he peered inside.

Silvie studied Hershel's veined hands as he examined the vehicle, running his fingers along the seam of the roof. He slid into the driver's seat, which seemed impossibly low for a man so tall, and his dark eyes roamed the dash and the instruments. He looked at the car as if it were a long-lost friend, and she wanted to touch him.

"I never gave this car a name," he said quietly, almost to himself.

"A name?"

"The Charger was Floyd."

She let out a small laugh. She'd expected that type of behavior from the guys back in Wyoming. She thought of Jacob, who hadn't named his car but called his genitalia the Club. She'd never been sure whether he meant the kind of club a caveman carried or he fancied that it was an invitation-only party. She didn't ask.

Hershel rummaged through the glove compartment.

"Why did you call it Floyd?"

He smiled but didn't answer. He took out the keys, removed one, and tossed it to her. She slid it into her pocket in anticipation of when she might use it.

13

Carl found Yolanda at the picnic table, gazing out across the fallow wheat field next to camp. The walk home had been dry, and the exercise had warmed his muscles. He'd carefully considered Hershel's question about the guns. It was a terrible business, the guns. But participation in this *victimless crime,* as Hershel once called it, was the price Carl paid for steady work close to home. Work that provided him with a sense of purpose in strange and oblique ways. It was best, he decided, to leave the question alone. Let Hershel puzzle it out if he could.

Yolanda spotted Carl and hastily wiped her sleeve across her face. "You okay?" he asked.

"Oh, Carlos, I'm fine."

"You sure?" He surveyed the camp. A familiar row of satellite receivers pointed south, a platoon of dutiful soldiers. "Look a little down to me."

She shook her head. "I miss my boys, that's all."

"They've only gone to Eugene—barely two hours away."

She said nothing. They'd been gone only three days, and it was routine for Manuel and Eduardo, two hopeless mama's boys in their late twenties, to roam as far as a day's drive away for the best work. Yolanda stayed at Campo Rojo, maintaining a tentative sense of family permanence by way of consistency.

Carl put his arm around her shoulder, and she leaned her head against him. They'd embraced like this before, and it was becoming familiar. Easy in its softness. But he was too cowardly to take the next step—to kiss her temple, to invite her into his home. Today would be no different. He couldn't bear the thought of her rejection, though he'd take the sweet scent of her perfume with him and lounge on his bed remembering the warmth of her body against his. For days he would find a secret joy in this small touch.

A door suddenly popped open, shuddering on its hinges, and a man shouted in Spanish. The boy Carl had seen there before ran out and plopped down on the step, looking over his shoulder furtively. His cheeks were ruddy and he'd been crying.

Yolanda pulled away, and as Carl turned to get a better look she put an apprehensive hand on his forearm. Her fingers were icy, and he could feel them through his shirtsleeve. "Leave him."

"Wasn't planning to do anything else."

"These are bad people. Mean."

"Yeah, I got that already."

"Did they threaten you?"

"Threaten me? Why would they do that?"

"I don't know. I . . . they wouldn't. I don't know why I said that."

The door opened again, and the hard little man stared out at Carl and Yolanda. He narrowed his eyes, and Yolanda jerked her hand away.

"We better go inside," she said, getting to her feet.

Carl stood also, and the man slammed the door, causing the boy to cower and bury his face between his knees.

"Carlos," Yolanda whispered. "Be careful. Please."

———

"I get tired a little easier than I used to," Hershel said over cold ham sandwiches. Silvie ate well tonight, and he noticed. "But I'll get new tires and a battery for that car tomorrow. We'll have it running by nightfall."

"How long has it been ... since your accident?"

"A little over three months."

"Does it still hurt?"

"I get some monster headaches. Keep hoping that'll go away, but they don't seem to." Hershel was coming to appreciate Silvie's careful questions.

"I'm sorry about yesterday," she said.

"What do you mean?"

"All that crying—I was a mess. I feel better today."

"I can tell. You're eating, anyway."

"It was the work. It did me good."

"Do you have anyone back home who's worrying about you?" Hershel asked. In a way, he hoped she was as alone as he was. It was comforting, the idea that she, too, might not have any discernible connections. He didn't really wish for her the sort of loneliness that he suffered.

"My mom, I suppose, is worried."

"She doesn't know where you are?"

"No one does."

"Do you want to call her?"

Silvie put down her sandwich and leaned heavily on her elbows. "I don't know what I would tell her."

"The truth?"

"Jacob Castor would be here in exactly the time it takes to drive from Wyoming to Oregon, maybe faster."

It was the first time she'd said the man's name, and Hershel rolled it over and over in his mind. He repeated it to himself, a chant. It was important not to forget this name the way he did all others. "So, I take it she doesn't know what he's done."

"She knows."

Hershel tried to fathom the idea. "How could she allow that to happen? He's a predator."

"Hmm ... *predator*." Silvie whispered the word. "That's an interesting way to call it."

"That's what it is—what *he* is."

"You think so?" Silvie took up her sandwich and ate as she waited for Hershel's response.

"Of course. Don't you?"

"I don't know. Maybe. I was pretty young."

"Silvie," he said, leaning across the table. "You said yourself that you didn't *let* him. And I'd say twelve is more than *pretty young*."

She shrugged. "Sometimes I don't know. That's what they say, you know? That girls are victims if they're under eighteen. He paid our heat bill lots of times. I think we would've been thrown out on the street if it weren't for Jacob. He was nice most of the time. I'm sure he paid the rent at least once, but my mom never would tell me."

"Was he dating your mother?" Hershel tried to piece together the circumstances of how Silvie had come to be at the mercy of a pedophile.

"No." She looked out the window for a few minutes, and Hershel waited for her to elaborate. "Is your mother still alive?"

"She lives in Baker City. Out on the eastern end of Oregon."

"Do you talk very often?"

"No." He struggled with the urge to change the subject. But maybe it would help her to know that she wasn't the only one with a messed-up family life. "They didn't even come to see me when I was in the hospital." He cringed as soon as he said it, realizing how trivial it sounded. She'd suffered worse things than he had. And Hershel was certain that he was responsible for the absence of family harmony, though he couldn't remember what he'd done that was terrible enough to keep them away in his hour of need.

"Wow, that's harsh."

"It didn't feel very good."

They sat quiet and comfortable in shared silence for a while. Finally Hershel said, "What kind of mother would tell this Jacob Castor where you are? Why would she do that?"

"She wouldn't do it on purpose. Not to hurt me, anyway. She drinks too much. She'd be all relieved to hear from me and tell everyone that I called and exactly where I am."

"You don't have to tell her where you are."

"I know. I should call her. I don't want her to worry, really. It's just that I know Jacob is asking her. He's probably stalking her, waiting for information, and she'll tell him. She will." Silvie finished her sandwich in silence. Then she sat back and smoothed her hair, lost in thought.

"Two lonely people, we are," Hershel said, as he stood and picked up the dishes. He set them in the sink and got down a pair of tumblers. "Brandy?"

"I've never had it."

He poured them each a drink and returned to the table. "It's your business. I won't bring it up again, but if you want to call you're welcome to use the phone."

"It's long-distance."

"I can afford it."

Silvie sipped her drink daintily, her nose wrinkled as if she wasn't sure whether she liked it. "Thanks for everything you're doing for me. Bet you didn't expect this much trouble when you stopped to help me that night on the road."

"Nope, not even half this much trouble." They both laughed. "It's okay. I wasn't doing anything important, anyway. Was sure as hell sick of my own company."

"Do you think Kyrellis will really try to blackmail Jacob?"

"If he figures out who he is? Yeah, I think he might."

"He's gonna lead Jacob straight here—straight to me. I should get as far away from here as I can as soon as I can."

"You're safer here. At least you have people to watch out for you."

"You're no match for Jacob."

Hershel felt his cheeks flush as her assessment of him sank in.

"I don't mean physically," she said, suddenly aware of how her statement must have sounded.

That was worse, he thought.

"I mean—" She waved a hand in the air, as if to wipe away her last comments. "He's sort of above the law. He can do what he wants, and there's no one to stop him."

"That's not true."

"Yes, it is."

"Well, maybe in Wyoming, but not here. Probably not even in most of Wyoming. How big is the town you come from?"

"Small. Six hundred people, about."

"Is he the only cop?"

"He covers the whole county. Jacob and two deputies. He doesn't even live in Hanley."

"You think he'll do anything to stop Kyrellis and come after you, but I think that's only true within the boundaries of his world. Why would he risk coming out here to hurt you?"

"Because that's how he is."

"No. He's a coward."

"He's not. Don't be fooled."

They stared across the table for a moment, neither backing down.

"I don't want you taking off because you're scared of this guy. If you want to leave, go for some other reason, like that you have some place you really want to be. But don't just go out of fear."

Silvie rolled her tongue across her lower lip, thinking.

He studied her. Was he making any impact? "If you're afraid now, how will you be any less afraid somewhere else?"

She bit into her lip, her eyes cast downward, masked by soft blond lashes.

"You'll never be able to stop running."

Her eyes came up to meet his, and she had tears.

"Don't," he said, getting to his feet and pulling her up. She leaned against him, and he hugged her. "I'm sorry. I shouldn't have said those things. I wasn't trying to upset you."

Her hair gave off the faint scent of apples. The unexpected touch of another person surprised him. Her softness against him made him unquenchably thirsty for more.

"You don't know," she said quietly. "You just don't know."

Silvie held Hershel's cellphone away from her ear and listened for signs that she'd roused him, but the house was still. The clock above the kitchen sink snapped out each second, and the moonlight cast an eerie blue sheen over the linoleum. The phone rang several times, and she knew that he wasn't going to answer. Still, she held on until the call was forwarded to Kyrellis's voice mail. She hoped she could appeal to his sense of decency. If not, she would persuade him through other avenues.

She heard a floor joist squeak above her and she paused a moment to listen. Then she wiped the phone off and set it on the counter, where she'd found it. She had to talk to Kyrellis. Had to understand him. They could negotiate. It was just a matter of laying out the ground rules. Or so she hoped.

"Everything okay?" Hershel startled her, and she jumped. He came into the kitchen barefoot, wearing a bathrobe. "I didn't mean to scare you."

She caught her breath, fluttering a hand over her heart. "Yeah, everything is fine. I just came down for some water."

He filled a glass and held it out to her like a gift. He watched her through the darkness as she drank. After a moment, she approached him, taking his hand, and the two slid quietly into each other's arms. She set the glass clumsily on the counter, and he muffed her ears with his hands, tilting her head back and kissing her. She encouraged him; it was what he expected for letting her stay. But she'd never been with any man but Jacob, and she didn't really know what to do. Sex in the movies was nothing like what she experienced in Jacob's bedroom. She often wondered which version was common and which was make-believe. As Hershel sucked her tongue deep into his mouth, she hoped he wouldn't ask her to strip for him. She hated that more than anything else.

Upstairs, he guided her to his bedroom but left the lights turned out. She assumed that he didn't want to see her naked. Was it the pictures? Was he imagining another woman as he stroked her?

He carefully undressed her, and she opened his robe, finding him erect. She knelt and took him in her mouth while he watched through the darkness. His deep-throated groan assured her that she was doing what he liked. But soon he was pulling her up onto her feet again, seeking her mouth. Had she done something wrong?

As his fingers roamed her breasts, she tensed. He noticed and stopped. "Is this okay?" he asked. "We don't have to."

"Yes. It's okay," she said, admonishing herself for interrupting him. "What do you want me to do?"

He caressed her hair. "Just let me make love to you." He kissed her again and eased her onto the bed. She couldn't quite get used to the soft touch. His skin against hers raised gooseflesh, and she mastered every muscle in her body to stop herself from trembling and making him think she didn't want to do this. When he entered her it was a sharp, painful breach. She sucked her breath in and held it there as he pulled her hips toward him and struck deeper into her core. When he finished, tears had leaked from the corners of her eyes, but she released a sigh in time with his.

14

Carl stepped out of his cabin before dawn, a dream—or, rather, a familiar nightmare of Vietnam—still gripping his subconscious. He scratched at his arms, pockmarked and now raw. No matter how long he abstained, the urge lay only beneath the surface. A simple dream away.

He wore a wool cap low over his ears, and an extra pair of socks. The landscape lay muted in shades of blue-gray. Rain drizzled out of a dark sky, and he buttoned his coat to the collar. He carried an old metal Tonka truck, dented and hard-used. He'd been saving it for the right kid, and the right kid was just across the muddy yard. Life in this place was too hard for children. There was no room for innocence here. Carl set the truck down on the step, assured that the boy would find it when his father next sent him out. Upon further consideration, he moved it to the ground next to the step, where the boy would see it but the father would not. Carl guessed that its beneficiary would need to hide it in order to keep it.

When he reached the highway, the rain was falling steadily with a west wind, stinging his nose and his fingers. He shoved his hands into his coat pockets and leaned into his stride.

"You! *Pendejo!*"

Carl turned to see who had shouted. Three shadowy figures followed twenty feet or so behind him. He glanced around for help, but the road was quiet at this hour. A tense unease came over him as he listened to their approaching footsteps. His dream of Vietnam, still fresh, reacquainted him with the idea that someone might kill him for reasons that were more ideas and principles than personal.

"What do you want?" he shouted back, pausing to face his pursuers.

"*Usted encuentra a la mujer* attractive."

Carl turned and trudged ahead, puzzling the words together.

"Hey you, fucker!" another shouted.

"I've done nothing to you," he said over his shoulder. "I'm making my way, the same as anyone."

"*Auséntese del Yolanda!*" Her name was spit at him with venom. The men broke into a run, the soft gravel along the shoulder of the highway spinning beneath their boots.

"She's a friend," he said, knowing he couldn't outrun them; he was twice their age. "*Amiga.*"

The short man Carl had seen with the boy lunged forward. Carl stepped back, but the man swung fast, catching him square in the jaw. His head spun, and he heard the bones of his neck pop as he went down. Pain spread across his ribs as one of the men buried a boot in his side. Carl struggled to get up, but he was knocked to the ground again. He took the toe of a boot square in the nose, sending brilliant yellow sparks through his vision. He lay in the gravel, recovering his sight as the three stood over him, staring down, their faces dark and their heads round against the chalky sky. The man who first hit him ran his index finger slowly across his own throat in a warning.

A pickup came around the corner, its headlights casting a yellow beam across the scene, and the men scattered, running into the brush along the river. Carl heard it pull off the road and idle there for a long moment; then a door slammed. He struggled to a sitting position and wiped blood from his nose.

The driver stood his distance and shouted, "You okay?"

Carl worked at getting his feet under him, finally staggering to a stand. "Yeah."

"You sure?" The man came closer now, but walked with rigid apprehension. "I called the police. I'll wait with you till they get here."

"You didn't need to do that." Carl felt along his side to assess the injury to his ribs. "I'm just bruised is all."

"Well, they might come back. I'm not leaving anyone out here to get the shit beat out of them. I don't care what you did."

"I didn't do anything. I was just minding my own business. Walking to work."

Carl pulled his hat off and used it to stanch the flow of blood from his nose. His jaw was aching powerfully, but his breath was finally coming back to him in slow bursts.

The man leaned against his truck. "Where d'you work?"

"Swift Consignment Auction."

"Oh, yeah," the man said with a vague nod. "He's back now, I hear."

The sky began whitening in the east, but the rain didn't let up. Carl wished the man would at least invite him to sit in the truck if he insisted on calling the police and waiting until they arrived. But he simply leaned against the tailgate, his broad cowboy hat shuttling the rain down the back of his waterproof jacket.

"Swift," the man said, as if remembering Hershel personally. "How long you worked for *that* son of a bitch?"

"A while."

"He's crooked."

Carl had heard it all before and didn't care to hear it again. "Been all right to me."

The sheriff's patrol arrived from the north, casting strobes of blue and red across the gray morning. Traffic was beginning to pick up, and a few drivers slowed and stared as they passed. The sheriff parked in front of the pickup and pulled his hat on before stepping out. He held his hand carefully centered over his gun.

Carl hated law-enforcement men. He believed the profession was a magnet for the worst sort of control freaks and insecure weirdos society had ever produced.

"Hear you two are having a fight," the sheriff said as he reached them.

The man who had stopped to help was suddenly outraged. "*We* aren't fighting. I came around the corner and found three Mexicans kicking the shit outta this guy." He gestured at Carl.

Carl shook his head, sending pain shuddering through his temples. There was no way the man could know those three were Mexican—not in this light. Today, however, would not be the day to stand on principle.

In Silvie's dream she was ten years old. A hot Wyoming summer had parched the ground to powdery dust. Sagebrush and prickly pear were all that survived out on the rocky plains, and the family had escaped to the Muddy River for the afternoon. Her father had stopped at the Gas 'n Go and let her pick out a small bag of chips and a soda. Silvie tucked them along the floorboard in the backseat of their Maverick, a treat to be savored, something to look forward to. Her father was an amateur fossil hunter who worked for the school district as a custodian. His hobby, which he preferred to pursue alone, had given him intimate knowledge of the southern Wyoming landscape. In Silvie's dream he took them to a remote, deserted stretch of river with a wide grassy slope and a deep pool. There she shrieked with delight and plunged into the tepid water, splashing wildly, while her mother situated herself on the bank. Melody carried a box of blush wine, something of a constant prop, and a romance novel. Her father disappeared up the slope to a rock quarry in search of fossils, despite his daughter's insistent pleas to watch her jumping into the water.

Silvie's dream was always the same. Her father wanders over

the low-flung bank, a canvas sack draped across his right shoulder. He never looks back. He never *comes* back, though Silvie waits.

Silvie woke in a strange place to the rumble of snoring. She stared up at the ceiling, the familiar dream still casting its gloomy pall—its suffocating sense of abandonment. She could feel his presence next to her. Her life had changed so suddenly. She was now a waitress at the South Store and expected to report to work that morning, and Hershel would be off to find tires and a battery for a car that was not hers but would be hers in the practical sense. As she stirred, thinking of a shower, trying to put this development into perspective, Hershel rolled over and wrapped his arms around her. It felt surprisingly nice there, warm and comforting. He pulled her against him so tight she could hardly breathe, her face buried in his hairy chest.

Jacob had come back to the tavern the week after they'd first met. She heard his voice echoing through the dining room as she bent over her schoolwork in her usual corner of the kitchen. Her skin had prickled with excitement at the sound of that distinct and confident tone.

"Where is she?" he asked. "Where is my little scholar?"

"She's home, where she belongs." Melody Thorne's voice was pleading. Silvie felt her mother's fear, and it somehow made his request more exhilarating.

Perhaps Jacob had seen Silvie slip in the back door earlier, or maybe he just had a way of knowing. A man like that knew things that weren't apparent to others, Silvie believed. Her initial disappointment rapidly turned to relief that her mother stood between this man and her.

"Nonsense," Jacob boomed. "She's in the kitchen. Send her out."

Melody poked her head around the corner, jerking her chin hard toward the dining room.

Silvie got up from the chair and smoothed her skirt, feeling somehow underdressed anyway, and slowly walked out to where Jacob waited. His eyes lingered on her for a long moment. He said nothing, just tilted his face to the side and appraised her. Then a smile spread over his lips, even while his eyes stayed firmly fixed, making Silvie feel even smaller than she was.

"There's my girl," he said. The phrase became his calling card. *My girl*. He would call her that so frequently in the coming years that Silvie would consider it a second name, but the resolute firmness of that first declaration remained to this day. *My girl*.

"She needs a break from the books, I think," Jacob announced. "An ice-cream cone is what she needs."

"But she's got schoolwork to finish," Melody protested.

Silvie turned and looked over her shoulder to see her mother chewing her lip, wringing her hands, and Charlie behind her looking grim. Finally her mother relented with a meek shrug. "I guess she can go."

Charlie neither relented nor stopped it. He simply stood in the doorway between the bar and the kitchen, a dark expression on his tired face. He kept shaking his head in a slow back-and-forth gesture that Silvie tried to puzzle out as she followed Jacob to his waiting truck. She thought about it many more times in the years that followed. He knew—Charlie knew.

Silvie tipped her head back and looked at the cleft in Hershel's chin. She felt dirty. She'd never cheated on Jacob before. She missed his familiarity, his warmth. She missed the way he talked to her. She missed breakfast at Alison's Café and the way Jacob always teased the waitresses. She missed his aftershave, and the way he smoothed her hair and twirled it around his fingers. It left a hard lump at the back of her throat, and she felt tears coming. But at least Hershel was more likely to let her stay now . . . to protect her.

"I'd better get in the shower," she said, and slid from Hershel's arms, wishing for something to cover her nakedness.

"Don't go," he said, pulling her back into bed. He peered at her with eyes blacker than she had imagined anyone's could be. He pressed his lips to her forehead, then her nose, and finally to her mouth. He thrust his tongue into her and explored. She let him, feeling helpless. Then he rolled on top of her and parted her legs, sliding inside. He was so much bigger than Jacob, and it took her breath away. He seemed to find new depths with each forward thrust, which she found invasive but not unpleasant.

After several minutes, Hershel groaned and fell against her, smothering her. "You're beautiful," he whispered.

He propped himself up on one elbow, gazing down at her. He gently smoothed the hair away from her eyes and kissed her nose. She smiled up at him, for no other reason than she'd never guessed that the quiet and sometimes curt man who'd rescued her on the highway would behave so tenderly.

"You do know it, don't you?"

She laughed, despite herself. "I have to get ready for work," she said. "It was your idea, remember?"

"What was I thinking? I could've had you in my bed all day, but instead I sent you down to the South Store to get a job. I will never cease to amaze myself. I must be the biggest moron roaming the planet."

She slid out from under him. He let her go, watching as she crossed the room in the nude, hugging her small breasts to herself as if to hide them. Wishing she could do the same about her ass.

Hershel found Carl at the sale barn, his face bruised. The left side of his jaw was swollen to twice its normal size, and there were crusts of blood around his nostrils. Dark streaks stained his shirt. The man limped around as if he were eighty.

"What happened to you?" he asked. But even this discovery couldn't dampen his jovial spirits. He felt like a new man.

Carl shrugged and winced as he hoisted a small box of canning jars onto his shoulder. "Couple of guys got me confused with someone else is all. I'm fine."

"What guys?"

Carl carried the box to the end of a long aisle of household goods. "Just some new guys in camp."

"Why would they confuse you with someone else?"

Carl dropped the box and turned to Hershel. "You never asked these sorts of questions before."

"I guess there are lots of things I never did before," he said to Carl. He smiled, unable to stop himself.

Carl stared, apprehensive. "You're in a good mood."

"Yeah, guess so." Hershel thought again about Silvie and how she'd walked into the restaurant that morning while he waited in the pickup, making sure she was safely inside the building, as if she might be abducted in broad daylight. So what if he never asked these questions before. That was a different Hershel. He would ask after his employees if he felt like it. He'd take an interest in why the only person who seemed to still be here, taking care of things and tending to business after all these months, was coming into work bloody and limping. Hell, he might even call his mother.

"I filed a police report. It's no big deal."

"Good."

"Kyrellis called," Carl said.

"What did he want?"

"Wanted to know if you'd be down here today."

He clenched his hands into fists. Perhaps the man had decided on a figure. "Wonder why he didn't just call my cell?"

Carl sorted through boxes, marking their contents on the flap with a grease pen so that it would be easy to work through the items during the sale. He'd delivered the message and couldn't be drawn into a conversation.

"He's got a box that belongs to Silvie," Hershel said, then wished he hadn't.

"I'm really sorry about that fuckup," Carl said. "It's been bugging me."

"Just did what you thought was right," he said, and started toward his office.

He tried to hold on to his good mood, but it was sifting away like fine mist. He'd made a phone call that morning to Trent Campbell, a local auto reseller, to find out if Trent had parts he could use to get the Porsche running again. Trent was terse on the phone, claimed he didn't have the parts and couldn't order them. Hershel asked him if he had any cars to put through the next sale, and Trent laughed without humor. They'd worked together in the past, but how long he couldn't pin down. A decade at least. Anything that stayed on Campbell's lot more than ninety days went to auction. But the man was gruff today, stating that he didn't think he'd be using Hershel's services in the future. Campbell thought he'd made that clear already. When Hershel inquired why, the man simply called him a "first-rate asshole" and hung up.

The first thing Hershel did when he got to his office was go to the file cabinet, pull open the top drawer, and begin to search for anything that had to do with Campbell's Auto Liquidators. He found nothing more recent than a two-year-old receipt for three cars. Campbell typically put the newer-model cars in reasonable condition through Hershel's auction, and the others went to the salvage yard for parts. He stared at the paper. Was it really two years ago that he'd last sold cars for Campbell? That's how he picked up Floyd, his Charger. Campbell had planned to part it out, but when Hershel saw the car, he talked the man into putting it through the sale. He could still remember the way it sat on the lot beckoning to him. The paint was oxidized, the weather stripping gone, the windshield cracked. But it was irresistible.

"It doesn't run," Campbell had told him. "I can get decent money for parts, though. It's a classic. The front end will bring a thousand bucks."

"Exactly," Hershel said. "Someone will want it to restore."

Campbell shook his head. "It'll need to bring at least eighteen hundred or I'm better off parting it out."

"It will." Hershel felt his skin prickle as he relived the conversation. He bought the car himself for six hundred dollars. And then he towed it to his house, where he restored it over the course of a year.

He looked down at the receipt. It was shortly after the date on that piece of paper that Campbell figured out that the newly restored Charger was the very same one he'd sold through Hershel's auction—at a loss. The brazenness with which he had taken advantage of Campbell and their business relationship astounded Hershel now. Did he think the man wouldn't find out? Why would he risk his business like that? It didn't make sense. There had to be more to it.

Silvie watched a spider scuttle across the kitchen floor at the South Store. It had a large brown abdomen with a triangular design that reminded her of a Navajo blanket. The summer she turned eighteen, she encountered a spider just like that one in Jacob's backyard. It had strung a perfectly symmetrical web in the space between his toolshed and a juniper bush. She'd watched it grow over the weeks, until it was monstrous in size, and though she had a particularly irrational fear of spiders, she left this one alone. It fascinated her, and it was confined to this place out in the open, honest about its intentions, not like the funnel spiders that tunneled along the walkway or under the decking.

One evening, as she waited for Jacob to finish up some work in his den, she sat in the garden sipping iced tea and watching the spider. A honeybee flew into the web, tearing it so badly that it was held in place by only two strands. The bee was nearly the size of the spider, but the predator pounced so rapidly that by the time Silvie was on her feet and bent over the scene it had already begun to spin its prey in circles. The bee fought hard, thrashing furiously, piercing the growing cocoon with its stinger over and over. It took minutes for the spider to finally subdue the bee—a fight that might have gone either way had the honeybee gotten just the right angle on the spider. When it was over, the bee was unrecognizable in its thick white shroud. A mummy, though still alive, still trying to break free.

Jacob appeared behind Silvie, startling her.

"What's so fascinating?" he asked, placing his hand on her hip, just above her buttocks.

"That spider caught a honeybee," she said. "You should've seen it. It fought so hard, and it took forever for the spider to win."

Jacob scowled at Silvie and said, "You didn't cut it loose? You just watched it die?" He traced her face with his eyes, clearly disturbed by her willingness to stand by and do nothing.

Silvie studied the cocoon, still quivering with life, and wondered what was going through the bee's mind right then. Terror? She had trouble reconciling her place in this event, her responsibility. Wasn't this life? The weak overtaken by the strong?

Jacob gave her a hard swat on the butt. "What's gotten into you?"

"You okay?" Karen asked, bringing Silvie back to the kitchen and the stack of dishes in her hands.

"Yeah," she said, and dropped them into the sink before washing up.

"Order up for table three."

Silvie dried her hands and collected the hot plates, balancing them precariously on her forearms as she stepped out into the warm dining room. The smell of freshly baked bread and the high-pitched whine of the espresso machine brought a smile to her face. The crowd was larger today and people were still coming in, dressed in fall fleece, their ears and noses reddened by the winter cold. They carried maps of Washington and Yamhill County wineries and discussed their routes. Where next? We can go out to McMinnville and circle back through Amity. Or up to Warden Hill in Dundee and then downvalley to Salem. Places with ro-

mantic names that she'd never heard of and could not fathom—
Oak Knoll, Vista Ridge, Sokol Blosser, Erath. They even chatted
across tables with strangers about where they'd been that morning, where they were headed, and which wineries they recommended. She wanted to be like these people, walk in their world,
experience life as they did. Unencumbered by the problems she
faced, these were the kind of people magazines like *Western Living*
and *Sunset* were written for. No doubt they had cloth napkins on
their tables, crystal in their china hutches, maybe even sleek-
coated horses in country stables. Their lifestyles were remote and
fascinating, nothing like hers. Still, the bustle of people swept
away all thoughts of Jacob or Hershel or Kyrellis. For the moment, she could imagine that she belonged here with these people, and it was a reprieve from the reality of her own life.

15

Hershel watched Kyrellis come in and speak briefly to Carl before finding his way to the open office door. Kyrellis paused there before stepping inside, smoothing the silver along his temples with his thick hand. His face was aged with soft lines, and his eyes made him look perpetually remorseful. He took the chair opposite Hershel's desk without waiting for an invitation, unbuttoning his coat as he sat.

"I heard on the police scanner there was a fight down at the migrant camp this morning. Looks like your man got the worst end of it."

Hershel leaned back in his chair and bent a paper clip between his fingers. It figured that Kyrellis listened to a police scanner.

"I don't mean to tell you how to run your business, but a loser like that will only cause trouble."

"He's been decent help," Hershel said.

Kyrellis glanced over his shoulder into the warehouse and shrugged. "At least he's white."

"What do you want, Kyrellis?"

He raised his eyebrows. "Why so unfriendly?"

"I don't like what you're doing."

Kyrellis dug through his coat pocket and dropped a photograph on Hershel's desk.

Hershel stared down at the little girl in the picture, her hair in ponytails, wearing knee socks and nothing else. She lay back on a bed, legs spread. Too young even to have breasts. His stomach lurched. Her flat stare couldn't hide her pain. He swiped up the picture and tore it into pieces.

"Hey!" Kyrellis came out of his seat. "That could've earned us both some money now."

"You sick fucker! You want to exploit her. I want to protect her."

"That's very admirable of you," Kyrellis said genuinely as he sat back again. "But a girl like that is too far gone to protect. You think you can undo what another man has done? Face it, Swift, she's damaged goods." He sighed heavily. "It's okay that you tore that one up. I was planning to give it to you, anyway. I have others at home."

"You bastard."

"I'm losing my patience with you." Kyrellis got to his feet again and stepped toward the door. "I know he's a cop. There's a badge on the dresser in one of the pictures. And I know she's from Wyoming. It's just a matter of time before I find the *right* cop."

"And then what?"

"And then he's going to pay me to keep these in a safe place. Unless you'd like to do that for him."

"I'll turn you in before I do that."

"No, you won't. If you turn me in I'll hand over the evidence that you murdered Albert Darling."

Hershel stared at Kyrellis, unable to find words for response.

"I thought you were just playing me, but I can see now that you really don't remember. You don't remember that you were coming back from disposing of his body the night you had your accident. The evidence is all over your car, which—" He looked solemnly at Hershel. "Which belongs to me."

Hershel's breath evacuated and his scar ached. He suffered a dark and fleeting image of the broad backs of hogs and mud. He could smell the stench. "That's not true," he said, completely unsure.

"Really? Then *you* tell *me* what happened that night? Where were you coming from?" Kyrellis waited for a response, but none came. "You'll go to prison for the rest of your life. How will you protect her then?"

———

A few customers lingered in the dining room as Silvie wiped down the empty tables, preparing for the end of her shift. Her feet were on fire. She'd have to get more comfortable shoes, and she guessed that she had enough in tip money between the two days to buy a pair if she was frugal. She would ask Karen to recommend a place once Hershel had the car running.

She didn't know why she'd seduced him. The first time she slept with Jacob, he'd been coming by the tavern to get her for nearly six weeks. He'd worked his way up to the big event. After the ice-cream cone that first day, he'd hinted that she might like to do something for him, but he didn't say what exactly. On the second afternoon that he took her out, he asked her to take off her top as she sipped the root-beer float he'd bought her. They were parked at the reservoir on a cold spring day, but the sun felt warm through the windshield of his pickup. She understood that it wasn't right. But what else could she do except comply with his wishes?

"Don't worry, sweetheart, everything is going to be okay," Jacob had told her, which confused her more than it comforted.

Kyrellis stood in the doorway and spied her, then surveyed the room, choosing a table in the corner near the window, where he chatted convivially with the next table. Silvie looked for Karen. Technically, her shift was over; she could pull her apron off and walk out. She peered through the service window into the kitchen.

"Got a new table out here," Silvie said.

Karen set down a large bucket of bleach water and pushed a strand of hair behind her ear. She looked exhausted. "Can you stay a little longer and handle it?"

Silvie glanced back at the man, who was watching her from the corner of his eye as he recommended wineries. "Sure."

"Afternoon, Silvie," he said as she approached.

She pulled an order pad from her pocket. "What can I get you?"

"Just coffee."

"Coming up." She set a cup in front of him on the buttery wood, but her hand shook and she spilled the coffee. She leaned in to wipe up the mess and he took a napkin from her, calmly finishing the job. When he was done he smiled up at her, and had he not stolen the most relevant and damning thing to her in the entire world, she would have thought him to be a warm, engaging gentleman. He had a way about him, incongruent with what she knew.

"Please return them," she said quietly.

"Who is he?"

"I'll tell him who *you* are before I tell you that."

"I know he's a cop." Kyrellis eyed the table next to him, but the couple were deep in conversation.

"What do you want?"

"I might be willing to trade some of them back to you for a favor or two," he said. "I'm sure we can work something out." His eyes slid across her shoulders and down her front.

She had hoped this man had a price, but being faced with the certainty of doing him favors made her stomach roll.

He turned his attention to the menu. "Certainly the idea isn't that distasteful. Is it?"

"Tell me exactly what it would take. For all of them. Not *some*. All!"

"I'll have to think about that." He poured sugar into his coffee and stirred slowly. "I think your friend, whoever he is, will pay a high price. Tell me his name and I'll give you back all the ones where we can tell it's you."

"He'll kill me. He'll hunt me down and kill me like a rat."

The couple at the next table went silent, the man eyeing Silvie and Kyrellis. Kyrellis smiled, as if to tell the man it was a joke, and he returned to his conversation.

"Then he'll kill *you*," she whispered.

"I don't think your judgment is reliable in this matter. After all, you're already sleeping with the most dangerous man you could possibly find."

Silvie struggled to follow him.

"Ask your new friend Hershel where he was coming from the night of his accident." Kyrellis lowered his voice. "Seems you have an appetite for murderers, I guess."

"What do you mean?"

Kyrellis stood and placed two dollars on the table. "That's for the coffee." He then pulled a twenty from his wallet and pressed it into her hand. "That's for the service I think you're capable of."

She tossed it on the table, but he was already on his way out. When she turned away, the couple at the other table were staring again. Silvie bit her lip, whisked up the twenty, and shoved it into her apron.

Hershel stood in the middle of his wrecked office, his knuckles bleeding and his head throbbing. He kicked the upturned file cabinet. The drawers of his desk were broken, mingled with the shattered remnants of a coffee cup.

Kyrellis had gotten the best of him—sent him searching vainly for anything to put this man, Albert Darling, back in his brain, back into the context of his life. But Hershel had found nothing, and the harder he'd looked, the more frantic he'd become, until he'd suffered a fury so deep that he couldn't stop himself. He had let loose three months of ineptitude, inability, lost identity.

Hershel slumped down in his office chair, spent and nauseated. A knock at the door, and a muffled voice. "Boss? You okay?"

Hershel closed his eyes. This wasn't the first attempt Carl had made. "Yeah," he said.

There was a silence on the other side. Then Carl said, "You need anything?"

"No." Hershel kicked at the pile of papers near his foot.

Carl swept the warehouse floor, preparing to lock up until Monday afternoon, when they would allow people in to preview the sale. The ad had run in the *Hillsboro Argus* the previous day, generating a slew of phone calls from dealers and collectors wanting specific details about the architectural items. Another would run in the Saturday *Oregonian* in the morning. It would be a good sale, with a big crowd, and he noticed that Hershel was assembling a long list of specific items in a particular order. Carl had found the list on Hershel's desk that morning, grateful, and endeavored to organize the merchandise into a systematic pattern to match the order in which Hershel would call it up.

The front door creaked open and Silvie came in, shaking rain off her jacket.

"Afternoon," Carl called.

She paused when she saw his face. "You okay?"

"Yeah, just got into a little scrape is all." He hoped the swelling would be gone by the Tuesday-evening sale. He was tired of the attention it drew.

"I've got feet to match your face," she said, taking a seat on a box near the door and pulling off one shoe. She peeled down her sock and exposed a red and oozing blister on her heel the size of a quarter.

He whistled. "That looks downright angry."

She picked at the skin around it, scrunching her face against the pain. "I'm not used to waiting tables. And these shoes are terrible."

Carl went into the concession stand and retrieved a small first-aid kit.

"Is Hershel here? I didn't see his truck."

He knelt down on the floor and unfolded a small wipe soaked in alcohol. "Went over to Les Schwab in Sherwood after some tires."

Silvie sucked her breath in as he laid the alcohol pad on the blister. "That stings."

"It's good for it. Hold it there a sec. How's your other foot?"

"Same as this one."

He felt her eyes on him and glanced up. She looked away and began unlacing her other shoe.

"Where was Hershel coming from the night he had his accident?"

Carl took his time cleaning the blister and covering it with a bandage. He started swabbing the matching blister on her other foot, carefully weighing his response. "Why?" he finally asked.

"I don't know. Something Kyrellis said."

"When did you talk to Kyrellis?"

"He stopped at the South Store. A special visit just for me."

"Hershel told me that he's got something that belongs to you," Carl said. When he saw her cheeks burn red, he wished he hadn't brought it up. "Did you get it back?"

"No."

"This is my fault. I can try and help you. Maybe talk to him."

"I suppose Hershel also told you what it is?" She sounded angry.

"He didn't."

"I don't think you can help with this."

"You don't know that. Maybe there's something I can do." He pressed a bandage over the second blister and sat back on his heels. "How's that?"

"Much better," she said, pulling her socks on. "Thank you."

"You know where to find me if you need anything," he said, returning the first-aid kit to the concession stand.

"If I tell you what Kyrellis has," she began slowly, "you'll think differently of me."

"I don't think any particular way now. How could it be different?"

"Believe me, it can."

"Silvie, there isn't much you can tell me that would shock or surprise me. I've seen and done worse things in my life than most people could even imagine. I try to make a general habit of not judging other people."

She pondered this so long that Carl stopped waiting for her and picked up the broom again and began sweeping.

"Do you think I can trust Hershel?"

The question wasn't what he'd expected. Carl sized her up, weighed her need against his experience with Hershel Swift.

———

Hershel turned the ignition and pulled onto Tualatin-Sherwood Road, past the cinema and across Highway 99. Sherwood was no longer the same town he'd grown up in. It had boomed in the past ten years, growing from six thousand to sixteen thousand residents. Where the Borscher farm once stood, there was now a Safeway. The open fields where Langers had grown onions and harvested walnuts were now strip malls with fast-food restaurants, a dry cleaner, gas stations, and a brewpub. New streetlights caused traffic congestion, backing up miles of SUVs and high-end sports cars that had never been part of *his* Sherwood. What was once a farming community was now one of the more affluent suburbs of Portland, despite the fact that it was more than twenty miles away from the city's center.

As he passed the mini-storage, he craned to see if Woody was at the counter. Should he stop? There was no reason to. Woody had asked if Albert Darling was still bothering him; clearly he believed Darling was alive. And maybe he was. But something about Darling was trapped in Hershel's blotted-over memory, like inky stains obliterating some critical fact. It left him to guess and extrapolate, question himself and Kyrellis. The man knew something, but was he telling the truth?

He turned onto Scholls-Sherwood Road, and the familiarity of the countryside returned to him. Rolling corn and onion fields, now dormant, stretched narrowly between hills of Christmas trees and filberts. A few more vineyards had sprung up, their clean lines and open space bringing a gentle order to things, even with the absence of leaves. He breathed in the cool, fresh air and promised to take Silvie to the top of Chehalem Mountain in the spring, when the trillium and wild dogwood bloomed white and dotted the misty hills.

Hershel glanced at his watch. It was nearly three o'clock. Silvie would be ready. The thought of her waiting for him at his warehouse—waiting to go home with him—caused the nagging sense of unease to evaporate.

When Hershel reached Scholls and the auction barn, the sun had broken through and he had momentarily forgotten about Kyrellis and Albert Darling. He anticipated an evening with Silvie. He'd grill a steak for her, he thought, then considered stopping by the grocery first. Or maybe he'd take her out for dinner. The occasion deserved celebration. When was the last time he'd felt this excited and optimistic about another human being—about *anything*, really?

A ray of sun penetrated the dusty window above the concession stand, and Silvie basked in it. How long since she'd experienced the sun? Winter was hard in Wyoming—hard in the cold sense—but the sun still showed up frequently. She thought she'd go out of her mind if she had to live in the overcast gray of Oregon, where the clouds scraped along the landscape, obliterating color and warmth.

Jacob was more on her mind today. She'd stolen from him,

caused him untold distress, and now she'd cheated on him. He'd forbidden her ever to be with another man. In fact, he had warned her so many times that she'd finally implored him to stop, that she understood. She promised she would never do that to him.

An engine outside returned her to this place. That would be Hershel. She hopped off the stool and collected her backpack, but paused with it slung over her shoulder. Jacob's face had been near hopeful, as if he wanted to believe her, but something stood in the way of full trust. In that moment, she'd been desperate to prove her devotion. It wasn't simply the threat of what he might do but a genuine desire to please the man who had pulled her from the muck of a ruined family and given her a strange new status as the sheriff's girl.

16

"Carlos," Yolanda shouted, running to meet him where the unmarked road to the migrant camp intersected the highway. He quickened his pace to meet her, and when she reached him she was breathless. "Carlos, they came. They took half the camp."

"What? Who?"

"Immigration came this morning, just after light. They went from cabin to cabin, checking our documents."

"Your sons?"

"Gracias Santa María." She crossed herself. "Away still."

Carl breathed relief, but Yolanda was no less tense.

"Don't come here tonight. They say it was you."

"Me what?"

"What called immigration. Even Jimmy Arndt is looking for you." As she spoke, she assessed his bruised face. She ran a cinnamon-scented hand gently along his jaw, but no words were necessary.

"I didn't call those bastards. I wouldn't!"

"I know. But listen to me; it's not safe."

"Yolanda, what am I supposed to do? Just leave? I live here."

She gave him a pained look. "Please, Carlos. I can't stand it for something to happen to you."

Carl tipped his face up to the gray sky and blew his breath out. His ribs ached. He'd been looking forward to the warmth of his woodstove and the softness of his bed.

"I hear them talking. Some men want to burn your cabin down while you sleep."

"Yolanda, I didn't do it."

"I know, Carlos. I know."

He shook his head and looked back up the highway, in the direction from which he'd just come. "I guess you better not be seen out here talking to me."

"Oh, Carlos." She put her hand to his cheek again, and he grasped hold of it. He pressed it to his lips and kissed her palm.

"I'll be at Swift's barn if you need anything." He looked into her dark eyes. "Anything at all." He let go and started up the highway. When he glanced back, she was still watching him.

Hershel took a back road to get to the restaurant, winding through steep and narrow canyons before cresting a low mountaintop, where he pulled onto the gravel shoulder and they took in the wide, velvety green-and-yellow valley. The coastal range stood blue and hazy to the west, hemming in the patchwork of farmland. A low ceiling of clouds scraped along the highest glens, leaving ragged tufts of mist in the crevices where deciduous trees stubbornly held on to the last of their summer foliage.

He seemed lost in his own thoughts, and she wondered if she'd done something wrong. His knuckles were scabbed, as if he'd beaten someone.

"That's Yamhill County," Hershel said quietly.

"It's beautiful." It reminded her of pictures of the English countryside. Everything lush and vibrant even though it was nearly winter.

"If it was a clear day, you'd be able to see Mount Hood right there." He pointed at the simple gray horizon. "It comes out when it feels like it."

He'd pulled back onto the road, which wound down a steep hillside with tight switchback curves, through a nameless town three times the size of Hanley, and up another mountain. This one was cultivated and pristine. Signs advertised wineries along the well-maintained road. And Silvie marveled at the beautiful buildings and perfectly groomed grounds of these establishments. Erath, Rex Hill, Alloro. The names were as exotic as the bright flowers that lined their entries, so unexpected in this late month.

"These look expensive," she said, hoping he didn't plan to take her inside one of these luxurious places with wrought-iron gates and cobblestoned driveways. She thought of the wine tasters she'd served that afternoon, with their crisp new jeans and turtleneck sweaters. Their sparkling Mercedeses and Acuras, and their still-soft suede shoes. Armani sunglasses. White teeth. Perfectly trimmed hair. She didn't belong.

To Silvie's relief, he continued on to Dundee, a town in transition from forgotten to the lucky recipient of new industry. The buildings along the main road were a hodgepodge of derelict houses and businesses with sagging porches and overgrown weeds, standing alongside brand-new bistros, gift shops, and tasting rooms with deep inset window boxes.

The restaurant was a refurbished Craftsman home with dark fir interior and wavy-paned windows. The dining room overlooked the mini-mart and the gas station, and a low-income neighborhood of small houses and trailers on the other side of the road. Hershel ordered a bottle of pinot noir, and she swirled the pale raspberry–colored liquid in her glass the way she'd seen wine tasters do on television cooking shows. Its flavor was tart and she couldn't manage more than a tiny sip at a time.

"Can I ask you something?" Hershel said, breaking the silence. "What happened to your father? I assume . . . he wasn't around." When she didn't immediately answer, he said, "I didn't mean to pry. It's okay if you'd rather not say."

"I don't ever know how to answer that question is all." She watched the way the liquid in her glass subtly changed color in the light as she swirled it.

"Is he dead?"

She snorted softly. "No." She braced up for the truth. "He left. Started over with another woman. He's got three kids with her."

"How old were you?"

"Ten."

"So you have brothers and sisters?" Hershel peered at her over the bottle of wine, solicitous but trepid.

"Technically they're my siblings, or half siblings, but I've never met them. They didn't *feel* like brothers. They didn't feel like anything. I don't know them."

Hershel poured himself another glass of wine. There was a strange barrier between them now.

"My dad just didn't come home one day. He called Mom from wherever he was staying to tell her that he wanted a divorce. Within a few months, he had a new wife. They had kids right away. All boys."

"What about your mother?"

Silvie could hear her father in that short period before he left. *You and your goddamn drinking. How much have you had tonight?* Her mother had cried inconsolably when he left. "Well, we lost the house. Mom had to file for bankruptcy. That's when we moved to town and she started waitressing at the bar."

"Didn't your father pay alimony or child support?"

Silvie felt tears beginning to rush forward. "You have to be sober long enough to file the paperwork and do all the stuff that's required to get money."

"Yeah, but . . ." Hershel shook his head.

"I only saw my dad once after he left. He arranged a visit, like he was supposed to. But it was weird. I didn't know what to say, and neither did he. He took me for a hamburger and watched me eat it." Her father had sat across the table at Denny's, drinking coffee, folding and refolding his napkin until it was a shredded mess. That he didn't eat with her seemed to be the loudest message. He lived in another world. When he looked at Silvie, he would quickly look away again. "We never said anything."

"And that was it?" Hershel was leaning forward now, as if frustrated by the absurdity of what she'd shared.

"That was it." She wanted to add the part that had slowly dawned on her over the years and cemented itself at her core, but she knew she would cry if she said it aloud. *I didn't matter.*

"Have the pasta—you need to put some meat on those bones." Hershel tried not to look too long at her.

She agreed a little too easily, and he wished he'd left it up to her to decide. Her story grew more tragic by the day. Every time she opened up and showed him a new little piece of her world, he found himself wanting to kill another man. First Jacob Castor, now Silvie's own father. It wasn't simply an *I'd like to kill that bastard* feeling but a genuine fingers-around-the-windpipe death grip that he craved. He could see the reddened face and the bulging eyes. Perhaps he was the killer Kyrellis claimed. He didn't care at this moment. Silvie, though. Silvie deserved better.

"What about *your* father?" she asked.

The question startled him a little. "He passed away about twenty years ago. Cancer."

"Sorry. Were you close?"

He shrugged. "Yeah."

She sipped her wine, and Hershel missed his father as if he had only just learned of his death.

"We hunted together." Hershel smiled down at his glass. "We didn't talk as much as I wish we had."

"What do you mean?"

"Just that . . . I don't know. We planned trips, prepared the gear, discussed routes and weather. That seemed to be the extent of it."

"Better than nothing." She swirled her wine as the pause stretched uncomfortably long between them. "I didn't mean that the way it sounded," she said.

"It's okay."

"I mean..."

"I think there must have been more there that I can't remember. I must have known more about his life—about him."

She picked daintily at the pasta, twisting more noodles around her plate than she put into her mouth.

He looked for something to convince this woman that those terrible days were over now. "Silvie," he said. "You're someone truly special. You've made my life a lot more interesting."

She laughed a girlish, giggly laugh.

"Interesting in a good way. I have been..." He reached for her hand and caressed her fingers. "Since my accident life has been... odd. It's like I woke up a different person. I don't know who that other guy was, but I think he was lonely and I don't want to be him."

"Kyrellis stopped by to see me today."

"He what?" Hershel jerked up from his chair to a near stand. "What did he want?"

"A name."

"Why didn't you tell me?"

"I just did."

"That man's dangerous. It's important you understand that." Hershel took her hand again, but the spark was gone and she rested it limply in his palm. "Silvie, I don't think you should be working down there where he can just drop in like that."

"What?" She pulled her hand away. "I need the money. Besides, it's nice to be around other people."

"I'll take care of the money—whatever you need."

"You sound like Jacob. I don't need some guy taking care of me."

"Some guy?" Hershel reeled. "That's all I am is *some guy*?"

"That's not what I meant. Besides, you told Carl about the box. That didn't feel too good, either."

Hershel closed his eyes. His head had begun to ache, and he could feel his temper rising. "I'm sorry. It slipped. I didn't tell him the details, just that Kyrellis has something that belongs to you. I've been thinking about Kyrellis. He knows Castor is a cop."

"I know. He told me."

"Let him figure it out—"

"Are you out of your mind?" Silvie leaned so far across the table that he could practically touch her face.

"Just hear me out."

She sat back with her arms crossed tightly, refusing to look at him. Her jaw was set in a hard line.

"Let him come. Let Castor come after Kyrellis, then we turn him in." He could feel her foot bouncing angrily under the table. "He's a felon, and once he's exposed he'll go to prison. It'll be over."

"What about Kyrellis? What about the photos?" Her words were sharp and direct. "What about the publicity? It's not you who'd have to suffer the scrutiny. Imagine how that'll be for me?"

Hershel swallowed the wine in his glass and refilled it, emptying the bottle. "Okay, maybe it's not the best idea. But there has to be a way. We just need to think it through."

"Hershel, Jacob is the one who's dangerous. You don't know him like I do. He won't go down easy. It isn't like calling the police and saying, 'Hey, this guy is breaking the law.' He *is* the law."

"Sweetheart, he's not. Not here."

17

Carl stomped the mud and gravel out of his boots on the cement stoop of the sale barn, then ducked inside. He'd throw a hot dog on the cooker and then borrow the apartment upstairs until things calmed down at Campo Rojo, which could be when this group of migrants moved on. That would be six weeks at the earliest.

After supper, he wandered upstairs and unfolded the sofa bed. The room was spacious and had running water and a flush toilet. He plugged the refrigerator in and tested it to see if it cooled. Satisfied, he unplugged it again. He had nothing that required refrigeration. He tinkered with the television, stringing up coat hangers and moving them around the room until he got a semi-decent signal with audio that he could actually understand, then tuned in to the news. In the last segment the anchorwoman mentioned the raid at Campo Rojo, stating that fourteen illegal immigrants had been detained following an assault. It *was* news, after all. With thousands of migrants shifting through the valley at any given time, people tended to tolerate their presence as if they weren't actually there. A raid always made a splash.

He settled onto the bed, hoping he'd find an old rerun of a seventies western. Maybe he'd get lucky and catch a Clint Eastwood flick. He wondered what Silvie had carried in her car that Kyrellis found valuable enough to keep. And why did she believe he would think differently of her if he knew? She was a mysterious girl. Arriving out of nowhere with a murky past and a guard around her so thick and impenetrable he could practically touch it. Was she a prostitute? He doubted it. She didn't look the part. Her face was still smooth and soft, the way it ought to be in your twenties. Had she lived that sort of life she'd look years older. She didn't look like a druggie, either. He could spot a fellow junkie a mile off, and she wasn't one. More likely a gun, given Kyrellis's line of work.

"People's troubles always seem biggest to themselves," he said aloud.

He got up and went downstairs, through the warehouse to Hershel's office, unlocking the door. He stood in the entryway and assessed the aftermath of his boss's violent temper. He'd never known the man to behave this way, and it had startled and concerned him that afternoon. And now Hershel was home with Silvie, a sweet girl in need of a rescuer.

Carl leaned down and picked up a file folder. He thumbed through it and then lifted the cabinet back into place. He put the folder in its rightful drawer and picked up another. Why did he work for this man? Why did he care if Hershel Swift's electricity was turned off or his house was broken into? What had Swift done for him that was a fraction so thoughtful? His arms began to itch.

Carl suffered a terrible night, but Hershel's office was put back together by morning. He had pondered Yolanda throughout the darkest hours, wishing he hadn't left her behind. He should have insisted that she come with him. He despised himself for abandoning her. He managed a little rest between five and eight, then lay in bed thinking again. At nine he made his way downstairs and put on a pot of coffee. He would go back to camp this morning and see for himself how things were. He wouldn't run away.

He had just sat down with his coffee when the doorknob jiggled and the large roll-up door shuddered.

"Hello?" a woman called from outside. "Carl?"

He unlocked the door and found Silvie, her shoes muddy and her coat wrapped around her as tight as she could make it.

"You're freezing. Get in here," he said, but realized it was scarcely warmer inside the building. "What are you doing here?"

"I came through the orchard. It's farther than it looks. I thought I was lost. You can go in circles out there in all those trees. Maybe never get out."

"Well, here you are."

"Yeah, it's due east." She spied the coffee in his hand. "Can I have one of those?"

Carl poured her a cup as she sat down at the counter. He wandered into the back hallway behind the concession stand and rummaged through the coats that hung in the closet there. He doubted that she would take one, but he pulled out the smallest three he could find. They weren't his, but they'd been there, untouched, for as long as he'd worked for Hershel.

"I left Hershel a note saying I'd gone out for a walk."

Carl laid out on the counter a down jacket that was so outdated even he recognized the fact, a firefighter's turnout, which seemed to weigh about eight pounds, and a flannel-lined plaid work shirt that was at least three sizes too big for her. "You need a better coat."

"You think I should walk around looking like I just came from a fire?"

"It's warm."

She took the plaid work shirt and pulled it on over her jacket. The sleeves hung several inches past the tips of her fingers.

He began rolling them up. "Better than freezing."

"I'm glad you were here," she said, adjusting the collar when he'd finished. "I forgot that it was Sunday until I was in the parking lot, then I figured I'd have to turn right around and start back."

He sipped his coffee, and they were both quiet for a moment. He could feel her working up to something as she fiddled with the buttons of her new garment.

"Remember what you said yesterday?"

"Barely."

"About not judging. About helping me out with Kyrellis?"

"Yeah. The offer is still here."

"Well . . ." She swirled her coffee. "That box Hershel told you about, it has a bunch of nude photos of me."

Carl worked to show no response, as if this were a common situation that he dealt with daily.

"Not just nude." She pushed her hair away from her face and took her time. "Pictures from when I was young. Like twelve."

He nodded slowly, unable to hide his surprise.

"And not just nude," she repeated. "They're really bad . . . if you know what I mean."

"Okay, you've managed to surprise me." His declaration hung between them like a hideous spider. Then Silvie burst out laughing. Confused, Carl looked over at her. Was she angry? But when their eyes met he laughed, too. Both were suddenly breathless with deep, bellyaching laughter, until tears crested over Silvie's cheeks.

As quickly as it started, it was gone. She looked away, her nose a brighter red than it was when she came in.

"And what does Kyrellis want with them?" Carl realized it was a stupid question.

"Well, that's the thing. He wants to know the name of the man who took them. So he can blackmail him."

"That sounds like the Kyrellis I know." Carl set his coffee down and faced Silvie. "Hershel hasn't had any luck getting them back?"

She shook her head.

"Do you want me to try?"

"Do you think you can?"

"I can try. I can't promise I'll be successful, but I might have something that will persuade him."

Silvie breathed a hard sigh and closed her eyes. "Please don't tell Hershel I asked you to help me."

"Okay. You can trust me."

The sun was peeking through the trees, a brilliant yellow that promised to scour away the cold. As she picked her way beneath the leafless canopy, she determined that once she had the box of photos she'd drive to California and mail them back to Jacob. Then she'd return here and work for a while. Long enough to save some money, get her feet under her. Jacob was angry with her, she knew, but the idea that she'd never see him again, which she was just now considering, made her heart ache.

As she emerged into Hershel's yard, the little orange Porsche still waiting for its new tires, he was standing on the porch looking out across the valley as if trying to see her.

"Morning," she said, gaining his attention. A look of relief came over his dark face.

"Good walk?"

"Yeah. The orchard is peaceful, but huge and muddy."

"I was worried."

"No need to be." She felt the warmth of the sun on her back now as she walked out into the open space next to the house. "I was just feeling a little antsy."

"You've been into my closet, I see."

She'd forgotten the work shirt, and paused to look down at it. Did he know she'd been to the auction barn?

He studied her. "You're very beautiful, Silvie."

Carl opened Hershel's office and left the door standing wide in case anyone came in. He routinely handled the man's affairs, and Hershel wouldn't be surprised or angry to find him here, leafing through his papers, but the information he sought today was precisely what he chose to overlook on every other day.

He easily worked the combination on the wall safe and pulled out a small wooden box. He fumbled through his keys, seeking the smallest one, inserted it into the lock, and pulled back the lid. It was full of various receipts and documents. Special information. Occasionally a seller would inadvertently leave a document that could be used to prove that Hershel sold guns without filing the federal paperwork required by law. Against Carl's advice, Hershel kept these receipts and documents rather than destroying them. Carl never asked why; he guessed he already knew.

Carl identified several guns that were sold directly to Kyrellis, marked on the bottom of the pages with the dates and the amounts. They were all cataloged this way, some to other dealers, some that were put through the auction to increase the price because Kyrellis, in particular, was cheap. Near the top of the stack was an inventory list that Albert Darling had filled out for State Farm Insurance, which prominently called out a rare antique Winchester rifle. He estimated its value at twenty-five thousand dollars. Darling had left the expired receipt in his storage unit with the gun, which was where Hershel had found it when he liquidated its contents.

Carl selected a few good examples and went to the copier, where he made duplicates. He returned the originals to the box and put it back in the safe. Then he called Kyrellis.

"This is Carl Abernathy."

"Who?"

"You know who I am."

Kyrellis snorted. "I thought Swift handled all the firearms transactions personally now that he's back."

"I'm not calling on his behalf today."

"Then why ever are you calling me, Mr. Abernathy?"

Kyrellis had always treated Carl as if he were common scum. People did, but Kyrellis was especially acidic. Carl had eventually come to understand that it was because he lived at Campo Rojo.

"I'm coming over to talk to you."

"I don't think that's a good idea. Why don't you just tell me what you have over the phone? You no doubt know what I'm looking for."

"This isn't about a gun. It's about Silvie's box."

"How does that concern you?"

"We'll talk about it when I get there." Carl hung up, his insides feeling dry.

Kyrellis's house was tucked along the base of Bull Mountain, on a road called Beef Bend. Carl hitchhiked from Scholls to Sherwood, catching a ride with a man who agreed to give him a lift if he sat in the bed of the truck with his border collie. The dog was overjoyed to have company, licking Carl's face. But once the driver reached speeds over thirty it abandoned him to zip back and forth between the wheel wells, pressing its face into the wind with rapt jubilation.

From Sherwood, Carl caught a TriMet bus into Tigard, then walked the last two miles. Kyrellis owned six acres, most of which were taken up with an array of greenhouses in various shapes and sizes that looked as though they'd been added over decades, without consideration for aesthetics or continuity. His home, a rambling brick ranch, had been built in the sixties. But it was upscale, with a stunning circular rose garden in front, flanked by rhododendron and laurel hedges for privacy. An old wisteria vine twisted up the front porch and ran across the entryway. With its leaves gone for the winter, its silver branches looked like hundreds of snakes in a hypnotic, intertwining embrace. As Carl waited for the man, he listened to a large chime sing out low, minor keys.

Kyrellis came to the door with a handgun strapped to his chest, visible through his cotton shirt. He scrutinized Carl for the same but eventually stepped aside, allowing him to enter. The house smelled of meat loaf and aftershave. Its dark interior was well appointed but outdated. The leather sofa in the living room appeared never to have been used.

"I heard about the incident down at the migrant camp yesterday," he said, studying Carl's eye and jaw. "You made the news."

"I'm not here about that."

"Are you the one who called immigration? I underestimated you, but it's good to know you're a red-blooded American after all."

The short hairs at the back of Carl's neck went up. "With a name like Kyrellis? Isn't that...what? Greek?"

"You know your linguistics; I'll give you that." Kyrellis led Carl into the kitchen and motioned for him to sit at the table. "Who are you, exactly, Carl Abernathy? Have we overlooked a scholar among us?"

"Hardly." Carl regretted the comment about Kyrellis's name. And though he knew the man mocked him, he would never let on that he had gone to Berkeley on a scholarship and completed his degree in literature. It didn't matter, either. That life was a kid's idealistic dream. Then came Vietnam, heroin, and reality.

"Well, then, let's get down to business. Why *are* you here?"

Carl reached into his breast pocket and pulled out the folded copies. He was careful and deliberate as he laid them out on the table. "Eighteen seventy-eight Frontier Colt. Seven hundred dollars. May 2004. Harpers Ferry M1842 musket. Twelve hundred. August 2006. Glock Model 23. Three hundred. December 2006." He went on through a list of twenty guns.

Kyrellis stood perfectly still, listening, eyeing the papers.

"Winchester Grand American—small-gauge. Forty thousand. April of this year." Carl laid the last sheet down. He stilled his face, preparing the sternest bluff he'd ever delivered. "I have a record of every single firearm. Its price. The date. Its origin. Its serial number." He looked at Kyrellis. "And its buyer."

"So you do," Kyrellis said quietly.

"I want the box. This information stays with me if you give me Silvie's box."

"And if I don't?"

"I go to the police."

"You know you'll ruin Hershel, too."

Carl stared at Kyrellis for a long serious moment, then gave him a simple nod. A flash of Vietnam went through his mind.

Kyrellis reached into his shirt and took the pistol from his holster.

Carl's dream beside the rice paddy flooded in on him. The oppressive heat.

"You forgot this one." He held up the gun so that Carl could see it. "Do you remember *this one*?"

That familiar sense of doom, intangible yet overwhelming.

"You called me about it yourself."

Carl stared at the Taurus semiautomatic. He remembered it. He'd sold it to Kyrellis while Hershel was in the hospital. Ironically, to pay the utilities at Hershel's house because the accountant wasn't authorized to handle his personal affairs.

Kyrellis pointed the gun at Carl's head.

He won't shoot me here, Carl told himself. Not in his kitchen, sitting at his dinner table. He closed his eyes and thought of Yolanda's smile, then a lightness, a release. No craving. No relentless urges. Nothing—just a small flash. Then nothing.

18

Kyrellis stood over Carl Abernathy, afraid to touch him. His breath was pinched and tight. "I'm having a heart attack," he stuttered as the gun clattered to the floor and skated across the polished linoleum. He grabbed at a side chair and collapsed into it, laying his head and shoulders on the table. "I'm . . . having . . . a . . . heart . . . attack," he wheezed.

He closed his eyes and cleared his head. After several minutes, the pains eased, leaving him shaky and ringed in sweat. He peered across the table at the man he'd just shot. The bullet hadn't exited Carl's skull. There wasn't much blood.

Kyrellis hadn't wanted to do that. He hadn't planned it. But Hershel Swift's flunky had proved himself a sly man, after all. The way he'd stated his demands with such cool deliberation; it was clear that he held no allegiance to Swift. He'd obviously been planning this for years to have kept such precise records.

Kyrellis rested his sweaty face against the wooden table. What would he do with the body? This had all gone wrong.

The dead man gurgled and blood suddenly poured from his nose onto the oak surface.

"Oh!" Kyrellis staggered up, his head pounding, and found a dish towel. He lifted the man's face and shoved the cloth under, watching it expand in scarlet. He ran his index finger down Carl's neck, seeking a pulse, but the skin was already cool and clammy.

Kyrellis slid into the chair once again and tried to organize his thoughts. It was a problem that the bullet hadn't come out the other side. It could be traced. Kyrellis nudged the corpse's leg with his foot. The bullet would be traced back only to the man who consigned the gun to Hershel and no further, assuming that this man slumped over his kitchen table hadn't left evidence behind. Even if he hadn't, this was too close to home. Kyrellis sized up the body, seeing it in pieces.

Something clicked for Kyrellis, seeing Carl's bruised face. He could tie this back to the fight at the migrant camp. It was his good luck that Carl had been involved, and that it had been both recent and reported. With an immigration raid that was likely this man's doing, who would question the link?

Kyrellis suffered a new shiver, recalling the way Carl had punctuated the Winchester in the list of guns he'd bought. It was rare, worth more than any gun he'd ever handled. It sold instantly to a private collector he'd been working with. The man paid sixty-two thousand dollars—more than its market value. Kyrellis had naïvely believed that its sale—the money—would bring an end to his troubles. Carl had been more dangerous than Kyrellis ever imagined, walking around with evidence like that. Kyrellis hadn't thought twice about the man all this time, even though he was well aware of Carl's involvement in Hershel's business. Who else might be lurking in the shadows, collecting damning evidence, preparing to blackmail him? It wasn't about the pictures, that was for damn sure. That was simply a test to see what he could get. Kyrellis knew it would never have stopped there. The man would have moved on to money, and he'd have done so rapidly. Kyrellis composed himself. He needed to clear his thoughts and figure out how to dispose of this body.

Silvie soaked up the sun in a wicker chair on Hershel's front porch. Billowy gray clouds formed and dissipated in the moody afternoon sky, occasionally stealing away the warmth, then bringing it back again like a sweet gift. She could hear Hershel tinkering with the Porsche, but so far he'd failed to get it running, despite its new tires and battery.

A red-tailed hawk sailed out over the river in search of food, and she studied the long driveway that emerged from the orchard a quarter mile or so from the house. This was a good place to be. She'd see Jacob coming long before he arrived, and she could slip into that same vast orchard that wrapped around the house. From the upstairs bedroom she had seen its southern boundary, where it marched into a wild blackberry thicket that folded into a ravine, then up another slope. Then it was forest and hills as far as she could see. Jacob would never find her.

After a time, Hershel joined her, wiping grease from his hands with a rag that looked as though it had once been a pair of boxer shorts. "Looks like you found a nice spot," he said. "Mind if I interrupt your solitude?"

"Want me to get you something to drink?"

"No, I'm okay." He eased into the chair, inspecting his clothes for grease stains.

"Carl seems like a generous person."

Hershel appeared to be completely lost in thought. "I should give him a raise, or something. Carl took care of things while I was...you know...recovering." Hershel sent Silvie a furtive glance before looking away again. "I've never been able to figure out why he lives like he does. I used to think he was a loser." He paused to press his fingers to his scar, absently, as he often did.

"That's pretty harsh judgment."

"Maybe. He lives in a migrant camp in a one-room shack, shoulder to shoulder with people who don't even speak English. He's got no plumbing. Just a woodstove and a shared latrine."

"I guess you *should* give him a raise."

"I doubt he'd move even if I did."

"What happened to his face yesterday?"

"Didn't say, exactly."

She scowled. Didn't he have some idea or opinion about what might have happened? Why didn't he find out? Had a friend of hers shown up with a battered face, she'd have gotten the story. Or...maybe Carl came to work looking like that all the time. How many times had she arrived bruised before Laree stopped interrogating her? After a while nothing needed saying. It was the same story, but at least her friend *knew* it.

"Is Carl married?"

Hershel looked surprised. "I don't think so."

"You don't know? How long has this guy been working for you? And you don't know if he's married?"

"It never came up."

She snorted.

"Why all the questions about Carl, anyway?"

"Just curious about him. Maybe his wife did that to his face."

"Maybe. Do you think he's married?"

"I don't know."

"Anything is possible."

Silvie pressed her head back against the chair and rolled her eyes. "Men are so strange."

Hershel reached between the chairs and took her hand. She hesitated.

"Kyrellis said something when he came by the South Store." She ran her finger lightly over his thumbnail, smoothing it, polishing it. "He told me...to ask you where you were coming from the night of your accident."

Hershel pulled his hand away and rested it in his lap, staring off at the northern horizon.

"He hinted that—" She waited through long seconds of agonizing silence. He didn't even move. She glanced over to see if he still breathed. "He'll say anything to get the information he wants, I suppose."

Hershel opened his mouth as if to speak but closed it again.

His eyes seemed fixed on a growing bank of dark thunderheads tinged purple at their base.

"He told you that I killed a man," he said finally.

"Not in so many words."

"Do you believe him?"

She shook her head, but he wouldn't look at her. "No."

He leaned forward and pressed his palms to his thighs, as if ready to get up. Then he turned his head and studied her. "I don't think I killed anyone."

It was a strange answer, she thought. Wouldn't you know? Even if you *had* suffered a brain injury, wouldn't you know in your gut?

"Look, Silvie. I'm not going to lie to you. I don't know where I was coming from the night I crashed my car. I've been trying to work out the days leading up to that wreck since I woke up in the hospital."

Silvie ran her hand down his arm, and he took her fingers in his.

"I don't think I killed anyone. And I don't trust Kyrellis to say what really happened."

"I'm sorry I brought it up."

"Don't be. I like the idea of not having any secrets between us. This is not easy. I've never been this open with anyone. But... your company—your trust—has become very important to me." He pressed her hand to his lips and brushed them lightly back and forth. "I won't hide anything from you."

Kyrellis carefully wiped up all the blood, then walked out and found a plastic tarp in his storage shed. He spread it across the kitchen floor, lifted Carl off the chair, and dragged his limp body onto the plastic, marveling at how thin and light the man was even as deadweight. He arranged Carl's skinny limbs into a straight line and gathered the tarp at the top, dragging it through the open patio door, across the cement, and out onto the gravel pathway that led between his greenhouses. The idea of leaving his kitchen with any traces of blood nagged him like an unanswered itch. He preferred to do this in stages, but he was gripped by the idea that maybe Carl had told someone where he was going. Had he shared his mission with Silvie? Would someone come looking for him? How long?

Kyrellis was breathless, and his fingers were cramping by the time he reached the pole barn at the back of his property. "Almost there," he said to the dead man, and gave the tarp a few hard tugs onto the top of the compost heap. He rolled Carl out onto the soil, where he dumped the spent potting dirt and turned under the rose clippings.

He returned with a common handsaw and a pair of sharp branch cutters and set to work removing Carl's head. Blood soaked into the rich ferment, and when he was finished Kyrellis used a pitchfork to churn it under for the worms.

By dark he'd scrubbed the kitchen with bleach, taking extra care with the tabletop. The saw and the clippers were returned to the shed, dipped in alcohol, and lightly oiled. The patio had been pressure-washed. He showered and bundled his clothing into the bottom of his burn barrel, covering it with a thick layer of dead brush, but he didn't light it. That would have to wait until the body, again wrapped in the tarp and waiting in the bed of his truck, was fully gone from here. He surveyed the scene where he'd murdered Carl Abernathy, looking for anything he might have missed.

Rain was both help and hindrance as Kyrellis backed his pickup down the narrow boat ramp along the Tualatin River, not a mile from the migrant camp. He was careful to stay on the gravel path and not to leave muddy footprints. His pulse raced and his chest ached as he climbed into the bed and dragged the headless body, stripped of any personal effects, down to the water. It would likely be found; Kyrellis knew that. Better to make it look like a hate crime and divert attention. He rolled the partially submerged corpse out into the scant current with his foot. The Tualatin was a silty river, opaque and dirty-looking year-round. It was littered with tree branches and debris, and Carl's body wouldn't float far before catching on something. But it would be difficult to find, nonetheless. Through the darkness Kyrellis watched the body disappear into the narrow channel.

It was just after one in the morning. The boat launch was far from farms or other signs of civilization, and not even an animal stirred tonight. A steady rain cleansed the landscape. When his breath had returned, he drove slowly up the ramp again, shifting as quietly as possible through the gears, and pulled onto the empty highway. He drove south toward the Willamette River, where he would drop Carl's head, now wrapped in a black garbage sack weighted with a cinder block, off the bridge near St. Paul. Carl had had ample opportunity to show his hand. Years of opportunity. Kyrellis questioned whether he'd murdered the man for something so harmless, a foolishly noble attempt to help a girl he barely knew. Kyrellis could see how a man might be talked into helping her. She had a look about her, helpless and in need, wrapped in a sexy package. Carl might have been more stupid than cunning. Still, Kyrellis told himself as the head made a faint splash, there was no way to know for sure. He had no choice but to protect himself.

Everyone knew too much. Carl knew about the guns, he knew about Silvie. How much had that girl shared with Carl? Did Hershel have any idea about her? In one of the photos she was tightly bound, hands and feet, with a gag in her mouth. A cascade of dark bruises showed along her hips and thighs. Someone had worked her over, and it looked to him like more than once. Kyrellis had separated the cache into categories. Photos of Silvie in sexy poses—poses that could arouse any man, which he arranged along the mirror above his bureau. The disturbing photos of abuse, which were few but stunning, he bound together with a rubber band and placed in the bottom of the box. These were the ones that the pervert who'd taken them would pay a premium for. There were three photos where the man had been careless. In one, Kyrellis could see his law-enforcement badge on the dresser. In the other two, he'd gotten vain and held the camera at arm's length and captured the child and himself together. It wasn't Silvie in both pictures. One of them was a dark-haired girl, much younger. Six, maybe. Those Kyrellis locked in his safe and took out only to examine with a magnifying glass, looking for clues to the man's identity. And the rest—the photos of assorted other girls ranging in age, printed on photo paper suggesting a span of decades—he set aside.

The way Kyrellis saw it, he stood to make money four ways: from the man in the photos—once for his identity and a second time for the bondage shots; from Hershel for Silvie's pictures; and from the perverts he could sell the others to. Kyrellis lit a cigarette, cracked the window, and blew the smoke out through the gap.

19

The sound of ringing on the other end of the line startled Silvie, and she almost hung up. She pressed the receiver to her ear and leaned against the wall between Hershel's kitchen and the dining room.

"Hello?"

"It's me," she said quietly.

"Silvie?" Her mother's voice came through now, urgent and awake. "Silvie, is that you?"

"Yes."

"Where are you? Oh God. I've been so worried."

Silvie sobbed quietly.

"Silvie, please. Where are you?"

"I'm okay," she squeaked.

"Please, baby. Tell me where you are—"

Silvie placed the receiver back on the phone dock and slid down the wall until she rested on the floor, her knees pulled tightly against her chest.

Hershel tried his keys in the door to the storage area under the bleachers. Turning each one back, inserting the next, feeling the barrier. His cheeks burned, and he kept an ear tuned for Carl. He had expected to spend the day restoring his office. What kind of man loses his temper and destroys his own business? And what would he say to Carl, who had cleaned up the mess?

He was down to two keys. Maybe he didn't have one for this door. What was in here? Finally, the lock snapped and he pushed the knob away. He was greeted by the musty smell of a long-sealed space and his heart leaped unexpectedly. New prospects? New clues? Had he hidden something here that would help him understand who he was?

He paused at the door, though. Would he find Albert Darling here? Or damning evidence to confirm Kyrellis's claim? He found the light switch. But, illuminated, the storage area was disappointingly empty. A sprung mousetrap in the corner and a box of *National Geographic* magazines. Hershel kicked it over, letting them spill out in the unlikely event he'd missed something. He closed the door, not bothering to lock it again.

The streets of Hillsboro were thick and congested, and Hershel cursed the way his fellow Oregonians dealt with water on the road. "It rains nine months out of the damn year," he shouted at the car in front of him, which had slowed to twenty, its wipers maniacally slapping away at the sudden downpour. "Learn to drive in it or move back to where you came from."

Peeling off Cornell, he took Main Street into downtown and looked at his map. Hershel wished he'd driven down to the migrant camp to see if Carl needed a ride to work instead of heading off on this pointless excursion. There were no set hours for previewing a sale, but Carl typically opened the doors around ten. At least that's what the yellow note in his office said. It was nine o'clock when Hershel looked up Albert Darling's last known address.

He took Third Street into a neighborhood of small homes from the 1940s and '50s. Most looked like rentals, the yards littered with toys and weeds. He searched the numbers, his head hurting in its familiar way, barely noticeable now. At last he found the one he sought and pulled up along the curb. Gray paint peeled off the house in long strips, revealing the aqua-green of a more optimistic era. One shutter was missing, and the other looked about ready to go. Someone peered through the dirty front window at him. Now seen, he slid out of his truck, which looked conspicuously extravagant here. He wandered up the front walk, stepping over a child's bicycle, past the boy who likely owned it, and knocked on the hollow door. As he waited, Hershel turned and looked at the kid. He stood in a mud puddle, his shoes black, the bottoms of his pants wet and ragged. The boy watched him, mouth slack, rain falling on his already soaked head. So this is what people mean when they say "not enough sense to come in out of the rain," Hershel thought.

A woman opened the front door a crack and peered out with one eye. "Can I help you?" She sounded defiant, and Hershel had a flash of Darling's in-your-face bluster.

"I'm looking for Albert Darling."

She opened the door about ten inches and looked Hershel up and down. Her hair was unwashed and hung in greasy dark strands almost to her waist. "Who are you?"

Hershel wondered if he should say. What did he have to hide? If only he knew. "Hershel Swift."

"Swift? You're that asshole that sold his stuff, aren't you?"

"He was delinquent on his payments. It was legal."

"Wasn't neither."

Hershel was already growing weary of her. "Is he around?"

She squinted at him. "No, he's not."

"You know when he'll be back?" Hershel basked in the relief that at least the man was still alive.

"I've got no idea. We ain't seen him since summer."

Hershel looked back at his fancy new truck. The boy was now standing inches from it, staring up at the grille.

"Git away from that, Caleb!" the woman shouted so shrilly that Hershel suffered a sharp pain through his left eye. "Look, mister, I don't know where Al is. I filed a missing-person report 'cuz he disappeared after trying to get his gun back from you."

Hershel experienced a strange melting sensation in his limbs.

"We figured you killed him."

"Why would I kill him?"

"I know how he can be." Her voice carried a hint of apology.

"I don't need to kill people. What I did was legal."

"Wasn't neither. You can't just sell a person's stuff like that. How was he supposed to get down there and pay you? He was in jail."

Hershel shook his head and stepped onto the sidewalk, heading for his truck.

"If you didn't kill him, I will when I get my hands on him. He's got three kids want to see their dad. And he owes me money...."

As Hershel climbed into his truck he glanced back at the woman, now on the step in her bathrobe and bare feet; then he pulled away from the curb. He felt nauseated. Where was Albert Darling if he'd been missing since summer? He'd gone only a few hundred yards when he hit the brakes hard and backed up until he was in front of the house again. The woman walked toward the truck.

"When, exactly, was the last time you saw him?"

She put her hands on her hips. "Middle of August."

"You have an exact date?"

She shot him a dark look. "Hang on." She disappeared inside the house.

After waiting several minutes, Hershel killed the engine. The boy was still admiring the truck, and Hershel smiled down at him, trying to put his mind on something less damning. The boy didn't smile, but stared at him as if he were growing a horn from the center of his forehead.

Finally she returned carrying a creased sheet of paper covered thickly with small-type print. She held it up. "August sixteenth. That was the last time."

Hershel felt struck by lightning. The sixteenth was the night of his accident. He started the engine and pulled away from the curb. "Thanks," he said. He rolled the window up and drove numbly toward the edge of town.

Silvie explored the outer perimeter of Hershel's farmhouse, examining the last remnants of autumn. He had border plants along the foundation, mere stalks now, some still clinging to seedpods like reluctant parents. Whatever they were, coralbells or columbine, they were unrecognizable without their leaves. It was cool and damp under the branchy canopy of the oak trees, and she wondered what it was like here in June or July, when the sun beat down and the shade of these giants was at a premium. She imagined the generations of children who might have grown up here, playing in the sprinkler and sucking on Popsicles. Was this Grandma's house? A place of happy memories and scrumptious food? She couldn't imagine that terrible things had ever happened here. It wasn't the sort of place where broken families lived. It could never have been a fatherless household. Not with the straightness of the eaves and the condition of its sturdy roof.

At the rear of the house next to the mudroom she found stone steps leading down to a storm cellar. Cautiously, she descended them, careful not to slip on the moss and the rotting leaves, and peered through the dusty window. It smelled of mushrooms and cedar, sweet organic decay. The door was locked, and she was relieved. Not because she wasn't curious about the things that might be left to languish in there but because someone might also use it as the perfect hiding place until Hershel was gone and she was alone.

The rain, which had momentarily dissipated, began to fall again, and she walked out to the tiny garage, past the little orange car that Hershel hadn't yet got running, in search of anything to explore. If this would be her home for the time being, even if it was just a possibility, she wanted to know every inch of it. Her eyes roamed the cobweb-covered shelves, skimming the common items collected over more than one person's lifetime: badminton rackets, camping gear, a single wooden oar without its boat. Three gasoline cans sat neatly in a row, the same size and color, but decades apart in design. There was nothing here to give her clues to who Hershel was; these things could have belonged to anyone and probably came with the house.

At the back of the garage, Silvie found another door. She tried the knob and with some effort pulled it open, revealing a walkway and another shed. It looked older than the garage, with a lean-to structure on one side, filled with disintegrating firewood, now so covered with wet moss that it would never light.

The shed door creaked, as if it hadn't been opened in a half century. She kept a constant inventory of the spiders, watching the direction in which they moved like an air-traffic controller alert for trouble. The building was shallow, and as her vision adjusted she found old cans and bottles with strange names she couldn't pronounce. She moved along a shelf row. They were forgotten chemicals used for agriculture. There was something charming about these relics of daily farming, untouched from the 1940s or '50s. She suspected that these chemicals had been long banned from modern production. But here they were, for anyone to discover.

An open sack of lime sat in the corner, used for sweetening acidic soil, she knew from her eighth-grade Western States history class. Most of the West had been built on cattle and farming, and her teacher had spent hours boring them senseless with small details like the importance of lime. She was surprised she remembered it. Silvie stepped close to examine a large metal drum, blowing the dust off the label, which was crowned with the silhouette of a tree.

"A-c-tylcho-lin-es-ter-ase," she enunciated. Her eyes traveled

down to the small print. Active ingredient: organophosphates.
"Hmm, organophosphates. That'll poison your dog." The same ingredient had been in the pesticide her mother had used to kill the
aphids on her flowers, which by accident had also killed Silvie's pet.

Returning to the house, Silvie washed her hands, letting the
water run over her skin, cleansing away the dust for long, long
minutes.

She opened a kitchen drawer filled with odds and ends, then another. She found Hershel's opened mail and reviewed the electric
bill, the phone bill, his Visa statement. She began an unfocused
search of information about him as she considered how she got
here.

She hadn't planned to leave Wyoming this way. She'd dreamed
of escaping to new places, but that's just what it was—dreaming.
The existence of the photos wasn't a surprise, but the revelation
that she was not his only victim carried a frightening edge that
had sent her into a blind panic. Those faces—those scared little
faces. So much like her own. She hadn't thought her plan
through—there was no plan.

It made her wary of everyone around her. Was anyone who he
seemed to be? Was Hershel keeping secrets, too, despite his declaration?

The old English roses were Kyrellis's favorites, even though the
nursery he had purchased had built its reputation on sturdy floribundas. He held a newly opened blossom to his nose and inhaled
the spicy-sweet aroma. Its petals were the soft pink of the inside
of a seashell, and they rippled back in delicate layers like folds of
luxurious silk. He held the flower in the crook of his thumb and
forefinger, gently resting it on his wide palm. He studied it a long

while, unable to tear his eyes away from the subtle color, so rich in the center, so mild at the edges. Perfection. It *was* perfection, though he knew that in six months he'd be standing in a rare spring light, bestowing the same honor on a floribunda. He could be so easily swayed between the two seasons. Floribundas were summer to him: large, bold, deliberate.

He released the stem and examined the tiny buds on the plant, looking for aphids. They were clean. This very rosebush had been plagued by a fungus that started at the trunk and marched upward, painting the undersides of the leaves with velvety orange as it went. He thought he'd have to toss the plant and fumigate the greenhouse. Once he'd switched to a systemic pesticide, however, the fungus disappeared and there wasn't an aphid in sight. Kyrellis knelt beside the plant to get a closer look at its underside, just to be sure.

Satisfied, he groaned to a stand once again. He'd cut these roses on short stems and float them in a crystal bowl of water on the kitchen table before going to bed. The kitchen needed brightening after the grim events of the previous day. He hadn't slept. He'd been afraid to sleep, walking over the scene a thousand more times upon his return. He'd stopped at the do-it-yourself car wash in Sherwood on his way home and sprayed out the bed of his truck, washing the last of Carl Abernathy down the city sewer. Still . . . Kyrellis wondered what he had missed. He worried that he was becoming careless; he needed sleep. Whatever he'd missed in his scrutiny was sure to come to him in his dreams.

Hershel pulled up to several people sitting in their cars, waiting for someone to open the sale barn so they could preview the upcoming sale. It was almost noon. Where was Carl? He parked next to Silvie's defunct Rabbit, wondering if she'd let him sell the damn thing tomorrow night. It had been a week since he found her walking up the highway. In some ways, some of them wonderful ways, it almost seemed like years.

He slid three keys from the silver ring that held them together and stepped out of the truck. As he strode across the parking lot, the men got out of their cars and trucks, and followed him to the door like a flock of gangly sheep. He gripped the three keys in his right hand, hoping that one of them would open the door and spare him the embarrassment of trying them all. As he shoved the first one into the lock and jiggled it, a line of onlookers formed behind him.

"Late opening up today," someone said.

Hershel ignored the comment, pocketing the first key and moving to the second. It worked, and he shoved the door open and stepped inside. Where the hell was Carl?

20

"This is Castor."

"Sheriff, I have something that belongs to you." Kyrellis waited through a long silence.

"Who is this?"

"In time, Sheriff."

"What is this? A prank?"

"I can call another time." He waited a beat, took a deep breath. "In the meantime, I can occupy myself with these photographs."

Castor went silent. The pause was drawn so long that Kyrellis thought perhaps the line had gone dead.

"Who is this?"

Kyrellis knew he had the right man now. There had been little doubt, though. He'd found an election photo of Jacob Castor on the county's website. Castor was the twelfth sheriff he'd researched in the past two days. When Castor's image popped onto his screen, his large white teeth bared at the camera, a jolt had rocketed through Kyrellis's center. There was no question that he was the one.

"I said, who is this?"

"In due time," Kyrellis repeated. "I've got these sorted out. I think we'll start with the bondage shots."

"What makes you think these . . . things you have . . . are mine?"

"Come now, Sheriff. How careless does a man have to be?"

The sheriff drew an audible breath, hissed it out through his teeth. "What do you want?"

"A million dollars."

"I don't have that kind of money."

"I bet Wilbur Huntington does." He flipped through the pictures loud enough that Castor might hear. "The Cheyenne *Tribune*?"

"You fucker."

"I'm a reasonable man. Let's talk this out."

"You have no idea who you're dealing with," Castor said. No wonder the girl was afraid of this man, Kyrellis thought. He had a voice that would silence songbirds. Nearly a minute passed. "Are you still there?" Castor said.

"I am."

"Where are you?"

"I'll be in touch," Kyrellis said.

"Is . . . ? Is she okay?"

"That's touching," Kyrellis said, and hung up. He stared down at the phone, his heart in his throat, hammering like a wood-pecker. His fingers had turned to rubber and he pressed his quaking hands to his temples.

Hershel had a vague sense that he'd squirreled away information about Albert Darling somewhere, but he knew that he wouldn't have put it in the obvious places. All the same, he sifted every file drawer, reviewed every sale list and bank log. Carl's presence was there in the neatly organized papers, bringing a sense of normalcy to the afternoon. Occasionally a firearm appeared, accompanied by a copy of the federal paperwork. These were dark thorns that tore at his psyche, opening glimpses into his past one ragged inch at a time.

The faces of various gun dealers began returning through the haze of his broken memory. Most were quiet, unremarkable men. These were family men, middle-aged men, working men. Hershel had never paused long to imagine what they did with the guns they purchased; to him, it was a victimless crime.

He now wished for the confidence he'd felt when he made that declaration. But disturbing signs to the contrary had begun to surface long before the accident. The crowd at his weekly auctions had shifted. Word about his practices had spread, and a younger, edgier group had begun to appear on Tuesday nights, standing alongside the farmers seeking used tractors and haybines. These newcomers carried an inner-city toughness.

This, in fact, had been his most pressing business concern in those past few months. He'd stood in the parking lot one evening before a sale, talking with a local man, when a large group of twentysomethings roared up in a 1970s Lincoln Continental with a refitted muffler. They blared their horn at another group nearby, then raucously poured from the car, red bandannas pulled tightly over their heads. Helen Cooper and her elderly mother, two women who sold antiques and collectibles in Hillsboro and had been attending Hershel's sales for several years, sat apprehensively behind the dashboard of their Toyota Tercel. They conversed quietly, their eyes crisscrossing the parking lot to the building and back. Then Helen started the engine and pulled away.

The man Hershel was talking with scanned the newcomers, and said pointedly, "You can't afford to lose good business. Can you, Swift?"

"Depends on what you consider good business," Hershel said, and walked away. No one told Hershel Swift how to run his business. The money he made on the sale of firearms was significant. But in private he'd begun to puzzle over the situation.

The narrow lane into the migrant camp was rutted and overgrown. Tree branches scraped the sides of Hershel's truck, and he tried to remember if he'd ever driven all the way back to where Carl lived.

He had fuzzy impressions of dropping Carl off at the highway where this road emerged, unnamed, from the brambles.

The camp was farther back into the woods than Hershel had imagined, but suddenly he came into a small parking lot with a handful of battered cars. He pulled in next to a late-seventies Pinto and sat with the engine idling. Which of the tiny, dilapidated buildings was Carl's? Doors cracked open, but only briefly, as suspicious faces peered out before disappearing again. A light, steady rain misted the scene, feeding the green fungus that crept up the exterior walls of the dozen or so run-down cabins. A wet rooster stood on the picnic table in the center of the yard, as if guarding the place against intruders. Hershel looked from one identical hut to the next, finally noticing the satellite dishes. Carl wouldn't pay for television; that he was sure of. He struggled with the urge to simply assume that the man no longer wanted employment or he would show up for work. Call it good. Hire someone else. But, as much as Hershel gravitated toward saying "To hell with him," he didn't believe that was the case. Carl had been too consistent, too loyal, especially through these tumultuous past few months. And Hershel had decided that afternoon as he searched his papers that he would set aside his pride and ask Carl about all these things. Ask him directly—what he knew about the guns, about Albert Darling. About all of it.

Hershel had the eerie sense that eyes were on him as he stood in the yard, a foreboding in his belly. He yearned for a six-shooter. The place felt deserted in the way Old West movie sets do as the loner rides into town. He glanced between the two shacks without satellite dishes, sitting directly across from each other. Exactly the same in every way, down to the rotting T1-11 siding. He chose the one on the right, which was backed up to a blackberry thicket protecting the muddy river beyond. He knocked twice, and as he waited he mulled over the declaration made by Albert Darling's girlfriend. He simply couldn't get it out of his mind. *We figured you killed him.*

Just then the door opened and a short round woman peered up at him. She looked frightened. "Can I help you?"

"I'm, uh, looking for Carl Abernathy. Do you know him?"

She stared suspiciously, as if trying to decide whether to answer.

"I'm Hershel Swift. He works for me."

Her eyes widened. "He's at your business. Where he works."

"I haven't seen him."

She crossed herself and mumbled something in Spanish that Hershel didn't understand.

"Can you tell me which cabin is his?"

She pointed at the one across the yard. "But he's not there. He tells me that he goes to stay at your business, where he works."

Hershel looked at Carl's cabin, wondering if the man had been in the upstairs apartment all the while. And why he wouldn't have come down to see to business. Something was wrong.

"He's not here," she said. Her face was creased with worry, and she watched him expectantly. Finally, she asked, "He is not there?"

"I didn't see him. I just came from there."

She sucked air audibly through the gap in her front teeth.

Hershel dug in his shirt pocket for a business card and handed it to her. "Here's my number."

She studied it.

"If you see him, would you tell him to call me?" He realized it was silly to give her the card; for all he knew she didn't have a phone. Carl knew how to reach him. But maybe she would call if she heard something.

"Yes, I will tell him."

Hershel thought of Carl's battered face, and suspected that there were things she knew but wasn't saying. He walked across the wet yard, past the rooster that was eyeing him with malice, and knocked loudly on Carl's door, but there was no answer. The woman didn't go inside, but watched. Hershel tried the knob; the place was locked. He wondered if he should ask her about the fight. He didn't know this woman. He had no idea how well Carl did, either. The interchange felt odd and unresolved, and she remained in the doorway, holding his business card as he turned his truck around and pulled out.

Kyrellis suffered a hard little knot at his core. Something he wanted to reach in and yank out, or massage until it relaxed and let go the tendons that ran up through his neck. He stacked the photos into piles, pulling down the ones he'd decorated his bedroom mirror with and returning them to their metal coffin. He still hadn't slept more than a couple of hours and his mind had begun to play tricks on him.

He reasoned that a sheriff could probably trace his call. He considered that Castor could find and kill him. Perhaps he'd been foolish and underestimated the kind of man this was—a man who could beat a child, then bind her up like that and take pictures. Why wouldn't someone capable of that also be a killer? And where were the other girls? He had the ominous feeling they lay in shallow graves along scenic Wyoming back roads.

He calmed himself in his greenhouse. A new rose with a spectacular saffron hue had finally come into bloom.

It was for the roses. Even as he loved them, he knew that his obsession had led him to this. Things never turn out the way one imagines they will. He'd set out to hybridize fungus-resistant roses. It would make him a millionaire. But he could not have foreseen the myriad obstacles. He could not have fathomed the true cost. A hundred thousand for this. Two hundred thousand for that. And not many willing to loan him the money, with his poor track record. For roses. To possess something of beauty.

It was Monday, and he wanted to go down to Swift's to see what would be in tomorrow's sale. In so many piles of junk, hidden in the bottom of a box, or the back of a drawer, there might be something wonderful. Something rare. Beautiful. Winona Free-hauf, the antiques dealer with the reserved seat next to his, once bought a battered old leather suitcase for seven dollars. Once she got it home, she found sixty five-dollar silver certificates from the 1950s carefully sewn into the lining. The bunch was worth more than a thousand dollars. It was that sort of intoxicating possibility that he and his fellow auction junkies craved. They were no better than gambling addicts, except that they always had *something* to show for their efforts.

The decadent aroma of chocolate cake permeated the house, giving it a warm and welcoming feel. She'd given up looking for Hershel's secrets when she found the box of cake mix in the cupboard, but not a single damning clue. Silvie wandered from room to room, imagining that the place was hers. It was so much like the home she had dreamed of owning when she was younger, and it was as though she just now recognized it.

Hershel's furniture was expensive. Nicer than she would have picked out, with its rich wood grains and delicate details. His sofa was shaped like a kidney bean and had carved feet with leaves and scrolls. Another dark band of wood ran the length of the backrest, with a scallop shell carved at its pinnacle. There was a matching chair, both in burgundy velvet. And the table between them was of the same dark wood but simpler in design, and topped with white marble. It looked elegantly old. Not like the trash her father had hauled home and called antique. His were musty, sagging copies of these sophisticated pieces. As she studied the intricate detail of the carving, she understood that what she'd thought of as good furniture had, in fact, been clumsy imitations. The revelation made her see herself as uneducated and backward. But the fact that she understood her backwardness also gave her a powerful new sense of direction. She could remake her life. She could become anybody she wanted, now that she was almost free of Jacob.

She would return the photos. She might scratch the faces off first, though. But then what would happen to the other girls? She didn't recognize them, and she'd spent her first night after leaving Wyoming in a roadside Motel 6, studying those little faces. It was the discovery of these girls that had propelled her into a frenzy of terror and a hasty run for it. Where were those girls now? Silvie believed they were dead. No different from the photos of missing people flashed on the evening news. Only to discover weeks, months, sometimes years later, that they had been murdered. Would she rob grieving families of some sense of closure when Jacob Castor finally died and was revealed for what he really was?

The chaos in her mind had finally crystallized into a hard nugget of honest recognition. She didn't fear running from Jacob the way she feared staying with him. The images of these girls had only reinforced what she subconsciously understood. Jacob Castor would eventually be finished with her. She was now fourteen years older than she was when they first met. She was no longer a little girl. No longer able to pretend to giggle and play, or wear her hair up in purple bows. And, while she wanted more than anything to live as the woman she'd grown into, she still painted her nails cotton-candy pink. She would eventually fail to interest him, and he wasn't the kind of man who would have his castoff lover fawned over by another man.

21

When Hershel found Silvie standing in the kitchen, frosting a chocolate layer cake, all concern about Carl's whereabouts evaporated. Who knew where the man was, whether he'd be back tomorrow, preparing for the sale. He'd wasted the afternoon, having gone looking for him. Carl was probably hanging out with friends somewhere and couldn't get a ride back to Scholls.

Silvie, though, was beautiful.

He suspected that she didn't even know it. She flashed an embarrassed smile his way when he looked over her shoulder at the confection she'd created.

"Thought you might like something sweet," she said.

Stay forever, he thought. *Stay forever.*

"Somebody named Marilyn Stromm called. She said she can't make it tomorrow. She pinched a nerve in her back."

"Damn."

"She was vaccinating sheep," Silvie added. "Said she got one by the hind legs and it kicked the crap out of her."

"Bet that hurt," Hershel said, peeling off his jacket. He didn't know that Marilyn, who had worked for him for more than five years, even raised sheep. Didn't know or had forgotten? No, he never knew. Hershel was coming to understand that forgotten things had a vague presence, like an oily sheen on the surface of his mind. There, but slippery and elusive. Unknown things were simply that: unknown.

"Who is Marilyn Stromm?"

"She's my clerk. Does the auctions."

"Oh. Who's going to be your clerk, then?"

"I'll think about that after cake."

Silvie licked the frosting from the spatula. "How about me? What would I have to do?"

Hershel sized her up. "Well, the clerk writes down every item that is sold, with the buyer's number and the price."

"That's all?"

"I guess there's a little more to it than that. You have to record the lot number. Helps if you can spell, but it's not a requirement. But your writing has to be legible. That *is* a requirement. And you have to pay close attention. If you space out you miss stuff, and I can't go back."

"I think I can do that, except maybe the spelling part."

"You would do that for me?"

"Sure. South Store doesn't need me until Thursday." Silvie dropped the dirty dishes into the sink.

"I'll pay you," he said.

She scowled down at the dishes in her hands. Had he been wrong to offer?

"You've done so much for me. I wouldn't feel right about that," she said.

"I would've paid Marilyn; there's no reason I wouldn't pay you. And you're helping me out hugely."

She shrugged noncommittally and began sudsing the dishes.

After supper they settled on the sofa and found an old movie starring Jack Nicholson. She snuggled against his side as if she'd been made for him. He wanted it to last forever.

"I called my mother," she said. "I wanted you to know so you aren't surprised by the phone bill."

"You don't have to account for everything you do."

She was quiet, and he wished he could see her face.

"But I'm glad you called. Is she okay?"

"I guess." Silvie twirled a lock of hair between her fingers, inspecting the ends. "I had to hang up when she begged me to tell her where I am. But . . . at least she knows I'm alive."

He squeezed her shoulder.

"Jacob knows I'm okay, too, now." She touched his hand lightly. "Do you think he can trace the call back here?"

Hershel hadn't thought of that. A sharp pain stabbed at his forehead. He's got the technology, he thought. And the authority to request a trace.

She pulled away to look at Hershel.

"I don't know," he admitted.

"Oh my God. What have I done?"

He pulled her in tight again. "I'm not going to let him hurt you. He'll have to deal with me." Hershel's mind worked through the scenarios. How would he know who this man was if he saw him?

"Hershel, I better go."

"Don't be silly. Where will you go?"

"I don't know. But he'll find me here."

"Then he'll find me, too." He lowered his voice to a whisper. "Silvie, you've become very important to me. I will protect you."

She pressed her nose against his windpipe. "He's a very dangerous man."

Hershel gave her his most reassuring smile. "There's every chance that I am, too."

———

Kyrellis scanned the auction barn. It was packed with soon-to-be bidders previewing the offerings, picking through boxes, inspecting and appraising merchandise. He couldn't remember when he'd seen this many people here. Stuart, one of Hershel's floor men, cussed his way through the growing crowd, his eyes darting from side to side. He nodded curtly at Kyrellis as he passed.

Hershel's office door stood open, and he was on the phone, leaning over his desk. Kyrellis wandered past the girl in the concession stand, who was too busy rushing about pouring coffee and sodas, scooping popcorn into small paper sacks, and ringing up sales to notice him. A line of ten or so people waited patiently to place their orders.

Kyrellis shut the door behind him, gaining Hershel's attention.

"Send anyone you've got. They just need to have strong backs and speak decent English." When he hung up, he stared at Kyrellis.

"Trouble?"

"Can't find Carl. Didn't show up yesterday. No sign of him today. I need him. We've got the biggest crowd we've ever had tonight, with all this architectural stuff. How does a man just go missing after years of consistency?"

"No idea," Kyrellis said. "He didn't seem the reliable type, anyway. You're probably better off."

"Why are you here? What do you want?"

"Our man, Jacob Castor..." He could tell by the look on Hershel's face that the name was familiar. "He's raising a million dollars for those pictures."

"You filthy son of a bitch."

"I'll sell them to you for half that. To protect the girl, of course."

"You're nothing but a predator."

"Welcome to the garden of predators, my friend." Kyrellis sat in the chair opposite Hershel's desk. He gazed sadly at his hands.

Silvie took her place on the auctioneer's stand, pulling the stool up to her new work space. She looked out over the crowd and her upper lip trembled. She'd had no idea all these people would be watching her. She opened the new package of pens sitting on the desk and studied the carbon-paper forms. They were long, narrow strips in quadruplicate: white, yellow, pink, with the cardboard copy on the bottom. Each form was laid out with spaces for ten items, encapsulating the things that Hershel had explained, with perforated lines for splitting them apart. She wondered how she'd know the lot number. Something to ask Hershel. She looked at the tiny clock pasted against the back of the podium, where only she and the auctioneer could see it. It was six-fifteen. Where was he? And where was Carl? She hadn't seen him among the floor men or the other employees. But she'd seen the bully, who had looked her up and down, not even bothering to close his mouth.

A red-haired girl appeared at Silvie's elbow, tiny from that perch four feet above the floor.

"This is for Hershel," the girl said, handing up a paper cup of orange soda. "What are you drinking?"

"Coke, I guess."

The girl nodded. "I'll bring it right out."

"Do you know where Hershel is?"

"He's trying to get more help for the floor. Carl didn't show." The girl disappeared before Silvie could ask any more questions.

She glimpsed Kyrellis as he took a seat in the front row. He nodded, keeping her in his sights.

"A newbie," the bully said, now standing where the concession girl had been. "What's your name?"

She considered him coolly but didn't answer, which she knew would piss him off. She'd been appraised by too many men, some twice the age and income of this asshole. He might as well understand right now that she wasn't giving what he was looking for.

He leaned an elbow against the lectern, too close to her thigh—a bold act. His beard was cropped short, and he rubbed it with his palm. "Haven't seen you around? Where you from?"

"Mars," she said.

He laughed, but his eyes darted around the floor now.

"Don't you have things to do, Stuart?" It was Hershel, and his voice boomed, even with the noise of the crowd. The man jumped.

"Just welcoming the new help, boss."

"She's not 'the help.' She's a friend of mine who was kind enough to do us a favor."

He nodded to Silvie. "Good luck."

Hershel took his place, squeezing Silvie's shoulder reassuringly. "Don't worry—you'll be able to keep up with me. It's a lot easier these days." He took up his microphone, thanked the crowd for coming, and opened the bidding on a tap-and-dye set.

22

The smooth rhythm of Hershel's auctioneering lulled Silvie, and she found herself losing track of the items and becoming swept up in the way he sang out the numbers. This man she'd come to know as hesitant in his speech and slow to find his words rolled through items with perfect tempo. Occasionally Stuart called out the name of an item when Hershel paused a beat too long, but they worked together like old partners. She scribbled down names, prices, lot numbers, and bidder numbers until her hand ached. Before she knew, it was nine o'clock. As she recorded the sales of glass doorknobs, six-panel fir doors, tin ceiling tiles, plaster molds, and dozens of other things she'd never heard of and had no idea how to spell properly, she began to see the potential in this weird business. In the run of ten minutes she guessed they'd sold a thousand dollars in merchandise, yielding more than three hundred dollars in commission. And all Hershel had to do was open his doors to bring it in and see it out again, in the span of a week. She glanced up at him as he called the numbers on a pristine porcelain sink from the 1930s. What she didn't know about this man.

"Okay, folks," Hershel said after wrapping up the bid. "We're doing something a little different tonight. We're taking a fifteen-minute break. Come down and look at what we've still got.

There's lots of stuff down here that's been hiding." He switched off the microphone and bent down to Silvie's ear. "You're doing great. How do you feel?"

She sat back, grateful for the pause in the frenetic pace. Her neck muscles were tense and her shoulders stiff. "I'm fine, but it's harder than it looks."

"We're halfway there."

Halfway? She tried to hide her dismay.

Silvie wound through the crowd that descended from the bleachers and mingled on the sale floor. She scanned the room for Kyrellis, keen to keep her distance. The girl in the concession stand was so busy she didn't notice Silvie, and Silvie didn't wait for her, pouring herself a cup of Coke and grabbing a bag of popcorn. It was a poor supper, but better than nothing. And the smell of it had been teasing her all evening.

Hershel wrapped up the sale at ten minutes to two. His head throbbed, but he'd gotten into a smooth pace where the names came back to him easily, and in his revelry he couldn't bring himself to end the event sooner. The temporary floor men had taken to leaning on boxes until it was their turn to move something. Only Stuart seemed to appreciate the long night, maintaining his stamina and even smiling.

Hershel could see that Silvie was exhausted. She sat back limply, yawning. "I'm sorry. I should have finished up earlier. You're tired."

"I'm okay," she said, straightening up in her seat.

He didn't have the heart to tell her that the real work had only just begun. Bidders had been checking out all evening, but the majority had remained for the exceptionally good merchandise tonight. And now they would line up to pay, find their items, and load them up. The crew in the back room would need Hershel's help in exchanging the receipts for items. There would be squabbles over what they did and did not buy, especially with first-timers. They didn't know they were paying by the piece and had taken all twenty, or they thought they'd bought one thing but in fact had bid on something else. Once everyone paid, Linda would tally the receipts, and Hershel and the crew would stay until everything balanced to the penny. Stuart would sweep up after he'd helped the buyers load their items. They had at least two hours of work ahead of them.

He handed Silvie his keys. "Why don't you take the truck and head home? I'll walk. You're tired, and I've got more work to do."

"I can stay," she said, yawning again. "What do you need me to do?"

"I need you to go home and get some rest."

She seemed relieved that he hadn't taken her up on the offer, and pulled on the work shirt she'd taken from his closet.

"Are you sure you want me to take the truck? I can go through the orchard."

"I don't want to have to send out a search party," he teased, but still he watched her walk to the door.

He stepped down onto the sale floor and headed toward the back room, but something caught his eye. An attorney's bookcase in oak, with leaded-glass doors and brass knobs. It was identical to the one in his living room. He must have walked past it a thousand times in the past few months, but something about its twin, sitting here on the sale floor, slid its origin into place. It was from the Pete Ellis estate, and Hershel didn't put the bookcase in the sale. He'd hauled it home and installed it in the living room. When Pete's widow asked how much it went for, knowing it should bring more than a thousand dollars, Hershel had shrugged and said, "Couple hundred. Didn't itemize everything."

She had insisted that it must have brought more.

"Maybe so. Can't remember exactly," he'd said. "Sold a lot of stuff."

Very little that Hershel had forgotten felt good to remember.

He stepped into the back room and helped the next person in line. He wandered into the catacombs in search of the shoe rack that number 361 had purchased for five dollars.

Kyrellis, leaning against his car door, watched for Silvie. He was about to give up when she emerged into the damp night. As she walked toward Hershel's truck he followed her, picking up his pace. She struggled with the lock in the dim light, and leaned a shoulder against the truck.

"Evening, Silvie. How was your first night?"

She started and let out a shriek.

"I'm sorry. I didn't mean to frighten you."

She kept a wary eye on him, but said nothing.

"Can we talk?"

She nodded.

"Why don't we go to my car?"

"I don't think that's a good idea." She brushed her hair over her shoulder and stood to her full height.

"It's around front. Where there are other people who can hear you scream." Kyrellis surveyed the empty back lot as if to make his point. "Besides, I have something for you."

He slid into the driver's seat of the big Impala and gestured toward the line of customers waiting to pay for their items. "See, nothing to fear."

"I'm not afraid of you," she said.

"I'm glad. I'm not going to hurt you." He leaned over and popped the glove box and took out a photograph.

She recognized it instantly and snatched it away from him, then rummaged through the open compartment, looking for others.

"It's the only one."

"Where are the rest?"

"In a safe place."

She shoved the picture into her backpack and zipped it tight.

"If you want them, there are some things you can do for me."

"Like what?" Her face had gone hard.

"Tell me about Jacob Castor."

"How do you—"

"I told you I'd get his name one way or another."

"Did Hershel tell you?"

"You're learning. Perhaps you can't trust him like you thought you could." Kyrellis seized on this opportunity. "He *is* all about money. I've know the man a long time, and he'll do anything for money."

Silvie turned away.

"He asked about you."

"Who?"

"Our friend Sheriff Castor, of course." Kyrellis took a pack of cigarettes from the dashboard and held it out to her. She shook her head, and he extracted one, taking his time lighting it. "You matter to him."

"He just wants to know where I am so he can kill me."

"I thought of that, too. Do you know any of the other girls in the photos?"

She bit her lip and shook her head.

"I won't tell him where you are. Unless you refuse to help me."

She wiped at her cheek, and he realized that she was crying.

"This doesn't have to be difficult." He rested his hand on her thigh. She tensed. "I'll give you a little time. Why don't you come see me tomorrow? After you've had some sleep. I can see you're tired."

"And then you'll give me the photos?"

"We can negotiate that. Here, I'll give you my card. It has my address on it." He glanced out at the dwindling line of bidders. "Hershel always spends Wednesdays here cleaning up. He won't even know you're gone."

She took the card and reached for the door handle.

"Did you care for him at all?"

She looked back as if she couldn't say for sure. It gave him hope. He didn't want the situation to be as bleak as it appeared. If there had been feelings between them, anything warm at all, it was better. She shoved the door open and got out, slamming it behind her.

———

At Hershel's house, Silvie looked at Kyrellis's card. *Oregon Premier Roses.* He sold roses? How bizarre and unexpected. She had assumed he was something like a crew boss for road construction or metalwork. Roses? Roses had never been her favorite flower. Jacob always offered her roses after doing unspeakable things to her.

She could still make out the scars on the insides of her elbows where he'd bound her too tightly, then gotten drunk while looking at her. The cords he'd used were thin and acrylic, and they cut into her flesh before he finally relented and let her go. He was horrified when he saw what he'd done, and he bought her roses. Silvie saw no romance in them.

Silvie stifled a wry smirk, thinking it was somehow appropriate and even poetic that a man who sold roses would blackmail Jacob Castor. What had they said to each other? Jacob probably shouted. He got verbally abusive when anyone confronted him. Kyrellis probably talked in that smooth, soft voice, believing he had the upper hand. Did Kyrellis regret his plan? Was he smart enough to realize that Jacob was a man who must always have the upper hand? He met every challenge as if it were a personal affront. When they were out together he would say to her, "See that man?" He'd point to any man; it didn't matter who. "He probably thinks he's hot shit. But he's nothing. He'll never accomplish half of what I've done in my lifetime." To Jacob, every man was someone to upstage.

She tucked the business card into her backpack and climbed the stairs to bed. She felt an eerie sense of calm, a sheer exhaustion in her bones that came from something deeper. She brushed her teeth and showered the cigarette smoke out of her hair. Walking down the hall she reached for the knob to the guest room, then kept going and slid into Hershel's bed. She couldn't risk alienating him. As she lay in bed, the sheets pulled up to her chin, her mind buzzed with the day ahead.

Kyrellis had no idea what he'd gotten into, and if Silvie didn't believe Jacob was planning to kill her she would call him herself and let him know where he could find his pictures. She lingered on the idea. What if she did call him? She could be gone before he got here. She let that scenario play out for a few minutes: Jacob would show up here and start questioning everyone as if he were the law wherever he went. He'd swagger through the Berry Barn and sneer at the locals as if they were beneath him. He would find her car at Hershel's business and pelt him with questions. She could see poor Hershel unable to answer them as quickly as they came at him. Jacob might become suspicious of him, and God knows what he would do. Kill him? It was not outside the realm of possibility.

She rolled onto her side, resigned to the fact that she didn't want to hurt the people here. Not Karen, not Carl, not anyone. Jacob Castor brought hurt wherever he went; there was nothing to be gained by bringing him here. She pressed her head back against the pillow and stared up at the ceiling. She closed her eyes and steeled her will to meet Kyrellis's request. If that's what it took to get the photos back, fine. That's what she would do.

23

Hershel left Silvie sleeping and prepped himself to head back to the auction barn. As he shaved, he studied his face in the mirror. The scar across his forehead was still purple-red, but fading. It gave him a gangster-like appearance that he suspected the old Hershel would appreciate much more than the new one. He'd changed so much in the past few months, but not as rapidly as in the past few days. He turned and gazed through the bedroom door at Silvie, strands of hair like corn silk cascading over the pillow, her hands drawn up in tight little fists beneath her chin. She slumbered so peacefully. She had made him look at his life differently, to see what was truly important. Had he ever been a predator, as Kyrellis had suggested, he was no longer. If he had murdered Albert Darling, and he questioned whether he had, *this* Hershel could not have done so. But these questions only left him wondering who he was. Could he ignore his past? Pretend it wasn't relevant?

He rinsed his razor in the sink, tapping the water out of the blades and toweling the moisture from his face. His mind felt sharp and clear today. He glanced around the bathroom, naming objects in his head: soap, mirror, sink, cologne, bath mat. *Bath mat*. He wouldn't have remembered that one a day ago.

On his way out, he bent over Silvie and kissed her cheek. She woke and stared up at him, looking bewildered.

"Go back to sleep," he whispered. "I'm heading to work."

"Can I borrow your truck?"

"I'll leave the keys on the counter."

"I need to get some new shoes for work." She smiled at him, and he melted inside.

"Go back to sleep," he said again. "It's still early."

Downstairs, he paused in front of the bookcase. This one was in better condition than the one at the sale barn; he kept only the very best for himself. He rummaged through his desk in the corner of the kitchen and wrote a check to Mary Ellis for a thousand dollars. He slipped it into his shirt pocket. He'd look up the paperwork and mail it when he got to work.

He found the place locked, no sign of Carl. Where had the man disappeared to? Something about his absence felt very wrong, and Hershel went inside with a sense of loss riding him. Stuart had agreed to work today, predicting that they'd seen the last of Carl Abernathy. He guessed the man had drifted on to a new place, but Hershel knew better.

In his office, Hershel looked up Carl's hire date and stared at the year in disbelief. The man had been in his employ for a decade. How could he have underestimated the man's commitment to him—to his business. Why? Hershel picked up the phone and called the police.

"I think I should report a missing person," he said.

The woman on the other end asked a series of questions in a rapid-fire manner that left Hershel fumbling for answers, but mostly admitting that he didn't know. Finally he explained that Carl had been a reliable, longtime employee who hadn't been seen in three days.

"Could he have just gone out of town?" the woman wanted to know.

Hershel supposed he could have. It didn't sound like much when he listened to himself try to explain his concern. But there was more to it, and he hoped it was nothing to do with some past transaction—something he was unknowingly responsible for.

"Can't someone just check into it?" he finally asked.

She agreed to file a report and took down Hershel's information.

After a few minutes, he picked up the phone and dialed a new number. It rang several times.

"Hello?"

Hershel's mouth went dry. "Mom?"

She hung up.

He listened to the dial tone, then gently set the phone down.

Kyrellis trimmed the rosebushes on his patio, deadheading the spent blossoms and carefully picking up the clippings. He would show his prized flowers to Silvie when she arrived, take her on a tour of his garden and greenhouses. He wondered if he should cut her a bouquet. She couldn't, of course, take it with her and risk questions from Hershel. Besides, he didn't like to part with such perfection. It was a fault he knew he must overcome if he was going to make this business profitable again. He'd become more collector than grower, obsessing about the new hybrids to the point of not returning phone calls from his customers about the varieties that had built the establishment. He'd nearly run this nursery, which he could scarcely afford when it was operating in the black, into the ground.

It was at Swift's auction that everything started to unravel for Kyrellis. The auction had seen a different type of clientele in the past year or so. Gangs, mostly, looking for guns. It had made them all uncomfortable. Not just the way these newcomers strutted around as if they owned the place, but their brazenness. The gun trading had been successful, in Kyrellis's opinion, because it was discreet.

One cozied up to Kyrellis, claiming he was eager to invest in hybrid flowers. Kyrellis wasn't stupid. He knew that his rose business was simply an opportunity to convert drug and gun money into something more legitimate. All he got in exchange for the loan was a first name and a post-office box in North Portland, where he was to send his payments.

But orders had continued their steady decline, despite the infusion of cash, and now there were only a handful of retail stores that still considered Kyrellis their primary supplier. The situation had caused his blood pressure to skyrocket. He admitted, as he trimmed the bushes, that he simply didn't know how to turn things around. He hated the sales aspect.

His doorbell rang, and he paused. It was early. He smiled to himself; she was anxious.

Kyrellis smoothed his hair back on his way to the door, glad that he'd been up early and showered. It was good that she'd come at this hour. He liked a freshly scrubbed girl and had planned on suggesting a bath first.

He opened the door, unable to hide his smile.

"Victor Kyrellis," said the man standing on the porch.

Kyrellis searched the visitor's face for recognition. He was tall, but the overriding trait was that he was solid. He wore a light cotton pullover that tightly contoured his pronounced muscles. He held his arms at his sides and his shoulders taut, in a hypervigilant manner. He flashed a smile, though not a friendly one and, against his black skin, the man's teeth seemed dazzling white. A rhinestone was embedded in his front tooth. Kyrellis couldn't see the gun, but he knew the man carried one.

"Do I know you?" Kyrellis asked.

"No, but you know the man I work for." He twisted a ragged white rose between his fingers, torn violently from the bush Kyrellis had set on the front porch that very morning for Silvie. The gray

Oregon winter could be so depressing. He'd thought the flowers would guide her to him.

Kyrellis's gut twisted. "I'll have the money within the month."

"Why don't you invite me in?"

"No, I don't think I will." The two eyed each other, and Kyrellis wished he had taken the same precaution this time that he had with Carl Abernathy. But his guns were in the cabinet, except for the single handgun he kept on the table next to his bed. "I have a line on a large sum. A month. Just give me a month."

"And what happens in a month if you don't have the money, Victor?"

"I will," he asserted. "It's just been a little dry this fall. But, like I said, I have a line."

"You said that the last time. Wasn't this note due a month ago?"

"I . . . no, I didn't say that. I didn't have a line on anything then. It was just hard luck. But things have changed. I just need a little time."

"Maybe. But he'd like some collateral this time. Just in case."

"Like what?"

"Well, how about we take a look at that gun collection."

"Oh, come on. Not that."

The man stared balefully at Kyrellis. "It could be much worse, and I think you know that."

"Please. Just a month."

"Even if I agree, I still need collateral."

Kyrellis closed his eyes. His guns were second only to his roses. He stood aside to let the man in.

"Wait here," he said in the living room. "I'll bring them out." He left the man and went to a small bedroom off the hallway, cursing under his breath. The room was lined on three walls with glass cabinets that showcased his numerous and rare specimens. Every time he came in here, though, he was reminded that he'd sold the very best gun that had ever passed through his hands: Albert Darling's Winchester rifle. The money was more important at the time, and for once he'd kept a cool head and sold it. But he never forgave himself for being in a situation where he had to let it go. And now...he would never again see whatever gun—or, worse, *guns*—he handed over today. This wasn't so much collateral as interest, and he knew it.

Kyrellis selected carefully, making sure the gun he chose was something he had a chance of replacing. A Smith shotgun, Eagle Grade, in fair condition. Not too rare. Not too expensive. But when he presented it to the man in his living room the man examined it carefully, set it on the coffee table, and asked what else he had. They repeated the ritual until there were five guns of graduating rarity and value, from the Smith to a Hammond Grant military automatic pistol in pristine condition, laid out between them.

"I'll take them all," the man announced, and stood to collect them.

Kyrellis wasn't surprised, and he watched with a sinking heart as the man went to his car and returned with a long blue duffel bag and began to seal them away. As the last gun disappeared from sight, a black pickup pulled into the driveway. They both peered out. Kyrellis realized it was Silvie.

"Expecting someone?" the man said.

Kyrellis didn't answer. He watched as she sat in the truck. Certainly she'd seen them both. Then she slowly backed out, turned around, and left.

"Guess it wasn't too important," the man said, returning to his task.

Kyrellis wanted to take up one of the guns he'd just handed over and shoot the man dead. His arrogance. The way he strutted around as if he were the man with the bucks. If he were half the gun expert he fancied himself, he would understand that Kyrellis had much better guns in his collection. Some worth up to thirty thousand dollars. This dolt was a fool to imagine he had any value to the one who had sent him.

"What's your name?" Kyrellis asked.

The man slid the duffel over his shoulder and stared at Kyrellis. He stepped closer and riveted his fist into Kyrellis's soft belly, doubling him over, making his mind go absolutely white. Kyrellis fell to his knees and fought for breath, dull pain blossoming through his center. He was sure he would vomit.

"I'll be back for the money in two weeks," the man said calmly. "Did you hear me, Victor? *Two weeks*."

———

At the auction barn, Hershel and Stuart spent the morning loading out sold merchandise to waiting pickup trucks, scrutinizing receipts, and marking items COLLECTED.

"Check those out," Stuart said, whistling to himself. He'd been commenting on the female customers' anatomy for the past few hours, but Hershel ignored him. "C'mon, boss, you couldn't have hit your head that hard—not to notice *those*."

"Just bring up the next load, will you, Stuart."

"Guess you're not interested since that new piece showed up, huh?" Stuart started back into the warehouse, but Hershel, in two quick steps, blocked his path. Stuart laughed tensely, stepping left and then right, trying to get around Hershel.

"I'm not just after her for some pussy."

Stuart stood back and looked at the ground. "Sorry, boss. Didn't mean nothing by it. You're just different now."

"I know it. Not a goddamn second goes by that I don't know I'm different." Hershel moved aside and let Stuart pass. Why the hell was he telling this man anything? Why can't a man be different?

There was a lull in traffic, and the place fell momentarily quiet. Hershel looked around at the items yet to be collected. Wednesday was old business, nothing fresh or interesting. He was forced to keep regular hours on this day because people had to arrange for transportation and help moving things. But it had all been sold, he'd collected the money, and this was just a day of cleanup.

"You can go," he said to Stuart. "I can manage the rest."

"No, I'll stay another hour or two. If you don't mind." He glanced at Hershel for permission. "Cost of gas these days is killing me. Almost not worth driving out here if I don't get in at least six hours."

"Fine with me." Hershel tried to conjure up where Stuart lived. He drew a blank, then wondered if it was an unknown or a forgotten. He must have known at some point. He realized that he was staring at Stuart as he puzzled it out, and walked away, heading for the concession stand to get a soda.

A middle-aged Mexican woman peered in through the open door, looking out of place and unsure. "Hello?" she called.

"C'mon in," he hollered. "Can I help you?"

As she neared, he recognized her as the woman from the migrant camp.

"My name is Yolanda," she said, holding up the business card he'd given her. "I met you before? You came to my house?"

"Yes, I remember."

She glanced around the large, nearly empty warehouse at the assortment of used items that were now stacked into neat piles, and winced. "Is Carl here?"

Hershel frowned. "No, I haven't seen him in three days."

She let out a wail that stunned him.

"What's wrong?"

She tipped her head back and howled again, then spoke rapidly in Spanish.

"Please," Hershel said, guiding her into his office. "Sit. Tell me what's wrong."

She went on in rapid Spanish, her voice pitched high and mournful.

"What is upsetting you?"

"I think it is him," she said, tears catching in her throat. "I think it is Carl."

"Who?"

"The body they took from the river."

Carl's bruised face and swollen jaw came to mind. The way he had limped around the day before he disappeared. Hershel had forgotten to mention that to the woman on the phone this morning.

"What body?"

"This morning they take a body out of the river. By Campo Rojo. A fisherman found it. I am fear that it is Carlos." She took a breath, her tears beyond control. "He tells me he is here."

Hershel shook his head, and Yolanda put her face in her hands and cried.

24

The new soft-soled shoes were rubbery under Silvie's feet. She'd driven down back roads, heading west from Kyrellis's place, into green valleys of farmland rimmed by low hills blue beneath the winter sky. She marveled at the way Oregon seemed to segregate its cities from its agriculture with abrupt, hard lines. A last row of close-in houses with tiny yards butted against an expanse of fallow strawberry fields. Hemmed in and cramped, as if they'd run out of room, when in fact all the space one could possibly want lay there for the taking. Driving the winding, narrow roads with names like Rood Bridge and Bald Peak, she'd find herself suddenly in the middle of a nameless community, and then, with as little warning, back into the open of a hay field or a dormant orchard. Nothing like the meandering businesses and homes, strung together like cheap beads, that contoured the highways between Wyoming and this odd, damp place. At last she found a sign directing her to Hillsboro. There she discovered a strip mall with a Payless shoe store. The sneakers would do for a while. As she navigated her way along the unfamiliar roads, trying to find Scholls again, she considered trying Kyrellis once more. It hadn't bothered her to find that he had company, but she knew the reprieve was only temporary. By the time she'd turned around and pulled onto the road again, she was already searching for another opportunity. She told herself that the task ahead was not important; it was the end goal that mattered. As she considered Kyrellis's demand, it was curse or cry. She cursed Jacob. And she pushed away a nagging doubt about Hershel. Had he shared information with Kyrellis? If she couldn't trust Hershel, she couldn't trust anyone, and while that might well be true, she needed the protection and shelter he provided. She would use him if necessary.

As she came up on Scholls Ferry Road, very near where she'd first met Hershel, instead of turning right onto the familiar road to the auction barn, she went straight, deciding that now was as good a time as any to negotiate the return of the photos.

Hershel had tried to persuade Yolanda to stay until he could give her a ride home, but she refused and walked down Scholls Ferry still crying and speaking Spanish in mournful tones.

Stuart had joined him at the front door, watching the sad little woman stumble away. He looked thoughtfully at Hershel and said, "I think she's in love with him."

"Does seem to be more there than meets the eye."

"Nice knockers," Stuart added, then gritted his teeth at his own remark.

"You're such an asshole."

"Oh, come on." Stuart shrugged and walked out to greet a customer who had pulled in and backed his truck up to the front of the building. A sheriff's patrol pulled in a minute later, and Hershel turned from the customer to meet the officer. He'd been half expecting this visit, since he'd called in a missing person on the same day that a body was found in the river—according to Yolanda, anyway. The grim coincidence hollowed out his center.

"This your place?" The officer started talking before he reached the door.

"It is. I'm Her..hel Swift."

"Your missing Abernathy the same one that lived at Campo Rojo?"

"Yeah. The last time I saw him, he was beat up pretty bad. His face was a mess, but he didn't say what happened."

"We've got that information. A passerby filed a report about a fight on the highway near the camp. We know Abernathy was involved, but the others were gone by the time the sheriff arrived, and no one at the camp would talk."

Hershel couldn't think of anything else he might add. "A woman from camp...she came by and said someone found a body."

"Yeah." The officer seemed reluctant to share information, pausing and looking out across the orchard. "We're still investigating."

"Was it him?"

He turned in the direction of Campo Rojo. "It was a male."

"When will you know for sure?"

"That'll be difficult. It's missing its head."

Hershel seemed unable to fully comprehend this information. Why would someone do that to Carl? He was such an easygoing man. Friendly to everyone. "Must be someone else," he said. "Nobody hated Carl Abernathy enough to kill him and...and do *that*."

"Immigration did a sweep of the camp after the fight. It's possible that this was retaliation."

"Retaliation?"

The officer handed Hershel a card. "Call me if he shows up, or if you hear anything you think would help us identify the body from the river."

Carl dead? He shoved the card into his back pocket. No one could want Carl Abernathy dead. Barely anyone knew that he was alive.

After a few wrong turns, Kyrellis's greenhouses appeared, then his driveway. Silvie's stomach tightened. She sat in the truck for a few minutes. The house appeared dark, no sign that he was home. She slid out and approached, pausing to touch the potted rosebush in full bloom on the front step. She bent to smell the flowers so out of place in the winter cold, and they brought Jacob to mind. A strange braid of longing and loathing twisted through her—a familiar confusion. She didn't know whether to curse him or beg his forgiveness. She pressed the doorbell and listened to the faint chime inside the house. After a moment Kyrellis appeared, looking pale, with his hair matted up on one side as if he'd been sleeping. He carried a pistol.

"I wasn't expecting you," he said, looking at the gun, then setting it down on a low table in the entryway.

"You invited me."

"Yes, but when you left earlier I assumed . . ." He stepped aside and motioned her in.

"I wasn't going to come inside while you had company." She was greeted by the smell of vomit. She turned and studied him.

"I'm not feeling well," he said somewhat indignantly.

"I'll come back another time, then. It's getting late, anyway. Hershel will be wondering."

"I suppose that's best."

"Let's just understand each other, though. What do I have to do to get my things back?"

He rubbed his hair and sighed. "Let's walk. I need some fresh air. I'll show you my garden."

"And you'll tell me the exact terms of this agreement." The force in her voice surprised her.

"Do you like roses?"

"They aren't my favorite."

"That's a shame. A woman who doesn't like roses," he said silkily. "You must be one of a kind." He led her through the kitchen to a back patio, which was covered with blooming bushes in a rainbow of colors. "I raise the finest floribundas in Oregon." He fondled a striking yellow flower. "This is called Southampton. And this"—he pointed to an apricot-colored rose—"is Chanelle." He let his eyes travel the length of her frame. "What woman doesn't love a rose?"

"They're nice, but they're just flowers."

He snorted in disgust. "Nice? You'll never see finer. Come see the greenhouse. I'm propagating a new variety."

She followed him out into the gray afternoon, searching for something to say. "My mother's roses always had bugs on them."

"Yes, there are ones that prey on new buds, snatching away their potential. You can kill the predator, but the flowers are ruined." He turned his eyes on her, and she flushed. Her cheeks were burning.

"What do you do about them?"

"The right poison will take care of any predator."

He was reverent about touching the petals of his roses. He whispered the names as they passed. "Sweet Promise. Virgo. Gentle Touch. Meteor." The bushes were lush and popping with buds where he kept them in the greenhouses. But the buildings were coated in green algae, and the plastic fabric was torn. Weeds sprouted through the gravel at their feet, and the long tables where he did his potting were angled downward in rot, as if the earth were pulling them into itself.

"How do they grow like this in the winter?"

Kyrellis lifted a bottle from a nearby table and handed it to Silvie. She unscrewed the cap and held it to her nose, but he yanked it back and resealed it. "It's several times more potent in liquid form and absorbs quickly. It can kill you, too, Silvie, not just bugs and fungus. You wouldn't want to get that on your skin. Goes right through. And you don't feel a thing." Then he laughed, and it sounded almost jolly.

———

When Kyrellis had shown her his propagation house and the hundreds of tiny stalks sprouting their first leaves, he seemed to have run out of things to talk about. The fresh air, or the roses, had invigorated him and he glanced often at her.

"Come tomorrow," he said. "We'll start our work."

"I'm waitressing tomorrow. Karen is short-staffed."

"Tell Swift you're going in early. Shower first. I want you fresh."

Her shoulder blades contracted tightly. "I want to know exactly what it's going to take to get all the pictures back."

"We'll discuss that tomorrow." He waved a hand in the air as if to dismiss her.

"No, today."

He sighed. "You'll get your photos."

"All of them. I won't agree to anything unless I get every single one back."

"If you insist. But not all at once. I like to savor the pleasure, if you know what I mean."

"Tell me what you have in mind."

"You're taking all the mystery out of this, my pet. How about one for one. A favor for a photo."

"What? No. There are at least thirty pictures in that box."

"No, there aren't. I gave one to you already. And I gave one to Hershel."

Hershel had one of her pictures? Why hadn't he said anything? Why hadn't he returned it?

"I wonder what he did with that one?" Kyrellis mused. "It was one of my favorites."

"I'm not going to fuck you thirty times," she said. "Or even twenty-eight. Not even once if you don't come up with a better deal than that."

"My, you *are* tough. Is that the Wyoming in you? I've heard girls from that part of the country are like rodeo ponies. Is it true?"

"You're a pig."

"Now now," he warned. "Let's not have that or there won't be a deal."

"I'll come Friday, when Hershel's receiving furniture for next

week's sale. After my shift at the South Store. I'll choose ten photos. Then you can have your way. But . . . no marks."

He shook his head. "Five. And I'm not the sort of man who
finds pleasure in pain."

She bit into her lip, considering him. Despite his soft-spoken
manner, he held the power. "Five, then. But you do what *I* say, the
way *I* say it."

"You're a tease," he said, smiling. "But I think I can wait until
Friday. It'll give me something to look forward to." He put his
broad hand on the small of her back, then ran it up to her shoulder blades. She tensed but remained still as he touched each ver-
tebra. He made his way back down her spine, as if counting to
make sure they were all in order. All the way to her tailbone,
where he let his hand linger. She swallowed, her throat dry, expecting his next move, anticipating that he'd drop his hand under
her, but he didn't. He smiled at her with dark, sharp eyes. "We
have an agreement, then. I'll expect you on Friday."

25

Hershel was preparing supper when he heard the truck pull up to the house. He'd been distracted enough to char the onions, spending his time scraping them off the frying pan and trying not to think about what might have happened to Silvie, or what decisions she might have made. He greeted her in the mudroom. "I was worried."

"I don't know the roads around here. I got lost." She brushed past him into the kitchen, scowling. She wore new shoes with gleaming white soles, slightly muddied around the toes and heels.

"Do you have my cell number?"

She halted in the center of the kitchen. "Did Kyrellis give you one of the pictures from Jacob's box?"

He struggled for what to say. "Yes. He did. I tore it up."

Silvie scrutinized him. "I don't believe you."

"It's . . . it's true."

"Why would you do that? You know I have to return those to Jacob before he'll leave me alone."

"I was . . . stunned by it. It disturbed me. I tore it up to make a point to Kyrellis." His mind slowly caught up with the implications of her accusation. "Where have you been? Talking to Kyrellis?"

She looked away. "How else am I going to get them back if I don't deal with him directly?"

"I said I would talk to him."

"Well, a lot of good that's done." Her eyes flared darkly.

Hershel's head pounded.

"And you told him who Jacob was! I thought I could trust you."

"I did not."

Her jaw was set in a hard line, and her nostrils blazed in and out with her breath.

"I didn't. And if you haven't figured out that you can trust me by now, I guess there's about nothing in the world I can do to prove it. Helping you on the highway, offering a place to stay..." He gestured at the house, at a loss for words. "How can you even say this?"

She threw her hands up. "I don't know. I'm confused. I don't know who to trust. You said you'd talk to Kyrellis. Carl said *he* would talk to Kyrellis. And when I talked to Kyrellis he tells me that you have one of the pictures. And that you gave him Jacob's name. And...that you murdered someone."

Hershel's mind lagged behind, stuck on her mention of Carl. "What do you mean Carl said he would talk to Kyrellis?"

She went to the sink, quiet, refusing to answer.

"Tell me about Carl," he demanded.

"He offered to help. He felt responsible."

"He went to talk to Kyrellis?"

"I don't know. We talked on Sunday, and—"

"Sunday?"

"Yeah, when I went out. I walked to the sale barn and Carl was there. We talked. He offered to help."

"Early in the morning? Carl was at the sale barn Sunday morning?"

She nodded. "I was surprised to find him there."

Hershel thought of Yolanda and her insistence that Carl was staying at his business. He *had* stayed there.

"What's wrong?" she asked.

Yolanda hadn't seen him, Hershel thought. Certainly if he'd returned home she would have known.

"Hershel, what's wrong?"

Hershel spoke slowly, quietly. "Why didn't you tell me you'd spoken to Carl about the pictures?"

"You don't think Kyrellis has something to do with Carl not showing up for work, do you?"

"They found a body in the river this morning," he whispered, his voice a coiled snake.

"What? No! It wasn't him! It wasn't him!"

"How do we know that?"

"Oh my God," she cried, as if Carl had been a brother—someone she'd known her entire life.

Kyrellis reviewed his business ledgers. His orders had evaporated. His receivables account was current, no big checks coming in. While he was an excellent horticulturist, he was a lousy businessman. If only he had a windfall. If he got himself clear of this mess he'd hire a manager with sales experience. But that was a big *if*. He picked up the phone and dialed the sheriff.

"Castor."

"Sheriff, this is your friend. Remember me?"

"Friend?" Castor's voice was quietly sarcastic.

"Have you thought about the figure?" Kyrellis asked, thinking of the amount he himself owed.

"Who do you think I am, anyway?" Castor's words were tight and controlled, but Kyrellis could feel the man's anger.

"You're a man who would rather avoid a scandal. Well, not just a scandal in your case. Prison time." Kyrellis drew out the last statement for effect. They both knew what was at stake. And it was worth a lot of money.

"I won't pay that much. I haven't got it. You'll have to come up with a better number or you'll get nothing."

"Hmm." Kyrellis stalled for time. "What about the girl?"

"What about her?"

"Is *she* worth a million dollars to you, Sheriff?"

There was a long pause. "You aren't holding her, are you?"

Kyrellis sensed a chink in the lawman's armor. "You love her, don't you?"

"Is she okay?"

"As well as can be expected, I guess."

"Let me speak to her."

"No—no, no. Not yet."

Castor drew a hard breath that sounded as if he'd sucked air through the phone line from Oregon all the way to Wyoming. "Don't hurt her. I'll pay what you want. Just don't hurt her."

"Very well. She'll be here waiting. When can we expect the money?"

"I need a few days. I'm working on it."

"I'll be in touch, then."

So, it was the girl after all. Her sheriff was not the killer she claimed him to be. Just an overly rough sugar daddy. One who would pay top dollar for his love.

———

Hershel stood in the doorway of the upstairs apartment of the sale barn. The bed was unfolded, not the way Silvie had left it. Carl's pocket knife was sitting on the table with some loose change, closed and abandoned. He envisioned the man's hard-crusted hands as he drew the blade of this knife across the tops of what might have been a thousand boxes in the time he'd worked for Hershel. Such a familiar object. Such a common movement.

He took it up and ran his fingers over the smooth, worn surface, then flipped open the blade. Sharp. Well maintained.

"The only tool necessary to man's existence," Hershel said quietly to himself, repeating a mantra Carl had used to describe his simple two-blade knife.

He suffered Carl's absence in a way that was familiar. The way he longed for the voices of his mother and his sister. The way one misses something that is invisible yet essential. He questioned again why Carl had worked for him for so long. A memory came to him, another horrible memory from a few years back, when the two of them were opening a small box of handguns late on a Sunday night, checking them for condition, making sure they were unloaded. Hershel picked up an automatic pistol, pulled the clip, and emptied it of its ammunition.

"Don't forget the chamber," Carl said.

Hershel had glared at him for a long moment, until Carl blinked and went back to his task. "You think I'm some kind of an idiot?"

"Sorry, it's habit."

"I know when a gun is loaded," Hershel said. He could still hear the vehemence in his tone. How dare this lowlife who couldn't even scrape together enough money for new shoes instruct him on the proper handling of a firearm? To prove his point, he aimed the gun at the calendar just above Carl's head.

Carl's eyes bulged. "Don't—"

He pulled the trigger, expecting the dull pop of an empty chamber. Instead, their ears rang, and a bullet pierced a hole in the month of September, lodging itself in the heavy beam behind. Hershel stared at the gun, startled. He'd checked the chamber; he'd thought it was empty. His hand trembled as he set the gun down.

"I'm different now," he said. It was one thing to be an arrogant asshole—and certainly he was that and worse. But the fact that he'd let Carl believe that he'd done it deliberately, as a reminder of his place—a warning to keep his mouth shut—*that* was unforgivable. Why couldn't he bring himself to simply apologize for his stupidity? Had he really thought so little of the man? It was a wonder Carl stayed on after that. "Thank God I'm different now," he whispered.

But if Castor didn't kill Kyrellis, Hershel would. It took less than ten minutes for him to find Jacob Castor's phone number. As he dialed it, he rehearsed his words. He couldn't lose his train of thought or forget a name in this conversation. He had to be completely credible and in control.

"Castor," a man answered in a tired voice.

"Sheriff Castor, I know who has your photos."

"Who is this?"

"Let's make a deal, you and me." The line was silent. Hershel forged ahead, not knowing what sort of man this was other than by Silvie's description. But the image of that little girl in the photograph hardened his will and gave him strength. "Those pictures will send you to prison, I'm sure you know that."

Castor breathed into the phone.

"How much are they worth to you?"

"Who is this?" Castor repeated.

"Do you think he'll stop after the first payment? That he'll just hand them over to you, and that's that?"

The man let out a strange, guttural noise that reminded Hershel of a wounded animal.

"He'll piece them out. Charging you for each one." He paused to let the sheriff think about it, if he hadn't already. "How much has he asked for?"

"What kind of deal?"

"The only way you'll rid yourself of him is to kill him."

"That can be arranged."

"That's the deal."

"What about Silvie? Is she with him?"

Hershel's scar prickled and his hands went hot. He suffered a sudden memory of Floyd, his red Charger, sitting in the gravel turnoff below the French Prairie Farm. The animals were frenzied, snorting and squealing and fighting over the body he'd dumped there. The sound of their jaws breaking the skull and bones, devouring the man, clothes and all, followed him to his waiting car. That's where he was coming from on the night of the accident.

"I want the girl back," Castor said. "Is she with him?"

"She's with me."

"You want this man dead, she's got to be part of the deal."

Hershel closed his eyes against the onslaught of memories: lighting a cigarette, traveling the dark highway, listening to Tom Petty. The cow in the road. He pressed his hand to his head. He could smell the stench of hogs as if they were here in the room. *Why now?*

"Bring me proof that Victor Kyrellis is dead and I'll give you the girl," Hershel said. "You'll find him at Oregon Premier Roses, in the city of Tigard."

"How will I get in touch?"

"Meet me in the filbert orchard on the west side of the French Prairie Farm. It's near St. Paul, on Butteville Road. Midnight Friday." Once a killer, always a killer.

"You don't give me much time."

"How much fucking time do you need?" Hershel's head seared with pain.

"Fine."

"I don't have to tell you to come alone."

"Midnight Friday," Castor repeated, and hung up.

Hershel dropped the phone and gripped his temples with both hands. The song echoed through the pain: *Don't come around here no more.* His arrogance felt familiar, the idea that he was brilliant. *I'm a fucking genius,* he'd said. It all came back now. The ache in his shoulders from dragging a man's deadweight. The spot on his jeans he couldn't distinguish from blood.

"I'm a killer," he said aloud. His words ricocheted around the quiet office, bouncing from metal file cabinet to cement floor to bare wall. "I am a killer," he repeated, louder. The words shocked him, setting his arms and legs tingling in a crawly, unpleasant way. Like thousands of spiders, the word danced across his skin. *Killer.* "So I'm going to kill *you*, Jacob Castor."

The pain eased and, oddly, the first thing that occurred to him was that his mother had known this about him. She could see exactly who he was, and now Hershel did, too.

26

Silvie's mind was hazy, and her eyes stung when she awoke on Thursday morning. The smell of bacon swirled through the house, making her stomach growl before she realized she was hungry. Dust motes floated in the golden air, and she lay in bed listening to the sound of Hershel cooking in the kitchen below her as she pieced together the events of the previous day. Carl gone. Why was she so certain Kyrellis had killed him? She told herself that it might not be true, but she wasn't convinced. Some things you just know, and the empty days ahead, she believed, would confirm it.

Downstairs, Hershel was hunched over the stove. He didn't hear her.

"May I use your truck?" she asked. "I'm working today."

He turned and looked at her, his face grayish, a stubbly beard beginning to show. His hair was uncombed.

"No." He turned back to the food.

She hesitated, then approached and stood next to him at the stove.

"I'll drop you off at work. I need the truck today." He pressed his lips together tightly and scowled. "Call me when your shift is done and I'll pick you up."

"When do you think you'll get that orange car running?"

He stared down into the pan, lost to his own thoughts, working through something.

"I want to go see where Carl lived. Will you take me there?"

He thought on it a long moment. "Get ready to go. You can eat this on the way." He laid the strips of bacon on a paper towel.

"I'm not going to eat. I can't."

He didn't argue, but wrapped the meat in the paper and set it next to his keys.

Silvie found Hershel outside next to the pickup, placing a box of canned food from the pantry in the bed. On top of that he laid several worn blankets and coats.

"What's that for?"

He got in and started the truck, waiting for Silvie to follow.

From Scholls Ferry Road they turned onto an unmarked and poorly maintained lane—just a pair of ruts, really. The truck bounced from side to side as Hershel dodged potholes, and the low-hanging branches scraped the roof. Silvie was beginning to regret her request when they suddenly emerged from the trees into a small parking lot. Sprawled out before them were several shed-like buildings in bright aqua-blue, running in two parallel rows. In the muddy common area between them was a picnic table, barely discernible beneath a mound of clutter. The two of them sat in the truck a moment, gazing out on the dilapidated community.

Hershel pointed at the first shack on the left. "That's Carl's."

Silvie slid out, stepped over a log, and waded through the wet grass and mud. The smell of fried tortillas drifted through the still air. She found his door covered with handwritten notes, most in Spanish. All addressed to Carl or Carlos. Many included hearts. Almost all had some form of the Madonna depicted, either with stickers or crude drawings. Silvie traced her fingers over the words "*Gracias, Carlos.*" A door creaked open behind her and a woman peered out, then closed it again.

Hershel, still ominously silent, joined Silvie.

"Look at this," she whispered. "They're thank-you notes. There must be a hundred of them here."

He sniffed hard, and she realized that he was trying to hold back tears. He returned to the truck, pulled out the things he'd brought, and carried them to the table. The woman opened the door again and, seeing Hershel there, stepped outside.

The picnic table was covered with spent candles, and wax had dripped over its surface, giving it an eerie shine. Tendrils of hardened paraffin were frozen down its sides like icicles, and in the center stood a cross made of thin wood. The name Carlos was carefully spelled out in ornate lettering on the crossbeam. Silvie ran her finger over it, and the woman stiffened. These people—Carl's neighbors—believed he was dead.

Silvie listened to Hershel's deliberate articulation of what he'd brought as he unloaded the items onto the bench of the picnic table. "Food. Blankets. Coats."

"Come inside," the woman said.

The woman motioned Silvie in also. The interior of her cabin was cramped and warm. It couldn't have been wider than twelve feet in either direction. Someone had painted it yellow, and put down a square of deep-blue shag carpet, now matted and muddy. Her dishes and cookery were lined up on open shelves above a small freestanding range, next to which stood a tiny table with three wooden chairs. One side of the room housed a twin-size bed, the other a pair of bunks.

"Sit," the woman said, motioning them to the table, and they obeyed. She then pulled down an old mixer and set it between them. "This is from Carlos. A gift."

Hershel smiled at it and nodded.

"He brings us many gifts." Next, she took out a serving plate and set it by the mixer. "From Carlos." And a stack of pretty dishes. "From Carlos."

"He was very generous," Silvie said.

Tears welled in the woman's eyes. "My sons go to find his killer."

"Tell them to leave it alone," Hershel warned.

"There were bad men here. But immigration took them away. We do not know who has done this." She wiped her face with the hem of her apron and stared longingly at the mixer. "Last night we have a memory gathering for Carlos with candles. People came from far away—people who lived here before. Some from Yakima and Medford. We wrote our thank-you notes and put them on his door in case by some miracle he comes home again."

Silvie found herself struggling against tears.

Hershel stood. "We can't stay."

The woman nodded, and Silvie realized that she had simply wanted them to understand who Carl was to them. When they stepped outside, she tipped her head up at the sky, its pale blue stinging deep in her retinas.

People had gathered around the table and were sifting through the things Hershel had brought. Yolanda said something in Spanish and gestured at Hershel, and they paused to look at him with awe. They smiled and exchanged comments.

"What did you say?" he asked.

"I tell them that Carlos worked for you. They know about your sale. It is where he got the things he gave to the people."

Hershel seemed disturbed by this and pressed his hand against Silvie's shoulder, guiding her back to the truck. But before he climbed in he said to the woman, "Send your sons to see me."

She neither agreed nor disagreed, but stood watching as they pulled away.

Kyrellis settled into his overstuffed chair and sipped a glass of Polish vodka. It wasn't particularly smooth; in fact, the first sip always elicited a hard shiver, but that's what he liked about it. He enjoyed the sensation of drinking something near caustic. It was early for liquor, but it always helped him think.

He had a little more time, though not a lot. He'd agreed to let

Silvie call the shots when they met tomorrow. That wouldn't do if he was going to capture her for Jacob Castor, though. The timing needed to be just right. Perhaps this first visit would be as she wanted it, and he would hand over five of the photos. Then he'd cut a new deal. The balance of the stash if she let him tie her up? A girl like that would agree. She'd had practice. And the pictures were of monumental importance to her. That was all he needed, an opportunity to restrain her, then give her to Castor in exchange for a million dollars. Even half of that would solve all his problems.

Back to the details. How would the transaction go down? He couldn't bring her with him to the meeting or Castor might simply kill him and leave with the money and the girl. No, Kyrellis needed to plan this out carefully. The pictures he'd keep. If Castor could raise a million dollars for his sweetheart, he could raise more for the photos.

Kyrellis took a long pull on his drink and studied the white rosebush through the foyer window. Then again, maybe it was best to let this one go. A million dollars was much more than he needed to repay his creditor, and he still had Hershel's Charger sitting in a heap behind the greenhouse.

He considered Hershel—a man who had cheated his way through life. A man whose business was bought and paid for with stolen guns, shady practices, and raw greed. In some ways they had traded places, he and Hershel. Kyrellis had never set out to get involved in gun sales. He had only ever wanted to be a horti-culturist and a collector. Somehow he'd gotten sidetracked after a string of bad business deals no more sinister than a failed lemon-ade stand. Nonetheless, failures add up. They begin to eat at the core of a man. And a man desperate to prove his worth is indeed a man at risk. Kyrellis understood this; he knew the path he'd taken, and he knew why. It was Swift who'd first suggested that a person could make a nice profit on a piece if there was no federal paperwork. It was after Kyrellis had confided that business was poor, and he couldn't support his gun-collecting habit. Swift was all greed in those days. Kyrellis believed he would have sold his own mother if she'd have brought a decent price.

The details were flooding back at Hershel so rapidly now that he wished he could retreat into his unknowing state once again. He drove out toward the coastal range, away from French Prairie, hoping to quell the onslaught. But still it came. Albert Darling's storage unit had been mostly packed with worthless garbage: old clothes, a mouse-infested sofa, a particleboard bedroom set that had been badly warped in a flood, a sack of putrid tennis shoes. The odor that issued from the room when they opened it caused them to stand back and look at each other, wondering if a dead body lay beneath the filth. It turned out to be an entire family of the mice decomposing inside the couch. Nothing was salvageable. Except for that one most unexpected item. It was a Winchester rifle in mint condition, well over a hundred years old. A Henry lever-action, .44-caliber rimfire. From the 1860s. Only thirteen thousand had been made, and this one looked as if it had never been fired. They almost missed it—almost sent it to the dump—because the idiot had wrapped it in a ratty old electric blanket the color of vomit.

Woody had gone back to the office for some trash bags when Carl unsheathed the beautiful gun. He and Hershel both stared openmouthed at the piece, a knowing glance passed between them, and Carl shunted it away to Hershel's truck.

When Woody returned, he was sweaty. "Why do people hold on to shit like this? Can you imagine wasting forty dollars a month just to keep this crap dry?"

"Apparently Darling can't, either," Hershel remarked. "Or he would've paid his bill."

A new name came to him now, as he neared McMinnville and turned back. Pauline Rainwater. She was a county clerk, and a woman who was overtly in love with Hershel. He took her out from time to time, but not because he liked her. She was homely, carrying thirty pounds more than her small frame could gracefully support. Her sallow skin bore the scars of teenage acne, and she wore tiny glasses that were neither in style nor flattering, perched above crooked teeth on a thick nose. Hershel strung her along just enough that she'd do him favors. He'd called her up that afternoon, in fact, cooing that she was his sweetheart and asking if she'd run an FBI check on his new Winchester. He didn't really have to use her, but the near-reachable promise of love that he held out as a carrot ensured that she didn't tell anyone which guns he'd checked over the years. Upon his request, she never kept a paper trail.

It struck him with absurd irony that not even *she* had visited him after his accident. Not even Pauline Rainwater would date a brain-damaged man.

And what of Carl Abernathy? The man his neighbors eulogized in hand-drawn notes commemorating his simple gifts. How had he justified his willing part in all of this? Hershel had been humbled that morning at the migrant camp. And he couldn't bear the faces that looked at him as if he were some good soul, like Carl. If they only knew the truth.

When he got home, he finished working on the Porsche and let it idle in the driveway for fifteen minutes before taking it out for a test drive. It was loose in the steering, and it rattled like a tin can, but he reckoned it was safe enough. The smell of fuel seemed to linger, and he made a mental note to check that. When he reached Scholls Ferry Road, he turned left before thinking about it. He hadn't planned to drive past the South Store, but then he guessed Silvie was too busy to notice the cars that passed the front of the building. He made a loop through Hillsboro, bypassing the store. He would not give her the car as he had promised—not yet. Things were going to get dangerous, and he needed to know exactly where she was every moment.

27

Silvie worked to hold back tears through the day. The lunch crowd at the South Store was light, and Karen had Silvie bleach down the tabletops. The visit to the migrant camp had made real for her that Carl was dead. Everyone seemed to know it, even though no one had proof. She wanted to call her mom, listen to her voice. In the early months after Silvie's father left, Melody had sung to her daughter at night. She had a soft voice that smoothed out the edges of the words, left them unarticulated and sleek, like strands of soft pearls—wet and indistinct syllables. It had eased their loneliness. For a time, anyway.

"I'm sorry I don't have more for you today," Karen said from behind the counter. "I wish I could keep you on for another hour or two, but there just isn't enough business."

"That's okay," Silvie said. The understanding that she'd sent Carl on his death errand was too large a burden for her to care about the job anymore. She'd spent the afternoon working out her plan for Kyrellis. All she needed was a car. She glanced at Karen. The soft lines at the corners of her eyes had been etched there by a million smiles. She was a kind woman.

"Do you think I could ask a really huge favor?"

"What's that?" Karen asked, retying her apron.

"Could I borrow your car to run up to the store?"

Karen didn't answer right away, taking her time to consider it. "Do you have a driver's license?"

"Sure, wanna see it?"

"No. That's fine. You won't be gone long, though, right?"

"An hour maybe. No more."

Karen disappeared into the kitchen, returning with her keys. "It's not much."

"Thanks. I promise to return it just like it is."

The ten-year-old Corolla was a stick shift and Silvie popped the clutch, spraying gravel across the parking lot as she pulled out. She hoped Karen wasn't standing at the window, regretting the favor.

Silvie missed a turn as she searched for the Walgreens store she'd passed on her way to find shoes, but after a few circles around the southern end of Hillsboro she found it again on the corner of Tualatin Valley Highway.

Inside, she wound her way to the personal items and inventoried tubes of lubricating jellies and massage oils. She gathered up three bottles of motion lotion in varying scents and colors.

As she returned, her purchase stashed in her backpack and fifteen minutes to spare on the hour she'd promised Karen, she glimpsed a small orange car, just like the one Hershel owned. As it neared, she craned to see the driver. It was him. He'd gotten it running finally.

The day remained dry and cloudless, a strange break in the Oregon winter, both unexpected and intensely rejuvenating to the landscape. The sweep of marshlands below Hershel's house colored up the way it looked in spring, with vibrant green and auburn. Branchy trees along the Tualatin River attracted a family of blue herons, which perched in the canopy today instead of wading the murky waters along the bank. Upstream from where the police had removed the body.

His phone rang. Kyrellis. He let it ring two more times, contemplating whether to let it go. "Swift," he said, flipping the phone open.

"Have you considered my offer?"

Hershel stiffened.

"Better they go to you, so you can destroy them, than back to Castor."

"They found a body in the river yesterday."

"I heard."

"You know goddamn well who it was," Hershel said, seething.

Kyrellis sighed into the phone.

"Why did you kill him?"

"Swift, listen to me. He was set to double-cross you. There was no loyalty there. You should be grateful to be rid of him."

"What did he threaten you with?"

"You never should've let a man like that into your business, Swift. He had records of every gun transaction you've ever made, and I'm not talking about the legitimate ones."

Hershel's chest tightened. He wanted to believe that Carl wouldn't have sold him down the river, but why wouldn't he? Hershel had never done a kind thing for the man.

"If you must know, he wanted some of the money for the photos...in exchange for his silence." Kyrellis exhaled, as if exhausted from trying to convince Hershel. "He threatened to go to the authorities if I didn't cooperate. But you and I both know it wouldn't have ended there. He'd have had us both over a barrel if we accepted those terms, and then what? Believe what you want about the man, Swift, but he was up to no good, and we both would've paid dearly."

"Why did you cut off his head?" Hershel's stomach lurched at the mention.

"Honestly, Swift. Must we? He was testing the water. If he could get the photos, he could get anything."

Hershel thought of the migrant camp, and the dozens of notes pasted to Carl's vacant door.

"I think you were mistaken," he said quietly.

"I guess we'll never know," Kyrellis replied. "But if you feel inclined to talk to the authorities, it'll behoove you to remember Albert Darling—if you *can* remember Albert Darling. Now, about the photos—"

"I don't want them. Sell them back to your sheriff in Wyoming." He hung up before Kyrellis could respond. Out along the river a pair of ravens were dive-bombing the herons, causing them to spread their enormous wings to stay afloat in the tree branches. The herons endured strike after strike, but they relinquished nothing.

Hershel fingered his cellphone, then punched in the numbers that had never been lost to him. Odd, he thought, that he could remember these when so much else was missing. He listened to the ringing on the other end as he repeated the numbers to himself, just in case.

"Hello?" Her voice was hoarse—a smoker's rasp, coupled with advancing age.

"Why didn't you come?"

An audible catching of breath as Hershel held his. A long strand of silence stretched between them, so fragile he could almost see it fray and pull apart.

"My heart was already broken," she said, and hung up.

She'd spoken to him.

Carl remained on Hershel's mind while he drove to the restaurant to pick up Silvie.

"Where is the car?" Silvie asked as they pulled in next to the house.

"I put it back in the garage," he said.

"You got it running."

"No. I think it's beyond repair."

She gazed at him curiously from the other side of the cab.

"We'll get you some wheels, don't worry."

Silvie wandered outside and sat on the front porch, quiet and downhearted. He watched her go, wishing he could recapture the excitement of only a day ago. Now they seemed a pair of perfect strangers, even in their shared pain.

She sat with her back against the window, looking out at the same river scene he'd inventoried earlier, her jacket wrapped around her and her hands tucked in. He joined her.

"It quit raining," Silvie said.

"I don't think you should go to work tomorrow."

She tipped her head back against the chair, unsurprised.

"Kyrellis is dangerous, and he's contacted—" The name fell away. He had trouble articulating it in her presence, as if its sound would crush her.

"Okay."

He smoothed her hair. Squeezed her shoulder. "Trust me. This will be over soon."

She turned her eyes on him, pale and full of worry. "What are you planning to do?"

"Just trust me."

"You won't hurt Jacob, will you?"

Her question sliced through the center of him, a burning sting.

"I mean, there's no reason to do that. If he gets his pictures back, he'll be satisfied."

"Will he?"

She stared through him. She wouldn't answer.

28

Kyrellis hadn't slept well, his limbs abuzz with anticipation of Silvie's smooth skin, mixed with erratic dreams of Carl Abernathy demanding money from him, as if the man would return from the dead and join forces with his creditor. He'd gotten up shortly after three and vacuumed, dusted, mopped. Pine cleaner mingled with the faint smell of leather conditioner.

He pulled down the shades at the front window, letting in a filtered light. It was almost a shame to block out the sun, so rare and uplifting this time of year. But she might be shy about these things. He'd laid ten photos out for her to choose from. He imagined that she wanted the bondage shots. They weren't his favorite. He'd spoken the truth when he told her that he didn't find pleasure in pain, and they gave him a bit of a sick stomach. All the same, he was careful in his selection; she wouldn't get the bondage photos. He needed to maximize his bargaining leverage.

Kyrellis's plan was set. After Silvie had performed her favor, he would offer her a second deal. Return Tuesday night while Hershel was conducting his sale, but this time she had to let him tie her up. In exchange, she'd receive the balance of the stash when he was finished. It sounded plausible, he thought. She'd let Castor tie her up, after all. It wasn't like he was the only man alive with *that* fantasy. The difference was that he wouldn't let her go. Castor could be here by then. They'd meet at the Starbucks on Murray Road, south of Portland. A public place with too many witnesses for the sheriff to get any stupid ideas. He'd collect the money and, in exchange, give Castor directions to the Kinton School, a derelict nineteenth-century relic on Scholls Ferry Road. It was now being used as a sheep barn. There Silvie would be waiting for him.

Kyrellis had decided to let Castor have the photos, too. The sheriff had taken on an Old West persona in Kyrellis's imagination, appearing in his dreams with his pistols drawn. Kyrellis figured he'd better not press his luck.

He hummed a tune from his childhood as he cooked himself an omelet stuffed with wild mushrooms and Swiss cheese. The aroma of melted butter made his mouth water. His appetite was finally returning, a good sign. He'd have the money for his creditor, and life could resume some semblance of normalcy. He'd hire a manager for the nursery, someone to call on his customers, take orders, oversee deliveries. He could make this work; he was certain of it. And when his new hybrids hit the market in the spring he'd be inundated with orders and he wouldn't be able to keep up with the demand.

"Ah, Silvie, we're going to have a wonderful time," he sang to himself.

Hershel listened from the living room as Silvie called the South Store and asked to be excused from her shift. She claimed an upset stomach and apologized for the inconvenience. He wished he could do the same, but if he didn't receive this load of furniture from the wholesale antiques shop that was going out of business there wouldn't be a sale on Tuesday. It was the bulk of his inventory this week, and he had already run the advertisements. The shop owner estimated six large truckloads and had a crew of four men and two vehicles. With travel time from Aurora to Scholls, it would likely take half the day to get everything in and organized. He'd tried to get Henry to come down and help, but the man was a Tuesday-night-only employee and claimed to have a previous engagement. Unlikely, but what could Hershel do?

He figured Castor was already in town; he'd have to handle his end of the agreement by tonight. Hershel toyed with the idea of calling Kyrellis to see if he was still alive. He'd suffered twinges of conscience over what he had done, which had caused him to sleep poorly—waking every twenty minutes, eyeing the clock. Did Kyrellis really have to die? Did anyone *have* to die? He wished he could see some other way through this mess, but he and Silvie were ensnared by these two men with no way out. And he couldn't fathom how the world could possibly be any worse without either of them. He'd thought this through. If Castor didn't kill Kyrellis, Hershel would have to do it himself.

Hershel rehearsed his plan. He would use the green Ford pickup that was on consignment at the sale barn. He had the keys as well as the title. He'd take that, along with John Wayne. At least one woman screamed every Tuesday when she discovered the movie star unexpectedly lounging against the wall with his eyes fixed on the ladies' room door. He would arrive at the agreed-upon place early enough to set up his decoy near the rim of the walnut orchard. It had occurred to Hershel that if Castor looked the place up and discovered that it was a hog farm he'd be suspicious. It was too late to change that, though. He hoped that deer poachers in Wyoming didn't feed the evidence of their crimes to the pigs the way they did in Oregon. Hogs were amazingly efficient at disposing of remains, leaving nothing behind. No hooves, no fur. And, in Darling's case, not even his clothing. Of course, a lawman would know that. Hershel felt uneasy. He'd already made at least one potentially fatal mistake. What else had he overlooked?

Silvie appeared in the doorway. "You okay?"

"Yeah." He laughed emptily.

"Well, I guess I'll just stay here today."

Hershel was relieved that she hadn't asked to go to the sale barn with him. He'd prepared an excuse, but she seemed content to remain where it was safe. At least he wouldn't have to worry about her.

"You'll be okay. You have my number, right?"

She nodded.

"Please stay here. I don't..." He felt near tears. It was the stress, not getting enough sleep. He was acting like an idiot. But what if he didn't say what was on his mind? It would be a sad-forever thought if anything happened to her.

"I love you," he blurted.

She looked up at him, unable to mask her surprise.

He kissed her hastily on the forehead, his lips grazing her still-damp, apple-scented hair, and gathered his keys. He felt the prick and sting of tears as he made his way to the back porch.

"Lock the doors," he said without looking back.

———

Silvie stood on the porch in the cool sunlight, watching Hershel's pickup cruise down the driveway. She didn't know how long he'd be gone, so she moved quickly, out to the little shed behind the garage. She pulled the door open to give herself as much light as possible, then tugged at the rubber gloves she'd found under the kitchen sink, pulling them snugly over her fingers. His declaration of love had surprised her, and she didn't know what to make of it exactly. It was an elusive idea, love. The movies made it out to be something magical, but she'd never felt it that way. Her mother drank herself into oblivion almost daily because of love. This wasn't the first time a man had told her he loved her; Jacob said it often.

She tied a bandanna over her nose and mouth, then invento-ried the cans and bottles of farm chemicals in the dusty shed. She came directly back to the drum of organophosphates. The others were mysterious; this one she understood personally. She'd arrived prepared for a challenge in getting the rusted lid open, and produced a hammer and a screwdriver. To her delight, it hadn't been properly secured and three sharp blows with the screwdriver under the lip popped it off. The drum was nearly empty, but Silvie knew that she didn't need much. She pulled a Ziploc bag and a spoon from the oversized shirt pocket. Careful not to get any of the crystals on her clothing, she held her breath, leaned in, and scooped several heaping spoonfuls of the powdery substance into the bag. She sealed it up with the spoon inside, replaced the lid, and went back to the house.

She detected no odor in the chemical, but she knew better than to test it by inhaling it. She picked the almond-scented bottle of motion lotion to mask any smell it might have. The transparent liquid had a mild golden hue as she poured a teaspoonful into a plastic bowl. She carefully spooned some of the crystals into the oily liquid and they dissolved into the solution. Silvie questioned its potency after all these years in Hershel's shed. A few drops of liquid organophosphates was enough to kill a large dog, but a grown man? And how quickly? She needed to make sure this worked, and more seemed better.

She poured off the top half of the bottle. Then, using a folded square of paper, she filled it again with crystals. She recapped the bottle and watched as the crystals merged into the liquid and dissolved, giving the lotion a slightly cloudy appearance. After contemplating her creation, she washed and dried the outside of the bottle with soap and placed it in a new Ziploc bag as an added precaution. She disposed of the materials in a plastic grocery bag, which she would later drop in a garbage can between here and Kyrellis's house. She was ready.

The Porsche drove better than her Rabbit had ever run, though this car rattled with every bump in the road. At the turnoff to Campo Rojo, she slowed and pulled in. It was small acknowledgment, she knew. Monumentally inadequate, in fact. The car bumped down the lane, scraping its underside on ruts and potholes. When she reached the parking lot, three children paused from their game of tag to gape at her. Even the rooster approached.

She sat inside, the sun warm through the windshield, and wrote her note on a piece of paper she'd found in Hershel's kitchen. Now she wished it didn't have SHERWOOD AUTO REPAIR emblazoned across the bottom, but it was too late to find something more suitable.

As she scribed, she remembered the concentration on Carl's face as he doctored her blistered feet. His head bent forward, his touch soft and caring. He'd treated her as if she were the only person in the world, taking his time, pausing from the more important business of preparing for the sale. He didn't ask if he could help but simply *did* help. It was an extraordinary moment, perhaps more so because of its ordinariness.

> *Carl,*
> *A kind man with a beautiful heart. If I could only know one person better in my lifetime, I would choose you. I'm so sorry. Please forgive me.*
> *S.T.*

She passed the rooster and the children on her way to Carl's door. There she touched the notes that adorned it, taking a moment to find the right place, where she posted her own. It looked so small in that sea of gratitude, and Silvie tried to fathom the number of people she had deprived of Carl's generosity and kindness with her selfish request. The burden that his death was her fault caused her to stumble and fall against the step, where she wept for him.

Kyrellis had learned his lesson the first time, and when the doorbell rang he didn't assume it was Silvie. He took his gun with him and peered through the window at the driveway, but it was empty.

The angle had never been quite right to see who stood on the doorstep through the foyer windows, and he considered things carefully. He didn't want to spoil the mood by showing up armed. Then it occurred to him that she wouldn't park in the driveway now that she knew where to find the shipping entrance to the nursery. She'd park behind one of the greenhouses to ensure that Hershel didn't see her there. Kyrellis relaxed; he was simply being paranoid. Who else *could* it be? His creditor had been appeased for the time being, and if it was a customer a gun would guarantee a non-sale. He set it down on the entry table and opened the door.

He instantly understood his stupidity, but it was already too late. A short man in jeans and cowboy boots stood on the doorstep, but it wasn't his attire that caught Kyrellis's attention. Rather, it was the pistol the man thrust in Kyrellis's face. He had a fleeting memory of Carl Abernathy.

"Victor Kyrellis?" the man asked with a distinct western twang. When Kyrellis didn't answer, he seemed to conclude that he had the correct man. "Step back."

Kyrellis obeyed, his heart thudding double time, his mind trying to make sense of his own carelessness.

"Where is she?" Castor asked as he stepped inside and closed the door.

This is what will save me, Kyrellis thought. "She isn't here right now."

Castor placed his gun between Kyrellis's eyes; the cold metal almost burned against his skin. The sheriff glimpsed the ten photos spread out across the coffee table, and his eyes made a slow sweep of the room.

"Where are the rest of them?"

"P-put the gun down," Kyrellis stammered. "So we can talk."

Castor studied him coldly, and Kyrellis did an accounting of the man's treachery. This was the man who'd beaten a child. This was the man who'd bound her. This was the man who'd threatened to kill her to keep her quiet. Why had he imagined that he could talk to such a man? Silvie had told him that Castor would hunt him down and kill him. Why in God's name hadn't he believed her?

Castor stepped back and picked up the gun Kyrellis had left in the entryway and stood with both pistols pointed at Kyrellis.

"Where is Silvie?" Castor repeated slowly.

"I told you, she's not here."

"You better start talking or you're a dead man."

"And what will stop you from killing me when I tell you?"

Castor considered this. "You never had her, did you?"

"I can tell you where she is. We have a deal. Let's just stick to our deal and you'll get your photos back as well as the girl."

Castor snorted. "Let's see, you want a million dollars for Silvie and the photos. And another man offers me Silvie to see you dead. *Who should I believe?*" he shouted. Castor's long white teeth gave him a vicious, canine appearance.

Kyrellis's mind went wild with the implications. He should've known he couldn't trust Hershel Swift.

A car pulled into the driveway; it sounded like an old Volkswagen Beetle. Castor stepped back again and craned through the foyer window, both guns still trained on Kyrellis.

"Expecting someone?" But no sooner had he said it than he smiled broadly. A smile that sent a shiver up Kyrellis's spine.

29

He hadn't been alone the night he killed Albert Darling; Kyrellis had been there, too. Hershel gripped the steering wheel so tensely that his knuckles ached. His head was too full to think straight. As he'd tried to focus on the details of his plan, his memory continued to plague him with random images. He was piecing it together now, in broken chunks. The two of them had lured Darling to the Willamette River west of St. Paul with the promise of telling him where his Winchester had gone. In exchange, Darling would leave them alone. That Winchester was the most beautiful gun Hershel had ever laid eyes on, and he should never have underestimated its owner's desire to see it returned. Darling had told him that it had been passed down through his family—a hundred years of pride, with its roots in postwar Mississippi. A treasure that set them apart. That was the difference between this and all other gun sales Hershel had taken a hand in. To Darling, the rifle was a proud symbol of who he was—his heritage. Hershel had not simply liquidated the man's storage unit, even legally; he'd stripped Darling of his identity, leaving him no way to reclaim it. Had they sold the gun through legal channels, Darling would have been on someone else's trail, looking for another way to retrieve his lost treasure. But that they claimed the gun had never been there—what else could the poor man do?

The irony was that the gun would have brought a high enough price through an auction sale. It would have gained national attention, possibly wider. There was no telling how much it might have brought in an international bidding contest. Hershel didn't have to do things the way he did. But Kyrellis had connections to a buyer who was looking for a gun like this, and he was willing to pay several times the market price. It came down to customer service, in a strange sort of way. That and greed. The same anonymous buyer—a man whose name Hershel never learned, or wanted to know—had already shuttled tens of thousands of untraceable, tax-free dollars their way. It wasn't just *this* gun but all the guns he would buy in the future. He was a veritable gold mine.

In the end, though, after Kyrellis's cut, Hershel gained only a few thousand dollars more. That and a tenacious little pitbull of a man, who was determined to ruin him. Darling had managed to make the connection between Hershel and Kyrellis, and he'd thrown around accusations and threats, drawing the attention of several gun buyers. He was poised to ruin everything.

As he approached the house, he tried to make up reasons why he would need to come back for a gun. He was completely inept—planning to kill a man and going off without his gun. What kind of killer was he? A poor one. A *stupid* one. He was ashamed of his cognitive deficiencies. He still hadn't found a suitable story that wouldn't frighten Silvie. But, above all, he was scared that he'd overlooked some other critical detail that would give Castor the upper hand. He might have given the man just enough information to find and destroy them all.

Silvie stood on Kyrellis's doorstep, her backpack slung over her shoulder, going over her plan one last time before turning the knob. She wondered if she should have parked in the driveway. Hershel might see the car. Then she thought about taking it and simply running. She could be in California by nightfall. Maybe she'd head east across the southern states. Find a place in Florida. Or drive up the coast from there to New York City. No one would ever find her in New York City.

"Come in," Kyrellis called a second time, louder than the first.

She wondered why he didn't open the door and hoped she wouldn't find him inside naked. He was just the kind of man who would do something like that. This was difficult enough. She'd need to work up to it.

It was dim inside, the shades drawn. Kyrellis stood in the middle of the living room, his eyes widened to the whites. He didn't say hello as she closed the door.

"Silvie," Jacob said, sending a jolt of lightning through her. He stood behind the door, two guns on Kyrellis, but his eyes on her.

"Jacob," she whispered. "I—"

He shook his head, eyes fierce. "Don't try to explain. Not yet."

"I was scared."

"I know you were, baby." Castor turned back to Kyrellis, and Silvie felt like a child again. She wanted to run to Jacob and beg him to forgive her. She wanted him to gather her up in his arms. This simple sweet acknowledgment that he understood could turn everything around. It could restore them.

"Did this man hurt you?" he said, gesturing toward Kyrellis.

She assessed her would-be victim, realizing with great relief that she wouldn't have to carry out her plan now. Jacob would take care of things for her.

Kyrellis shook his head, pleading with her. His eyes imploring. "I didn't touch her," he said. "Tell him, Silvie. Tell him that I didn't touch you."

"No, but he was going to," she said. She had no sympathy for Kyrellis. "He was going to make me do things in return for your . . . for the—" She spied the ten photos carefully laid out on the coffee table. Jacob had undoubtedly seen them, too.

"Was he, now?" Jacob stepped closer to Kyrellis, who closed his eyes as if expecting him to pull the trigger. "Tell her where the others are."

"Look, we can work this out. It's not too late."

"Tell her!"

Silvie winced.

"In the freezer," Kyrellis said.

Jacob snapped his head to the side, ordering her to retrieve them. She scrambled into the kitchen, her hands shaking. She fumbled through the contents of Kyrellis's freezer, finally dragging everything out onto the counter before finding the icy metal box underneath two large bags of frozen blackberries. She brought it to the living room, her fingers aching, and tried to open it, but it was locked.

"Where's the key?" she said, breathless, trying to appear helpful to Jacob. His ally.

"Are you going to kill me?" Kyrellis asked. His eyes glistened, and Silvie could hear his fear. For an instant, she pitied him.

"What do *you* think, you stupid fool," Jacob said.

———

Hershel parked in front of the garage, deciding that he'd tell Silvie there was a coyote prowling around the auction barn. It would prevent any idea of walking over there, as well as explain his need to take his gun. He'd take the rifle as well as his pistol.

The sun had brightened everything, but instead of giving him a new sense of purpose, as it usually did, it only sharpened his headache. When this was over—when he'd killed Jacob Castor and was rid of Kyrellis, too—he would suggest that they move somewhere new. Idaho, maybe. Or Colorado. A mountain state, with a rugged landscape and more days of sun. They didn't have to stay here. A new start would be good for both of them. He had no choice in what he was about to do, but his future—their future—could be different. And maybe then these damn headaches would finally go away.

As he stepped down he noticed that the doors to the garage were slightly open, not the way he thought he'd left them. He didn't want Silvie trying to start the car and discovering that it ran. She thought she could outsmart Kyrellis, but she was wrong. Look what had come of her efforts. He didn't blame her for Carl's death, but neither could he trust her judgment on this. He should never have given Silvie a key to the Porsche. Another example of his abysmal capacity for thinking ahead, anticipating what problems might arise. But as he pushed the door closed the empty space inside registered. The car was gone.

Hershel sprinted to the house, bursting inside, calling Silvie's name as he took the stairs two at a time. He went directly to his bedroom and gathered his pistol from the nightstand. He skidded back down the wooden steps on one foot, thumping against the wall at the bottom and knocking his sister's oil painting to the floor. He stepped over it and went to the kitchen, still calling after her in vain, knowing that she wasn't there. What kind of crazy idea had she gotten in her head to do?

He rustled through his utility drawer, looking for ammunition, scooping up one box for his pistol and another for his rifle. In the mudroom he took his rifle and was peeling down the driveway in seconds, his arsenal flung out on the seat next to him, heading for Kyrellis's.

Kyrellis dropped to his knees, begging. "Please. You don't have to do this. I'll give you my gun collection. I have beautiful guns. Guns like you've never seen before. You can take them. Take them all. But, please, don't kill me."

"Tell her where the key is," Jacob said again, his lips tight with impatience. The knuckles on his right hand had purpled.

"Under the yellow rosebush on the patio," Kyrellis said, relenting.

Silvie hustled from the room after it. When she found it, she wondered if Jacob would make her watch him kill Kyrellis. He might consider that punishment for running off with his pictures. As terrible as the idea was, she doubted that would be the extent of her reprimand. She returned to the living room with the key and struggled with the frozen lock, finally springing it and pulling the lid back. She dumped the contents of the box onto the coffee table and began counting the photos.

"He's going to kill you, too, Silvie," Kyrellis said, trying to win her over. "You told me so yourself."

She locked eyes with him for an instant. He was terrified, and it was familiar to her. But she would not sacrifice herself for this man.

"Ask him where those other girls are. Do you think, even for a minute, that he didn't kill them?"

Her eyes darted to Castor before she could stop herself.

"Don't listen to him," Castor said. "You know how much I love you."

She smiled weakly; she wanted to believe him.

"Ask him," Kyrellis urged.

"Shut up!" Castor said, stepping toward him. He turned to Silvie. "Are they all there?"

"I—I think so."

"Lay them out so I can see them."

She obeyed, making a disturbing sexual collage across the coffee table. He glanced over them, but she refused to look. The faces of those mysterious girls only deepened her doubt.

"He *bound* you, he *beat* you, he threatened to *kill* you," Kyrellis said, just loud enough to get to her.

She stared back at him, incredulous. "You would have done the same. You were *going* to do the same."

Castor placed the gun against Kyrellis's forehead. Then he held the other gun out to Silvie. "Take it," he said.

She walked slowly to Castor's side. He gestured toward the gun with his chin. Her hand shook as she reached for it, the metal warm against her frozen fingers.

"Put it to his head."

"I—I can't."

"Do it," Castor said, his tone harsh and unbending.

She pressed the metal barrel against Kyrellis's temple. It wobbled and bucked in her trembling grip.

"Does it feel good to hold a gun to this man's head?"

She couldn't answer. Couldn't find words or solidify her thoughts.

"Maybe I'll let you do the honors. But first," Castor said. "Who is the other man?"

Her breath caught in her throat. "I don't know who you mean."

He studied her.

"Really, Jacob. This is the only man."

He turned to Kyrellis. "Then you tell me the name of the other man, the man who wants you dead."

"What's in it for me?" Kyrellis rasped.

"Do you hate him as much as he hates you? Do you want him dead, too?"

Silvie's stomach rolled. Hershel, she thought. Her Good Samaritan, her savior. His kiss was still fresh on her forehead. I love you, he'd said. *I love you.*

Kyrellis opened his mouth to speak, and Silvie squeezed the trigger. The sharp explosion erupted in her ears, and she saw Kyrellis's head blow back. Blood sprayed across the leather armchair. She shrieked and dropped the gun.

Castor stood over Kyrellis's limp body, a hard, angry scowl on his face.

Hershel slowed as he passed Kyrellis's house. The Porsche sat in the driveway. His chest went tight. He pulled into the delivery entrance and eased the pickup between the rows of greenhouses. When he reached the service road that ran between the propagation house and the back of the property, he saw the other pickup.

A big Ford 4x4. Early nineties. Tan and white, with a crew cab. Wyoming plates.

He swung a wide U-turn, heading toward the equipment sheds behind Kyrellis's house. He pulled the truck inside a gaping pole barn that housed a tractor with a scoop and a forklift. Quietly shutting the door, pulling the rifle with him, Hershel surveyed the area. His truck was well hidden from the back of the house and Castor's pickup. He looked around, scouting for a position from which he could see the pathway between the back patio door and the waiting vehicle. Castor wouldn't kill Silvie here. He'd take her with him. Hershel's best chance was to lie in wait and shoot the man as he got into his truck. He took a practice aim, using the scope and imagining his bullet zinging through the back window and into Castor's head. The hunk of metal beneath him, he finally noticed, was Floyd.

Hershel focused on the patio door, then scanned the back of Kyrellis's house, searching for alternative routes. They would have to come through the patio door or walk around from the front. He guessed they wouldn't do that; the front was exposed to the highway. Either way, he'd have Castor when the man got to his truck.

Floyd was warm beneath him, the black tarp soaking up the winter sun like a thirsty sponge. The car felt almost alive. He wondered what they were doing inside, and for an instant he considered going down to the house. What if Castor did kill Silvie here? Hershel would never forgive himself if he allowed that to happen. He let the gun drop an inch or two and looked more closely, trying to catch any glimpse of movement through the windows.

The patio door slid open, and Silvie stepped out. Her skin grayish, her gait stiff and halting. She looked around, as if sensing his eyes on her. But upon seeing Castor's truck she started for it at a fast clip. Hershel stood, and she caught sight of him, wincing.

"Silvie," he called in a hoarse whisper. She was about fifty yards away, and he instantly worried that the sound of his voice had traveled into the house.

She looked startled, then glanced over her shoulder at the patio door.

"Thank God you're okay. Where's Castor?"

"Hershel, get out of here." Her face was set hard. Her backpack swayed at her knee. "He's going to kill you."

"Come with me." He held a hand out to her as she approached, preparing to pull her to safety—to ensconce her in the armor of his truck.

"No!"

The resolution in her voice startled him.

"Just go," she snapped, reminding him of someone chasing off an unwanted animal. "Kyrellis is dead." A look of anguish crossed her face, making him wonder if she'd witnessed it. "I shot him."

"You what?"

"I shot him," she said fiercely. "Before he could give Jacob your name."

"Silvie," he said. "It will be okay. Just come with me. I'll protect you."

"I can't." She looked furtively at the house. "Jacob is coming. I have to go."

"Please, just get behind the car," he said, gesturing toward Floyd. "I'm going to finish this."

"No!" Her blue eyes sent icy daggers at him.

"Get behind the car," he demanded. "I'm going to kill that fucker."

"You can't do that," she said through tears. "I . . . I love him." She headed toward Castor's truck. When she reached the passenger door she turned and looked back at him, her brows pressed together with worry. Then she climbed inside. A moment later Castor came through the patio door, carrying the small metal box that had consumed Hershel's days since he'd met Silvie.

Hershel crouched and sighted the man with his rifle scope. He followed him along the pathway to his pickup, an easy target. One that he could hit in his sleep. He fingered the trigger, Silvie's words swelling in his head.

"Now," he whispered. But his finger would not obey his command. "Now," he said again.

Castor started the engine, the back of his head squarely in the crosshairs of Hershel's rifle scope. "Now."

The truck pulled forward, and Castor made the same arcing U-turn that Hershel had. He sighted the man's face as he came back in this direction. "Now."

The truck turned down the lane between the greenhouses. Hershel laid the rifle across Floyd's buckled hood and drew a breath.

30

Hershel lay on his sofa, his head aching in its familiar, maddening way. His muscles echoed the pain, now a day after he'd retrieved the Porsche and returned it to its dusty tomb. He'd paused to sit in it after backing it into the garage, running his fingers over the steering wheel. Its name had revealed itself as Silvie. The car would never be of use to him now. It would only remind him of their all too brief encounter and its tragic end. The haunted eyes of that little girl, and the sweetness of the woman she'd become. He thought he might sell the car. But something about the idea warned him that it would only add to his list of regrets.

He'd made two trips back to Kyrellis's yesterday. Both with the flatbed truck that he kept at his auction barn, which he used to bring Floyd home. It was where the Charger should always have been. The work had served to keep him busy and postpone the promised emptiness ahead. After running the flatbed to the sale barn and hiking through the orchard for the second time that day, he'd stood in the driveway and bravely unsheathed the ruined car. Its windshield gaped at him in the cool evening sunshine. The brightness of the afternoon—its out-of-the-ordinariness—had already lent a surreal feeling to the events of the day. He went back over what had happened. Had he been able to carry out his plan, he'd be just hours from meeting Castor in the orchard. And, likely, hours away from death. The car reminded him that he'd been there before, wandering the line between this world and the next. He tried the trunk, but the bent frame had sealed it tight. What secrets Floyd harbored would remain secrets for now.

Hershel hadn't gone inside Kyrellis's house on either of his trips. He knew that someone would find the body in time. A driver looking for a shipment of roses, perhaps. A friend, if Kyrellis had any. Hershel reasoned that he hadn't actually killed the man—not directly. He told himself that he had nothing to fear from the law. If questioned, he would simply explain that he'd been at Kyrellis's to collect the Charger. A buy-back. He'd taken the time to draw up a false receipt in case he needed to prove it. But, even as he prepared his story, the truth that he'd hastened the man's death couldn't be avoided.

As he listened to the tick of the kitchen clock in the empty house, he parsed Silvie's declaration that *she* had killed Kyrellis. Had he misunderstood her? Had she said that Castor shot him, and somehow the shock of her leaving with the same man who had enslaved her caused Hershel to get it wrong? He'd gotten so many things wrong; it could be just one more item on that long list. And yet her voice, taut with emotion, rang so clear, even a day later.

One thing had become clear to Hershel, though. As he'd stood looking at Floyd, running his fingers over the crushed-in roof, he knew that he had not killed Albert Darling. Like the oily sheen of those things lost to him, there was also a void—a wide, empty space inside his brain—that by its very presence confirmed that some things never were. Whatever Kyrellis had convinced him of, however Darling's body had come to him for disposing, a true killer would have pulled the trigger and killed Castor. He was not a killer. He had never been a killer.

———

On Monday morning, after another difficult night of unrest, Hershel went to the auction barn. The day was as dark as his mood, a heavy rain pelting his skin through the leafless tree branches. Its icy sting was punishing, but he neither put on the hat he carried in his hand nor turned back for his pickup. At the doorstep he sifted through his keys, calling out each one in his mind: truck, house, storage, post office, warehouse. How could he remember these unimportant keys now and not the other details of his past life? How had he broken his mother's heart? How had Albert Darling departed this world?

Inside, he found the furniture that Stuart had received on Friday stored haphazardly. A china hutch and a bedroom set were both turned to face the wall. "I should fire that stupid son of a bitch," he muttered. "How will anyone know what they're bidding on if they can't even see the damn things?"

Carl would have known that. He would have taken the time to think about the arrangement, placing it for maximum bidding potential. He would have put the dining set together—table, chairs, sideboard, hutch—so that a woman yet to arrive would see it and instantly fall in love. Carl had understood that auctions were an emotional affair. And his absence here was bitingly real for Hershel. They would never again work together in that comfortable side-by-side silence.

Hershel wandered into the concession stand, which stood quiet, everything washed and put away just as the girl had left it last week. By now Carl would have eaten the leftover hot dogs and started on the fresh ones. The cooker would be greasy and in need of another cleaning before the upcoming sale. The coffeemaker would be covered with brown splatters and used grounds. It was the only benefit Hershel offered—all you can eat and drink. And still he'd found the capacity to resent Carl for taking too much.

The idea was so absurd that Hershel almost laughed at his own meanness. Was anyone that stingy? It was funny, and it was sick. The epiphany that he'd valued all the wrong things in his life shamed him. And the nagging question that had pestered him all morning only grew in intensity. Why was he here today? Why was he here at all? How could he imagine that life would just go on, as if nothing had happened?

He slid his hand into his pocket and ran a finger over Carl's worn knife. It had become his constant companion. As he pondered whether to close his business forever—one last liquidation sale and be finished—someone knocked at the front door.

"C'min," he called.

Two young Mexican men peered in through the door. " 'Ello?" Behind them the rain was furiously hitting the ground, filling the parking lot with puddles and bringing them to life with motion.

"Can I help you?"

"Our mother," one of the men called above the roar of pounding rain. "She sent us. You asked us to come?"

Yolanda's sons; he'd forgotten his request of the woman in the migrant camp. He worried about how she was getting along and motioned the men inside. They introduced themselves in broken English. Manuel and Eduardo. They both stood barely five and a half feet tall, with wide, muscular shoulders and worn, calloused hands. Eduardo, the younger and darker of the two, wore his hair long and tied back in a ponytail. Manuel's was cropped short in a crew cut, and he sported a gold front tooth.

"About Carl Abernathy," Hershel said.

"*Sí.*" They both nodded. "Carlos."

"She said you were looking for the person who … who killed him."

"*Sí.*" He took care of our mother," Manuel said. "He was a good friend to her."

"His killer—" Hershel stopped. As far as he knew, he reminded himself, he didn't know if Carl Abernathy was dead or just on a long vacation. He didn't know that Kyrellis wasn't at his nursery propagating roses as they spoke. He had never known about any photos, or the name of a Wyoming sheriff. He knew nothing.

The two listened intently, waiting for Hershel to continue.

"Forget about his killer."

Eduardo shook his head defiantly. "We will find him and kill him."

"No," Hershel said.

"Those that did this will pay," Eduardo said. His mouth had hardened into a grim line. "They don't know who they're dealing with."

"You don't even know who did it."

"Yes, we have an idea. The men that were here in camp—the new ones. They don't like how Carlos spends time with our mother," Eduardo said.

Manuel flushed and shoved his hands into his pockets.

"It wasn't them," Hershel said.

Eduardo shook his head. "No. But they know who it was. They *sent* who it was. They were getting even with Carlos."

Hershel held his hands up in the air to stop the conversation. These two young men were going to kill someone in retaliation for Carl's murder—someone who had nothing to do with it.

"Listen to me; it won't bring him back."

Manuel studied his boots as Eduardo puffed out his chest like a bantam rooster.

"You'll only get yourselves thrown in prison, or worse." Hershel thought of Yolanda the day she came looking for Carl and how she walked back down Scholls Ferry Road in the rain, her shoulders hunched, her face wet with tears. Her grief had touched him. "Think of what it will do to your mother."

The two men fidgeted and glanced awkwardly around the building. Obviously his request would be ignored.

"I need help," Hershel said at last. "I have jobs. If...you want them."

They both took new interest.

"It's hard work. Moving furniture. Boxes. Heavy stuff. It's what Carl did for me...these past ten years."

Manuel shrugged. "We are strong."

"How long is the job?" Eduardo asked. "We prune grapevines in February, and we pick strawberries in spring."

Hershel looked around at the giant warehouse that, despite its clutter, felt as vacant and lonely as his own house. What else had he to do? If he sold everything, what would be different about his life? Silvie would still be gone. His mother would still hang up when he called.

"Until I go out of business," he said.

The two looked at each other, perplexed.

"There is no end. You work for me every day. Forty hours each week. Sometimes more. It depends on the week. Depends on the sale."

"Ah," Manuel said, a smile dawning over his face. "All the time. Like Carlos."

"Yes. But . . . but I'm not hiring a couple of killers. You've got to leave this business alone if you want to work here. Agreed?"

They both thought on this a long moment—so long, in fact, that Hershel was ready to withdraw the offer. Finally Manuel stepped forward, nodded solemnly, and shook Hershel's hand. Eduardo took his time, but eventually joined his brother. They each thanked Hershel quietly in English and again in Spanish.

"Can you start today? I need to arrange all this stuff." He swept a hand out at the furniture. "It has to be easy to see for the people who want to buy it."

"We start now," Eduardo said.

The picture of Silvie that was stuck in Hershel's mind was the last he'd seen her, as she looked at him before climbing into Castor's pickup. Her hair, golden-blond, had ruffled in the breezy sunlight. She wore his flannel work shirt over her jacket and jeans, as if she had just stopped by the nursery to pick up a rosebush and would be home planting it soon. Though she had been more than fifty yards away, he believed he could see the blue of her frightened eyes. Those same haunted eyes that belonged to the girl in the photograph.

This was the vision he had as he closed his eyes at night,

the image that persisted in his mind, both sleeping and awake. He knew that she was scared, but was it because she'd killed Kyrellis or because she feared Castor? Why had she claimed to love Castor if she hadn't wanted to go with him? Had he missed something? A hidden message to follow? To rescue? Her words were spoken with such clarity he knew that to believe anything but what she'd said would be a fabrication.

She'd said she *loved* him. How could she *love* him?

Hershel sat up in bed, swung his legs off the side of the mattress, and pressed his feet against the cool floor. The clock glowed twelve forty-five. He could estimate the sleep he'd managed over the past three days in mere minutes. If he continued this way he'd die of exhaustion. And yet sleep evaded him.

"Why didn't I shoot?" He gripped his temples in his hands and squeezed. "I should have just killed him. I could go kill him now." Hershel went to the window and peered down at the yard and his dark truck. "I can still kill him."

The sale barn was quiet on Tuesday morning. Too early for bidders to preview the sale that evening. Eduardo and Manuel had done a good job the previous day, arranging the furniture so that it could be appraised properly by potential buyers. He had instructed them only once on the goal of their task, and they managed from there, though Hershel had stepped in and worked alongside them. The two seemed nervous about this in the beginning, as if they thought he didn't trust them. Quiet glances bounced between them, then furtively at Hershel. But it was his business, and he had always taken a hands-on approach. There was no reason to stop now, and every reason to continue. He needed the physical work more than they could possibly know.

He sat at his desk, sifting through the mail that Carl used to manage for him. He sorted the envelopes into piles, dreading the coming evening. He was too tired to think straight. But at least his clerk would be back tonight. Stuart had surmised that Marilyn had made a speedy recovery in response to the ease with which Hershel had found her replacement—a good-looking replacement, at that.

He considered firing Stuart. The man was vile. He couldn't be trusted. He leered at the women when they weren't looking and sometimes when they were. The man offended his customers with his trashy mouth, and made Hershel look like an imbecile every opportunity he got. But he saw something of his former self in Stuart. It was both repulsive and endearing. He couldn't throw the man away for these things.

He opened his safe and sifted through its contents. The wooden box was familiar, but he didn't remember what it held, so he dragged it out and placed it on the desk, then examined his keys for one that might work. When he'd found the right one, he opened the lid and withdrew a jumble of papers. He pressed the first one flat across the surface of the desk and a prickle raced over his scalp. It was Albert Darling's insurance list—the Winchester rifle proudly called out on the first line. Why had he kept this? He leafed through the others, all damning evidence of past gun sales. Why? Had he planned to blackmail the buyers?

Hershel's phone rang, and he picked it up. "Hello."

"Any guns in the sale tonight?"

Hershel froze. Was Kyrellis alive? No, the voice was wrong, too high. Younger. Another man, familiar and unfamiliar in that frustrating way.

"Yes," he said. "Two small pistols. Did you see the ad in the paper?"

"That's all?"

"I advertise all my guns."

The man snorted. "Since when?"

"Since today."

There was a long silence on the other end.

"I file my paperwork as required by law. If you're looking for something else, you won't find it here."

"If you say so." The man's voice was flat with disappointment as he hung up.

Hershel dropped the phone back into its cradle. How many of these men were out there? How often would he have this conversation?

He gathered up the papers and slipped them into a large manila envelope. He would carry them home and burn them today. He would turn his business and his home upside down in the week ahead, searching for evidence like this, and destroy it. His mission was simple—eradicate the man who had once possessed this place, this body. This soul.

He dialed the phone.

"Hello," she answered.

"I've changed."

She drew an audible breath.

"Please don't hang up. Please."

She seemed frozen, and Hershel didn't know what more to say. He simply wanted to hold this connection like a fragile, beautiful glass thread.

"I'm different. Why don't you want anything to do with me?"

"I—I can't."

"I don't remember what happened." He expected her to hang up, but the line was simply quiet now. Was she still there? "I don't remember a lot of my life before. It's gone. I'm... I'm different."

She sniffed hard, and he heard her muffled sob. He was breaking her heart. He was killing her.

"I need you, Mom," he whispered.

She hung up.

31

Silvie slept for hours, days—maybe even weeks. She'd lost track. Time wadded up around her like a thick, dark cocoon. The room was light. Then dark. Then light. Now dark. She staggered to the bathroom, squinting away from the harsh light, and peered at her reflection. Her face was puffy and red. The worst of her bruises had begun the slow migration from purple to green. The least of them had yellowed. The swelling had finally gone down. Her hair hung limply around her shoulders, oily. When had she last bathed?

"Silvie?" Jacob called.

She closed her eyes against his voice. "I'm in the bathroom." Her voice was hoarse with fatigue.

Once she'd emptied her bladder and washed her hands, rubbing at the deep grooving around her wrists that was still visible, she returned to bed, feeling exhausted. Jacob sat on the edge, waiting. He pulled the covers back for her and waited as she climbed in. Then he drew the blankets up around her again and kissed her forehead. He smelled of alcohol still.

"Take this," he said, reaching for a tablet and a glass of water.

She shook her head.

"Do like I ask."

"Please, Jacob. I've been sleeping too much." She rubbed her hands over her puffy, hot skin. "When can I see my mother?"

He looked at her sadly. He had deep creases under his eyes, and he looked older than she remembered. He'd always seemed old, but now he *looked* old. After a moment to contemplate her request, he pressed the pill into her palm. "Take it."

"Jacob?"

He waited patiently. He was in one of his caretaking moods, when he treated her like a child, seeing to her every need. This was the Jacob she had missed, though now she couldn't quite grasp why.

He hadn't even waited until they were back in Wyoming before he began the beatings. The first few hours of the trip, she'd huddled against the passenger door, wiping away silent tears. Those Portland streets, the wide band of interstate that curled its way through the heart of the city—a city radiant in its cloak of green velvet that sunny day—were unreal. It was as if time had suddenly stopped. She felt numb, her mind unable to grasp reality. She'd killed a man. It was shocking in such a way that it simply wouldn't stop surprising her. At every turn, every light, she realized again, as if it were the first time, that she'd killed a man.

But, as the city faded into the background and the Columbia River Gorge opened its arms to them, the fear that she'd carried with her when she arrived in Oregon crept back. She glanced at Jacob from time to time, trying to get a sense about things. Was it okay that he'd found her? She'd missed him. What would he do? How angry was he? Had he had time to yearn for her before he'd come? She studied the side of his face, working at reading his mood. But that was just the problem; she'd never been able to do that. He startled her with his affection and he startled her with his brutality. She never saw either one coming.

He waited until Idaho Falls, some ten hours on the road, before he began to question her. She turned her face to the window to deal with her tears and simply remained silent. He didn't persist, not until they'd reached the motel.

"I'm sorry for what I did," she said, holding the pill in her hand, stalling for time.

He nodded, almost to himself.

"When can I see my mom?"

His eyes came up to meet hers, but they were guarded and un-readable. He'd been drinking consistently since they returned. Her stomach instinctively clenched down on itself. He set the water glass on the nightstand.

"Why don't you have a bath? You can take that later." He took the pill back and set it next to the glass.

"How long have we been home?"

"Don't worry about that," he said. "Just take a hot bath. Take your time. Get cleaned up."

She knew what this meant. She rose, having no choice but to comply. She couldn't change the course of his plans twice, and she wasn't foolish enough to try. She stepped gingerly into the bath-room again.

Silvie slid into the hot water, wishing she had taken the drug. She'd be asleep by now. Instead, she was preparing herself for him like a sacrificial lamb.

She wondered why Hershel hadn't rescued her by now. And a bigger part of her wondered why he hadn't shot Jacob when he had the chance. She'd seen him point his rifle at Jacob's face as they turned around and started out of Kyrellis's nursery. She'd watched the long barrel of his gun as it followed the movement of the truck. She'd held her breath, expecting Jacob's brains to splat-ter across her lap at any moment. And then they were turning onto Scholls Ferry Road, her heart sinking. Jacob was reaching for her, pulling her closer to him, telling her how happy he was that he'd found her alive. She was struggling with the cruel realization that she didn't want to go with him. She wanted to stay.

She wished, above all, that she hadn't told Hershel she loved Jacob. At the moment, she had believed it was true. Or true enough that she didn't want Hershel to kill him. But her parting words sounded so ugly now. He would never know that he had meant anything to her at all.

The phone rang, and Jacob answered it. Though the door was

open only a crack, she had always been able to hear him conduct his business from this room, even when it was closed.

"No," he said. "I haven't heard from her."

Silvie perked up. Was he talking about her?

"I promise, Melody. The first I know I will call you." There was a long pause. Silvie chased her breath, unable to catch it. "How are you doing? Do you need anything? Are you current on your rent?"

She cried out, a small moan. He was speaking to her mother. He was lying to her mother. Why, though? It wasn't as if her mother didn't know Jacob beat her. The first time it happened, Silvie went to her for help. It was the day before her thirteenth birthday. He'd hit Silvie before that, but this was a bona-fide beating with his fists that seemed to go on forever, until she threw up. When she showed her mother the bruises, Melody made indignant noises and horrified faces. She had sympathized, telling her daughter that she shouldn't have done that. Then she made Silvie a cup of hot cocoa, sat her down, and explained to her that everyone had a cross to bear. Life was hard. We don't always get what we want, and everyone has to do their part. Especially now that her father was gone. This was simply Silvie's cross—and God wouldn't give her more than she could handle.

"You almost done in there, sweetie?" Jacob called. "Silvie?" He opened the door and peered in.

"I'm still kind of tired," she said, through slit eyes. The sight of him struck fear anew in her. She could imagine only one reason why he would lie to her mother: he was finally going to kill her.

He took up the large bath towel, holding it out for her, hugging her against him as if she were a little girl. He smelled sourly of some strange liquor. She was stiff in his embrace, and he ran his hands up and down her arms through the cotton shroud, as if to soften her.

"Come on," he whispered. "I've laid out your nightie."

On the bed, Silvie found a silky blue negligee with lace trim.

The bra was transparent and gauzy. The gown itself barely long enough to cover her rear. He would do one of two things: he'd have her dance for him, or he'd tie her up. Either way, he would masturbate first, and then they would screw. She would moan to make it all seem believable. That was the way it always went.

She turned to him, and he nodded at the outfit, his momentary softness now gone. She noticed the bottle on the nightstand. Moutai—a Chinese whiskey that he boasted to friends was 102 proof. She couldn't see how much he'd drunk; the bottle was opaque white. The more he drank, though, the meaner he would be. He was a bad drunk that way. Her backpack was next to the overstuffed chair by the bed.

"Ready for me to dance, Jacob?"

"I have questions first."

"I have a surprise for you. It's in my backpack."

He ignored her, binding her hands to the headboard with an electric cord. He then arranged her on the mattress in a position that was less painful than it was humiliating. He tied her ankles but left six or eight inches of slack in the line between them. He pushed her knees up over her breasts, then pulled them apart so that her hips opened and she was fully exposed.

"You'll be here awhile," he said, placing a pillow under each hip. "Might as well be as comfortable as possible."

I'll survive this. It's what she always told herself. But this seemed different. She wished that Hershel had killed him, that she hadn't stood in the way. She wanted Jacob dead now; she was certain. No amount of distance or time would let her forget that again.

He staggered a little as he worked. And when he was finished setting things up he gazed at her for a long time.

"This is for stealing from me," he said. "And running away." His eyes were crazy, slightly out of alignment. Silvie waited, expecting to be beaten, but he slumped into the armchair next to the bed and took up his drink. He sipped it slowly at first, then gulped down the remainder. He listed to the side as he reached again for the bottle. He poured himself another drink and tortured her with silence for a while.

"Haven't I always given you what you needed?"

"Yes," she said, the picture of compliance.

He bent and lifted up her backpack. He'd obviously been through it, because he drew out the bottle of motion lotion and assessed it. He removed it from the extra bag and rolled it between his hands.

Silvie watched. How would she do this? How would she prevent him from poisoning her, too?

"You found my surprise for you." The words sounded false.

"For me? Or was this intended for Hershel Swift?" Jacob asked.

She closed her eyes.

"Darling, don't make me hurt you."

"It was for you," she said quietly. "Before I found the box...before I ran away. Jacob, I was scared. Please forgive me. I was just scared."

"Who is Hershel?"

"I don't know."

"Of course you do. You were driving his car."

She didn't respond, and Jacob reached over and pinched her hard on the leg.

"Kyrellis gave me the car. I didn't know it belonged to someone else."

"Why would he give you a car?"

"He didn't *give* it to me. He let me borrow it. The Rabbit died. That's how he found me. I was stranded on the side of the road."

"But why would he lend you a car? You could've just left."

"He had your box. I couldn't leave it behind. I wouldn't do that to you, Jacob, and he knew it."

"Did you tell him my name?"

"No! Of course not."

He shook the lotion and held it up. "I just don't know if I can believe you, darling."

"Please, Jacob. I didn't run away from him because I was trying to get the pictures back." Her story was thin and didn't add up. She was grateful that he was drunk. If he weren't, this would invoke a beating until she provided a story that made sense.

Jacob seemed to consider her plea. He finished his drink and had trouble getting the glass onto the nightstand, clattering it against the clock and knocking a bottle of Valium to the floor. He stared down at the carpet, but Silvie couldn't see what he looked at. He leaned down and picked up a tablet but lost his grip on it. It rolled into his lap and he got up, looking for it.

"What would happen if I took this while I was drinking?" he asked, retrieving the pill. "Bet that would put me out for a little bit, don't you?"

He studied it, as if Silvie no longer existed. "You'd be in a bad position if that happened," he observed.

Silvie believed that spending the night bound as she was would still be better than what he would do to her if he stayed awake.

He set the pill on the nightstand and resumed his seat. "I'll save that for you."

"Why don't you let me dance for you? You know how I love to do that." It was risky to suggest this, but he liked for her to strip, and he'd had enough to drink to make it a reasonable offer. "I'll go real slow."

He was quiet, and she waited with her eyes closed. The faces of those other girls were flashing through her mind as if projected onto the insides of her lids. Solemn faces. Freckled faces. Peering out at her in the faded colors of aged photo paper.

"Wouldn't you like that? Wouldn't you like me to dance for you? I can feel your cock already."

Jacob made a strange noise, and Silvie turned in his direction. He had poured some of the lotion into the palm of his hand and was smoothing it with his fingers.

"Wouldn't you like me to perform for you? Huh?"

"You're so beautiful, Silvie. I always loved you," he said. "I might let you do that for me one last time."

He stood and worked the cords that bound her wrists. With

every brush of his skin against hers, she imagined the poison transferring to her body. Finally, he loosened them enough that she could slide one wrist out; then she worked on the other.

As she got to her feet, she said, "Let me help you with your belt." She carefully removed his pants, deliberately slow, rubbing against his bulging crotch. "Sit on the bed and relax a little. Show me the Club." She leaned down and kissed his cheek. "I'll do my very best for you tonight, Jacob."

32

Hershel stood on his front porch, a heavy rain driving down the valley from the west in sheets of steel gray. A chill wind bit at his skin and he shoved his hands into his pockets for warmth. Clouds scraped the treetops, giving the day a hard and unforgiving feel.

"When was the last time you saw Victor Kyrellis?" the officer asked from the bottom of the step. He was the same one who had come to the sale barn the day Hershel reported Carl missing. The rain collected in the wide brim of the man's hat, and when he tipped his head up for Hershel's response a stream of water poured off his back.

"Oh, I don't know," Hershel said, looking at the underside of his porch roof, trying to remember. "He attended the Tuesday sale last week, but he wasn't there this week."

"So last Tuesday?"

"Yeah. That was the last time. Has something happened to him?"

"Someone shot him in his home. He'd been dead a few days when we found him."

Hershel scowled. "Do you have any suspects?"

"Might have been a robbery. He had a nice gun collection. Someone broke the glass on a couple of the cases and it looked like a few guns were missing." The officer took in Hershel's well-maintained yard. "Something must have scared them off, though; they left an awful lot of nice guns behind."

"I'm sorry to hear about this," Hershel said.

"He didn't tell you he was expecting anyone? Nothing like that?"

"I don't really know him very well."

"He called your cellphone several times," the officer said. He looked at Hershel suspiciously. "We've got the records."

"He buys stuff at my sale. Has my number and calls about what's coming up. But we were never friendly, really. Honestly? I found him to be kind of creepy."

The officer shook the rain off himself. "What sorts of things did he buy from you?"

"I don't know. Odds and ends. Bought a Volkswagen Rabbit a couple weeks ago, but it didn't have clear title, so I had to buy it back. Think he bought a dresser and some tools before. He might have bought a rifle or two. I'd have to look back through my records." He looked the man dead in the eye. "You're welcome to come down to my business. Check my books."

"I just might." The officer shifted back and forth. A puddle had formed beneath his shoes. "Guess winter is upon us, huh?"

"Looks that way."

"Well, thanks for the info." He turned toward his cruiser.

"No problem. Let me know if I can help with anything." Hershel ran his hand over his stubbly chin. He hadn't shaved in three days. "You ever find out who that body was they pulled from the Tualatin?"

The officer stopped. "Yeah. It was Abernathy. A boater in the Willamette pulled up anchor along with a decomposed head. Pretty gruesome sight, from what I understand." He marveled, as if trying to imagine it. "Didn't anyone tell you?"

"No," Hershel said, his voice cracking, his stomach turning sour. Though he already knew Carl was dead, this confirmation hollowed him out in a new way.

"Dental records matched. Now we're trying to locate his family, but he doesn't appear to have any. They don't know who to give the body to."

"I'll take it. Who should I call?"

"Sorry?"

"He was the best employee I ever had—ten years of service. He was a good man. I'll see to a burial."

Silvie sat in the emergency room waiting area. Jacob's senior deputy, Walter Erickson, tapped his foot next to her. On her lap she cradled her backpack, which held the box of photos.

"I could arrest you right now," Walter said.

She ignored him. The nurse at the reception desk was on the phone, eyeing Silvie's bruises.

"Tell me what happened," Walter demanded. It was the fourth time he'd tried to get her to talk.

"I'll only talk to the district attorney," she said again. She didn't know if the district attorney was the right person. When she first called for the ambulance, she'd asked the 911 operator to call the attorney general, too. She wished she'd paid better attention in school and knew who could protect her.

"We don't need to involve the district attorney," Walter said. "You know that. Jacob will be furious . . . if he lives."

She turned to Walter so that he could get a full view of her bruised face. She rolled her sleeves up, and held out her purpled wrists. "Furious?"

He flushed and turned away. He'd known her as long as Jacob had. If he wasn't fully aware of what Jacob had done to her over the years, he was deaf and blind. He had some culpability in this, she knew. And that was why he was pushing her to tell him what had happened.

She'd given only the information she needed to when the paramedics asked what had happened to Jacob. She'd simply said,

"He's been poisoned with organophosphates." Then she requested to ride in the ambulance, stating that she had information about a crime that would put her at risk if she stayed behind. They didn't seem to know what to say, shaking their heads. But she climbed in with Jacob anyway, and no one stopped her.

When the emergency room doctor asked how Jacob had been poisoned, she said she needed to speak with the attorney general. It was the nurse who suggested the district attorney after getting a good look at Silvie's face. She put an arm around Silvie and led her back to the waiting room, assuring her that she'd get him out here right away. Walter showed up six minutes later, breathless, as if he'd run from Hanley to Rawlings on foot.

When the district attorney burst through the door at Rawlings Medical Center, he spoke first to the nurse at the desk, who whispered and gestured toward Silvie. Then he approached, smiling softly, saying her name.

"Excuse us," he said to Walter, who had gotten up to follow them. "We need a word alone."

Walter stared after them, tall and lanky, looking guilty and sick to his stomach as they left the room.

His name was Mr. Pane, which Silvie found ironic. He led her to an empty office down the corridor. Silvie felt oddly calm, amazingly strong all of a sudden.

"Now, tell me what's going on," Mr. Pane said.

Silvie opened her backpack and took out the box of photos. She watched as he opened it, his face turning gray, his lips pressed in a hard frown.

"Jacob Castor took those. *Sheriff* Jacob Castor." She pointed out the ones of herself. "He's been hurting me since I was twelve."

The man looked up, his eyes meeting hers. She saw a flicker in them, a split second of doubt or disbelief, but then he steadied them. She took the photos and found the ones with Jacob.

"See?" She wondered if he knew Jacob well enough to recognize him. Were they friends? Did they have drinks together?

"What I want to know is where these other girls are." She leafed through the pictures, immune to them now. She handed him the older images. The little girls who stared out with hollow eyes, haunting her. "He was going to kill me, too."

Mr. Pane gathered the photos up and placed them in the box, closing the lid. "Did he give you those bruises?"

"Yes." She showed him her wrists, and he winced. "The bruises are worse on my back."

"Did you poison him?"

"Yes." She dug in her backpack again, this time taking out the motion lotion. "I mixed organophosphates in this, and he used it to stroke himself." She could have sworn that she saw the briefest smile cross Mr. Pane's face.

"Why did you call an ambulance if you meant to kill him?"

"I don't know." She squirmed a little in her chair, wondering the same thing. Jacob had been too drunk to get himself help. He'd reached orgasm while watching her dance, and then passed out. She guessed it was from the booze, and she changed into her street clothes while trying to think of what she should do. If she left him like this, she would never know if he was alive or dead. She'd be looking over her shoulder for the rest of her life. She considered stabbing him, but she knew that she didn't have it in her to do that. Then she thought she could shoot him. She'd shot Kyrellis, why not him? But by then he'd come awake again, and he was having some sort of seizure, convulsing on the bed. Then he began to vomit, just as her dog had, and he lost control of his bowels.

"When I saw him like that...you know...puking all over the place and shaking..." Tears prickled her eyes, but she ignored them. "I realized that he wasn't that tough, really."

Mr. Pane touched her shoulder.

"Am I going to jail?"

He drew a long breath and considered this. "I think we can probably avoid that. I know these pictures are going to help us.

But you'll need to see the doctor right away. He'll take more pictures...of your bruises and your injuries. We're going to need them for evidence. Okay?"

"Okay."

"Silvie, where did you get the poison?"

"It's a common pesticide," she said. "Most people use it to kill bugs on their roses. I only knew about it because my mom poisoned our dog once." She committed the statement to memory. That was all that she would ever say about it. She would never tell about Oregon, Hershel, Carl, or Kyrellis. If they pieced it together, she would claim that Jacob killed Kyrellis. But she wouldn't bring it up. If Jacob lived, he would never tell anyone about Oregon, either; she was certain of that. The gun he'd handed her, the one she'd used to kill Kyrellis, was Jacob's.

Chehalem View Cemetery was packed with mourners, despite the rain. Even the Channel 6 news had shown up for the graveside service of Carl Abernathy. He was being hailed as a modern-day saint among some in the migrant community, and word of his extraordinary generosity had spread to the cultural center in Hillsboro and outward into the rest of the community. When Hershel had told Yolanda about the service barely a day ago, he had expected a handful of people from Campo Rojo. The funeral notice in the *Oregonian* that morning had been small, and he didn't think it would garner much attention. But this crowd of several hundred—not only Mexican migrants but farmers and auctiongoers and people in professional attire—had shocked and humbled him. Some had driven down from Seattle to attend. Both sides of Highway 219 were jammed with cars, trucks, and vans. A pyramid of handmade and store-bought bouquets at the foot of the grave site offered the only color on that misty morning near the summit of Chehalem Mountain.

Hershel had prepared a few words, but, looking out at the faces, he felt his knees go rubbery. Who was he to eulogize Carl Abernathy? As the minister finished his prayer, the faces turned to Hershel. He shook his head, wanting to retreat and knowing that he couldn't.

"There are no words that can describe the man that Carl was," he began. "Loyal, generous, unselfish. These are mere impressions of a deeper, more complex person. Carl worked for me for ten years. It has taken this loss for me to understand that he didn't work *for* me but *with* me. Side by side, he was a partner in all that I did."

A soft rain had begun to fall, and a few umbrellas popped up. Some of the migrant workers pulled their hoods up, but no one left. What more could he say? The people waited for Hershel to continue.

"I suffered a serious brain injury earlier this year. Had it not been for Carl, I might have had nothing to return home for. He took care of my business, my home, and, more important, me. See…the truth is…I wasn't a very nice man. Carl deserved better than to work for someone like me. But that's just it, I guess— he didn't *have* to work for me. He chose to so that he could help others. What little he made, he spent at my sales. He bought small things no one else wanted, or had left behind. Like coats, old appliances, hand tools—damaged goods, mostly. I was a man consumed by money, incapable of understanding a man like Carl. I didn't know or care what he did with these things. I assumed that he was selling them, but I never guessed that he was giving them away." Hershel paused for a much-needed breath. "Carl Abernathy taught me what was important in life. He taught me what it means to be a human being."

Hershel stepped back, an enormous lump taking over his airway.

One by one, people stepped forward, migrants mostly, and recounted the gifts they had received from Carl. A pair of rubber boots in the heart of February for a man who worked in the vineyards. A used carburetor for another man's broken-down van. A set of almost-new roller skates for one woman's little girl, three days before Christmas. They went on for several minutes as the onlookers dabbed at their eyes. Then it fell quiet, and after a minute or two everyone began to file out of the cemetery, leaving Hershel standing in the pouring rain. He stared down at the casket, ready to be sealed away. A simple wooden capsule of polished pine. Carl would have said it was too much. Hershel believed it wasn't enough.

When he got home, he changed his clothes, pulled on his raincoat, and went outside. There he used a crowbar to pry open Floyd's trunk. The carpeting was stained dark, and smeared with dried mud. He felt around inside, but it was empty. Then his eye caught the glint of a brass shell casing lodged in the crease near the wheel well. He picked it up and rolled it in his palm. A shell casing from Kyrellis's gun. He remembered now. Kyrellis had insisted that Hershel take the body in the trunk of his car because he'd driven a pickup and it could be easily seen. Hershel had wanted to dump the body in the river, not risk contaminating his car with evidence. But Kyrellis was insistent, saying they would dredge the river when they found Darling's car at the remote park near St. Paul. It was used mostly by fishermen, and they'd chosen the place because they knew no one would be around. Too far from anywhere to draw attention. Kyrellis had arrived early and scouted the best location. He was to cover Hershel in case things didn't go as planned. Darling believed he was meeting Hershel alone.

"Why did you kill him?" Hershel had asked, standing over Darling's crumpled body.

Kyrellis hadn't allowed the man to say a single word, but had shot him three times as he walked up to Hershel.

"We agreed not to kill him."

"Don't be stupid, Swift. Do you really think we could've bribed this guy to leave us alone?"

Kyrellis had left immediately after they loaded the body into the trunk and agreed on what Hershel planned to do with it. He said that he didn't want anyone to see them together, and that suited Hershel just fine. He stayed at the park for ten minutes after Kyrellis left, and he used the time to retrieve the shells. He disposed of the body the way he disposed of his poached elk carcasses, by feeding Darling to the hogs at French Prairie Farm.

Hershel had driven back toward Newberg with an odd sense of lightness, as if released from a binding contract. He'd marveled at his own genius, because he had deposited the shells in Darling's shirt pocket. The evidence would point to Kyrellis if it came down to that.

He closed the trunk. "Some fucking genius."

The question now was what to do about this mess. Darling was dead. Kyrellis was dead. He hadn't killed either of them. Not technically, anyway. He could turn himself in. He'd go to prison, he guessed, but there was no way to know for how long. He thought of Silvie. He was in too deep. If he told anything, he'd have to tell everything, and that would put her at risk.

He walked to the edge of the filbert orchard and threw the shell casing as hard as he could into the trees. Silvie had voluntarily returned with Castor. Said she loved him, even. There was nothing Hershel could do to save her. Kyrellis had been right about one thing: he couldn't undo the damage that another man had done. They were both irreparably damaged people.

Inside, Hershel's house was mournfully silent. He'd spent the next several hours reviewing his finances and drawing up instructions for his accountant to set up a fund for the migrant families in Carl Abernathy's name. It would provide simple things like school supplies and clothing. Household items. It would serve as an emergency fund for people who were behind on their utilities or in need of minor medical assistance. He had an idea for a vocational-training scholarship, too. Something he'd look into. It gave him some comfort, but it didn't feel like enough. It was something he should have done years ago.

33

The phone rang early, and Hershel stumbled downstairs to reach it. He could scarcely remember the last time someone had called him at home.

"Hello?" he said. It was just past seven in the morning.

"Hershel?"

A hot spark raced through him. "Silvie? Is that you?"

"Yes. Hershel—"

"Are you okay? Do you need me to come get you?"

"I'm . . . I'm—"

"What is it? Are you hurt?"

"I'm going to be here awhile. I—I poisoned Jacob."

"You what?"

"He's okay. I called an ambulance in time, and he's going to be okay. But . . . I turned him in for all the other stuff. The district attorney is pressing charges against him. I have to testify."

"My God, Silvie. I'm proud of you."

She was quiet.

"Did you hear me? I'm so proud of you."

"Hershel," she said, and he could hear that she was crying. "I didn't mean what I said. About loving him. I just didn't want you to shoot him."

It was all he needed to hear.

"I miss you," she said.

"Do you want me to come be with you?"

"I can do this. I'm okay." She paused. "Yes, please come. I need you."

EPILOGUE

Hershel held his breath as he dialed the phone number that was still in his memory. It had been months since he'd last called, and he believed that he could do this only once more. His heart was breaking a little more each time.

"Hello," she answered. She sounded as if she'd been laughing.

"Mom?"

She went silent, the joy he'd felt from her having evaporated like mist. But she didn't hang up.

"I've met a woman and . . . I would like you to meet her, too."

She made a strange sound, almost like a hard little "Huh."

"She's seen some rough life: Kind of like me, only she didn't bring it on herself like I did." He looked out the front window at the coming spring. The herons were flocking to the river by the dozens as the leaves were starting to come on. The wetlands were a vibrant green, and the magnolia in his front yard held hundreds of purple blossoms still conically tight. Silvie was heading down the driveway in the Porsche, kicking up dust from the recent dry spell, headed for her shift at the South Store. "I think you'd like her."

"I promised myself that I would never give you another chance to hurt me, Hershel. Can you understand how much you've hurt me?"

The words stung, but they also felt good. He let them wash over him like icy water. He knew he'd hurt her, but he still didn't remember the details.

"One more time and you'll kill me. I can't have my heart broken again. One more time and you *will* kill me. I'd have been better off if God had ripped my heart from my chest the moment you were born."

"I'm different now. I promise I am."

She sucked in air and remained quiet for a long time.

"Please forgive me. Give me a chance to prove that I'm different."

"Oh, Hershel . . . I don't know."

He waited for her to hang up, his heart sinking.

"What is her name?"

ACKNOWLEDGMENTS

Special thanks to Holli Mason, MD, my dear sister, who tirelessly provides the medical details of trauma, various diseases and conditions, as well as the effects and treatments of poisons. This book would not be what it is without her.

During the final draft of *Damaged Goods* I was fortunate to work with Jess Row at Vermont College of Fine Arts. His critical eye and strong teaching helped clear away the unnecessary debris that inevitably piles up during the writing process.

My editor Randall Klein's keen perception and brilliant editing have improved this work exponentially. I am grateful for the privilege to work with such a thoughtful and patient professional.

Others who contributed to the shaping of this work are Jason Clark, Tina Ricks, and Anita Gutierrez. Thank you each for the ongoing support and repeated readings. Thank you also to my family, without whose help this could not be possible.

ABOUT THE AUTHOR

HEATHER SHARFEDDIN is the acclaimed author of *Sweetwater Burning* (originally released as *Blackbelly*), proclaimed one of the top novels of 2005 by New Hampshire's *Portsmouth Herald*. It has also been honored by the Eric Hoffer Awards and the San Francisco Book Festival. It was named a "Best of the Northwest" title by the Pacific Northwest Booksellers Association. Her other books include *Mineral Spirits*, which also received a "Best of the Northwest" title, and *Windless Summer*, honored at the 2010 New York Book Festival.

Sharfeddin holds an MFA in writing from Vermont College of Fine Arts. Raised in Idaho and western Montana, she now lives near Portland in Oregon's Yamhill Valley.